CHARLIE, PRESUMED DEAD

CHARLIE, PRESUMED DEAD

BY ANNE HELTZEL

Houghton Mifflin Harcourt
Boston   New York

Text set in Adobe Garamond

Library of Congress Cataloging-in-Publication Data
Heltzel, Anne, author.
Charlie, presumed dead / by Anne Heltzel.
p. cm.
Summary: Told in the separate voices of Lena and Aubrey, each hiding her own
secrets, who set off in search of the truth about Charlie, including if he is really
dead, after meeting at his funeral and learning that he was dating both of them.
ISBN 978-0-544-38849-9
[1. Secrets—Fiction. 2. Dating (Social customs)—Fiction. 3. Voyages and travels—
Fiction. 4. Missing persons—Fiction. 5. Mystery and detective stories.] I. Title.
PZ7.H3762Ch 2015
[Fic]—dc23
2014023458

Manufactured in the United States of America
DOC 10 9 8 7 6 5 4 3 2 1
4500530706

CHARLIE, PRESUMED DEAD

1

Aubrey

THE GIRL WITH THE SHIMMERY TIGHTS and fringed, calf-high boots is staring in my direction again. She looks like she's been crying for days now. Exactly twelve, if I were to guess—because that's the time that's passed between now and the day Charlie went missing. It's been twelve days since he took his parents' Cessna for a joyride —ten since initial debris from the wreckage was found in the North Sea off the coast of Durham, where the Prices have an estate. No one knows why he took the plane out; he'd never done it before, and he didn't have a license. But the bits of recovered debris have convinced police that the plane exploded. They think it happened in the air, before the plane went down—some sort of fuel leak. Now Charlie is presumed dead.

The girl's eyes are a startling blue against the blotchy skin of her face; they stand out even from all the way across the room. She's in the foyer, a few feet north of the entrance to the actual room where we're supposed to pay our respects. She leans up against a faux wood table while I stand opposite, nearer to the building's entrance. The table is the foldaway kind they use in cheap offices and cafeterias, and it looks like the girl needs it to support her frame. The table itself buckles a little under her weight, giving the impression that one of them—it or her—is about to collapse. Her black leather jacket has zippered sleeves, and her hair is the kind of blond that's almost white. It's long and wavy like a fairy's or maybe an elf's, and it floats in a halo around her bloated red face. It's difficult to look at her grief. Seeing it makes it harder to force back my own.

I'm chewing on some gum. It's my worst habit when I'm anxious, and I've been feeling frayed for the past few months at least. I'm putting off the moment when I'll have to walk inside the main room, where the service is being held. I can tell she's doing the same. It's in her body language: the way she pushes her heels against the floor and leans back. I wonder who she is and why she doesn't look familiar. I think about how maybe she's a cousin—maybe Kate, Charlie's mom's sister's daughter. Kate had straight brown hair in the picture he showed me, but people go through changes; they do funny things with boxes of hair dye and curling irons and magenta lipstick. I look inside the room that contains Charlie's empty casket, and the pit in my stomach deepens and twists.

My eyes dart back to the girl, and I have to make efforts not to stare too hard. I watch her resist as an older woman tugs at her wrist and pulls her in the direction of the larger room. Strains of tinny classical music emanating from overhead speakers surround me. My jaw opens and closes rhythmically around my wintergreen gum. It's beginning to lose its flavor. The girl turns toward me again, staring hard. She meets my eyes, and in that brief second I realize: I could be looking into a mirror. My messy dark hair, cut short with bangs, is the opposite of the ethereal image she projects. I wince. I hate looking at my reflection. I haven't been able to look at myself for months now without feeling sick inside. But I can tell without having to look that my eyes are puffy like hers; my shoulders droop in the same way; my guilt and grief are in evidence all over me, just like hers.

More people are filtering in. There are lots of official government-looking types, probably Charlie's dad's colleagues—he's a British diplomat. Hundreds of people have come to Paris for the memorial. Even though his dad moved around every couple of years, they always kept a home here. Charlie said they considered it home base, since it's where most of the extended family lives.

Someone must have turned up the sound system, because the music is suddenly drowning out everyone's soft murmurs. I can't explain why the girl's gaze is making me uncomfortable, or why mine keeps returning to her face with magnetic force. I'm jet-lagged and my whole face feels heavy from crying. My boyfriend is presumed dead and I'm alone in Paris for the first time ever. I could be on another planet for how strange it all feels.

I slip into a group of people who look about my age—a guy in a blue blazer and a girl in a black shift dress who are entering with some older people, probably their parents—and follow them from the foyer into the main room. The room is bare despite all the fancy architectural finishes that I'm beginning to recognize are common in Paris: ornate moldings in the shape of flowers, swoops and swirls fashioned from plaster. Other than that, it's a modestly decorated space with just a photo display set up in one corner, a bunch of folding chairs facing a podium, and a projector screen up front. Charlie's casket is next to the podium. My heart accelerates at the sight of it, and I blink back the tears that threaten to obscure my vision.

I realize with a pang that I really don't know any of Charlie's friends, not personally. I met his old roommate Adam from his senior year in Mumbai, when I visited Charlie once in D.C. — but I don't see Adam here now. I can't tell whether I'm disappointed or relieved. Everyone else I only knew from pictures; Adam would have been someone to lean on during all of this. At least someone to know — to legitimize my presence here. When I first met Adam, it was a comfort to know that Charlie was friends with such a good guy. Knowing Adam was Charlie's friend — when we didn't have any friends in common who could vouch for him — had made me rest easy.

I didn't even know about Charlie's disappearance or the memorial service until three days ago. A week before that, I had noticed he wasn't answering my texts. He always took a little time, sometimes forgot to get back; so it didn't seem unusual for that first week. And then my texts and calls became more panicked, and he still didn't reply. Charlie wasn't on Facebook or Twitter. I didn't have his parents' numbers. Then I got the news blast in my email from the local paper in Oxford, something Charlie had suggested I sign up for. And there it was: "University Student Missing," one of the first headlines on the list. The student in question was unnamed. After that, there was nothing I could do but Google him. I'd hoped to find some phone numbers, someone I could contact.

I found a more detailed article instead.

It still hurts, knowing that after a year, no one knew me well enough to reach out. It hurts that I found out the way I did. That I almost missed the service altogether. But why would I know anybody? I only knew Adam. Charlie and I always met up at such random places, spots that were in between Chicago and Oxford and easy for both of us to reach. He paid for most of those trips, and I saved up for the rest with my babysitting money. My parents weren't too happy about it. None of it ever seemed strange to me. But now, looking around and seeing all the people who knew Charlie—all the people I *don't* know—I wonder how I didn't see it before. He was meeting me in the middle, but also holding me at arm's length.

I can feel the fairy-elf's eyes on my back as I pass the row of chairs where she sits. The room is mostly filled. It's so big it could be a concert venue. There's a slideshow of Charlie's face flashing across the front of the room. I look at his eyes and can't accept that this is all that's left of him.

It's hard to comprehend what his memorial service really means. All I can feel is that he's not *here*. But he's never been present for me the way other people are readily available to one another. Charlie is road trips with pit stops at the Mars Cheese Castle and weekends away in New York City. He's not breakfast, lunch, and dinner or anything else regular. He never has been.

I walk over to the photo display, keeping his mother and father in my periphery. I haven't met Charlie's parents, and I can't help feeling that now isn't the moment to introduce myself. I wrote them a letter the minute I discovered Charlie was missing, shortly after the news reports started making their way around the Internet. They would have received the letter by now. But he's no longer just missing—he's *presumed dead*. As of four days ago—when more wreckage was found off the coast of Durham—the investigation was closed. His body hasn't been recovered and no one knows what really happened when the plane went down; but between plane debris and the charred and bloodstained remnants of his navy Oxford blazer—still marked with an engraved class pin—there was finally enough physical evidence to shut the investigation down. All that was missing was a reason and a body. A short blurb in the *Oxford*

Times mentioned the discoveries, and it wasn't even on the front page. Closed just like that, with a memorial service thrown together so quickly it barely left me time to get out here from Chicago. I can't figure out why and how his family could give up on him so quickly.

His mom is crying hysterically, and some of my resentment melts. I notice the elfin girl from the foyer sidle over; she gives Mrs. Price a long hug and whispers something in her ear. I feel a sharp pang of something like discomfort for reasons I don't understand. I turn back to the pictures, chalking it up to grief and exhaustion —I'm not thinking clearly.

Charlie sparkles in every shot, his dark hair flopping across his forehead. There's one in front of his high school in Bangkok: his arms are slung around both of his parents, his grin—angled higher on one side—just barely showing, like he's suppressing a laugh. There's one of him as a kid in a swimming pool in what must have been Paris—he spent most of his childhood there. His eyes are so wide you can see the flecks of gold in the blue, and his arms are stuffed into floaties.

The pictures show Charlie with friends, Charlie with his parents. Charlie with the basset hound they used to have. My favorite is one of Charlie caught off-guard: he's somewhere beachy—I can see a stretch of white sand like a long blanket wrapping itself around him in the background. The expression on his face is playful, like he's teasing the person behind the camera. There's one of Charlie and Adam wearing wide grins, their arms slung around each other's shoulders against the backdrop of their dorm room, and it ignites something sharp in my heart. There's an open checkerboard on the coffee table behind them. The memory that follows leaves me breathless.

Charlie places the checkerboard between us. We're in the corridor outside a hospital room; my little brother has just gotten his appendix out.

Charlie banned checkers from our relationship shortly after we began dating, when he realized that I'm basically a checkers savant and win every single time. Checkers, however, keeps me calm and focused. On the checkerboard, I feel in control.

"Like a lamb to the slaughter," I inform him in a serious tone, and he laughs loudly.

"I like that. Well, I'm happy to dig my own grave as long as you'll lie in it too," he says. Then he winks, and his whole face lights up with this mix of things: playfulness, secrecy, confidence, charm. When Charlie's playing nice guy, he's at his best.

The problem is, he's always playing.

The thought crosses my mind before I can help it, and I react by reaching across the board and squeezing him again, extra tight.

"I love you," I whisper. I desperately need to hear it back.

"You sweetheart," he says instead, and I feel my heart sink.

I pull away and look him in the eyes, hoping to catch a glimpse of what he's thinking. But there it is again: that smile. Charlie being playful.

The image leaves me shaking. My armpits are damp, and I realize I've been lingering too long in front of the photo that triggered the memory. I push forward, shaking my head in an effort to clear my thoughts. There aren't any pictures of Charlie and me in the photo display—not even the one he kept in a frame next to his bed in the dorm. We'd have been dating for over a year by now. Still, a lot has changed in the past few months.

I don't even notice that I'm the only one still examining the

photos until a man in a navy blue suit—maybe a funeral coor-
dinator—taps me on the shoulder. "Miss, could you please take
your seat? The ceremony is about to start." He gestures toward
the seats, which are almost all filled.

"Thanks," I tell him as I scan for an empty chair. I'm about to
take the one closest to me, right on the end by the aisle, when I
see an older lady walking with a cane a few paces behind me. She's
clearly moving toward the same chair; so instead I squeeze halfway
down the row behind this one, where there's one remaining seat
toward the center, next to a middle-aged couple that I'd mistake for
siblings if they weren't holding hands. The woman keeps clearing
her throat loudly and blowing her nose into an elaborately embroidered handkerchief. I reach for my bag and hand her my extra pack
of tissues, just in case.

The service passes in a blur: a few thoughtful words, some psalms.
Then Charlie's philosophy teacher from high school is at the podium
saying a few nice and funny things about how Charlie once wrote
an entire term paper in a series of haikus and still managed to hit
on the relevant arguments; so technically, the teacher couldn't fail
him even though it wasn't exactly a scholarly essay. That produces a
chuckle. And an uncle tells a story about how when Charlie was a
kid and crashing at his place, he'd had a hell of a time keeping Charlie away from the tree that stretched past the second-story terrace,
and how Charlie had been found more than once clambering down
it to the 7th arrondissement sidewalk, and how he'd never met a kid
cleverer or sneakier. I laugh at that one because it's so true. Charlie
was always catching me off-guard—it was one of the reasons I cared
about him.

After an hour of listening to other people's memories, I'm

exhausted. My boyfriend was beloved by more people than just me — that much is clear. It's one of the main reasons I was drawn to him — at first, Charlie was a perfect fit. It doesn't occur to me to offer some memories of my own, though; I feel like an outsider here. My throat constricts as it hits me: I'll never see him again. The tears come from somewhere deep and indecipherable.

I blink rapidly, eyes stinging. I reach for my purse and rummage around for my other pack of tissues. I've just found them when I hear murmurs. When I look up to see the elfin girl stepping up to the podium. She smiles in the direction of Charlie's mom, and for some reason my heart goes cold. She's gripping the sides of the wooden frame like it's a lifeline. I watch her draw in a breath. And then she begins to talk.

2

Lena

"I'M LENA," I SAY, GRIPPING THE PODIUM tight with both hands. The wooden elevated surface where I'm standing creaks under me as I shift my weight. "Most of you know me as Charlie's girlfriend." The second I say it, all I can think about is the pack of cigarettes in my bag and how the only thing I want to do is run straight out of here and continue on to a grungy dive bar in Pigalle and take a shot or three and smoke up a storm. There's all this pressure to say something important now, and all I wanted was for everyone to know who I am. That's it. Because I'm selfish like that. I wonder what would happen if I pulled out a cigarette right here, but then I hear Charlie's voice in my ear: *You're making it all about you again, Lena.* And it pisses me off so much that for a second I'm glad I won't ever have to hear the phrase again or see the smug expression that always went along with it.

"Charlie and I were in love," I say, hating myself as the words dump out. I sound like a stupid American greeting card with traces of a British accent, leftovers from a life spent in U.K. boarding schools. There's a sharp intake of breath from somewhere, and I scan the crowd. Charlie's mom is looking at me with desperate eyes, like

I'm some sort of flotation device. After a long struggle, she finally accepted he was dead, given the myriad evidence and the fact that the police said there was no way he could have survived the explosion. I pry my gaze from her grief-racked face with difficulty. A few feet to her right, Charlie's friend Max looks bored. Max is all cozied up to his new girlfriend like it's a movie date and he can't wait to go home and make out.

My eyes settle on the girl in the third row, the really beautiful but kind of cagey-looking one, sitting with the family even though she's *not* family—I know it because I've met all the family at birthday parties and anniversaries and reunions. The family is close like that. The girl's face is pale. Her mouth is hanging open. She looks like someone just told her that her father murdered her puppy.

That's when I know it. It's so obvious, I almost laugh. The way she looked at me in the hallway. The way she's looking at me now.

"Charlie and I dated for three years," I say aloud, not because there's any point to it, but because I want to see her reaction. Red splotches are appearing on her cheeks. "We talked about marriage." We hadn't, really—I'm nineteen and he was twenty, for Christ's sake—but now that I'm watching her react, I can't stop myself. It's like orchestrating a multicar collision—one designed for revenge. The feeling makes me heady, and I have to grip the podium tighter for support.

The words escaping my mouth are saccharine. I know if Charlie could see us (which he can't, because I know there's no heaven and thus no more Charlie), he'd make a gagging noise in the back of his throat and accuse me of being melodramatic.

"I really believe I'll be promised to Charlie in my heart forever,"

I conclude a minute later. I know I've provoked tears because I can hear the sounds of noses blowing and muted sobs, and I have to control the instinct to roll my eyes. I train my eyes on *her*; she looks like some kind of ghoul under those jet-black bangs and that wavy, messy bob. I wait for her to crack. To bolt upright and run away. The challenge hangs there for a minute; but she stares back at me, unflinching despite the horror written all over her face. She's tougher than she looks. I return to my seat and face front, forcing myself not to turn back. This weird, lightheaded feeling washes over me, like I was just two seconds from fainting up there.

As soon as the minister says some final words and invites everyone to a luncheon immediately following the service, I allow myself to turn halfway around in my chair as though I'm reaching for my purse. I look for her. She's not there. But the door to the foyer is just now swinging closed.

I run in the direction of the exit as fast as I can in my suede booties.

When I reach the foyer she's not there. I push through the glass-paned door and into the courtyard and trip over the cobblestones as I whisper a string of *shit*s to myself—how could she have disappeared so quickly? And then I spot her by the big, gated door that leads to the street. Twining yellow and pink roses stretch around the door frame. She's tugging on the handle like the tourist she probably is, and I almost laugh when she actually kicks the door with her prissy black pump. She mutters something under her breath as I approach.

"You have to press *Porte*," I go. "See, right here." I indicate the button on the stone wall to the left of the door. She moves toward it but I'm too quick. I step in front of the set of buttons—*Lumière* being the other option—and block them with my body. "It's weird, the way doors work here," I continue. "They're all the same. High-tech security. Serious stuff." I reach for my black leather tote and rummage for a cigarette. She's standing there, arms crossed over her chest, looking a mixture of angry and frightened. She still hasn't said anything. "Want one?" I extend the pack toward her. One of us has to make this less awkward, and it looks like it's going to be me.

"I don't smoke," she says in an American accent. It confirms my suspicions—an American like me, but without the international experiences that have rendered my own accent difficult to place. "Can you please step aside so I can go?" Her jaw is tight and her eyes are cloaked in dark circles. Far away she looked exotic and devastated. Up close she just looks tired and snotty.

"No," I mimic her. "I cannot."

"What do you want?"

"I can only guess from the way you were staring in there that you didn't know about me," I say matter-of-factly.

"What are you talking about?" she says, but her eyes dart downward. She knows—she must, after my speech. I peer at her closely before I continue, giving her a minute to be upfront. I'm not sure what game she's playing.

"You're the other girl," I say, when it becomes obvious she's determined to be silent. "I always knew he was cheating," I continue. "I just can't believe you had the balls to show up here. Oh . . ." I finish, deliberately trailing off. I'm sure she can't know how calculated my words are. She's definitely the sheltered type. "Don't tell me you were in love with him."

"Charlie was my *boyfriend*," she hisses, almost defensively. "Of course I loved him. I don't even know who you are." I didn't think she could shock me; now my blood runs cold. I knew Charlie had a thing with another American girl when he was spending the summer at NYU the year before. I'd even suspected maybe there'd been one or two more incidents. But someone he was serious enough about to consider his girlfriend? Not possible. I'd have known.

"You're delusional," I tell her. I suck at my cigarette and wait for the smoke to calm me. It doesn't. The girl's face turns into two faces and then a blurry blob before my line of vision. These are angry tears. I always cry when I'm pissed off. "Charlie and I dated for three years."

"We were together for a year," she tells me in an uncertain voice. "We just had our anniversary."

"You say that like he's still alive." I'm testing her, trying to gauge if she has the same suspicions I do.

"That's ridiculous," she snaps back, her eyes narrowing. "Of course he's dead."

I'm taken aback by her vehemence. There's a silence. There's the sound of her breathing hard, of me expelling more smoke. I breathe it in. I breathe it out. I hope when it leaves my lungs it'll take my pain with it.

"When?" I want to know. I have to know.

"When what?" She's stopped sniffling and is mopping her mess of a face with a tissue.

"When did you celebrate?" Charlie went water-skiing with some friends the second weekend of July. He'd canceled on a concert with me and I'd tried not to be angry. But it was an important concert, Vampire Weekend. Neither of us even liked them anymore, but it still meant something to me.

"July twelfth," she says. "We met up in Milwaukee."

I slump against the wall.

• • •

The first concert Charlie and I went to together was Vampire Week-end. That night, we had sex for the first time in a little room behind the sound pit. We could be as loud as we wanted because the mu-sic drowned us out; and the cacophony actually wound up forming a weird kind of silent bubble between us. It was the same sensation as when something's so cold it's hot — your body no longer knows how to sort out the sensations. Actually, that's how I always felt around Charlie.

Charlie's friend Derek hooked him up with the room, back near where the bands get ready. Derek's dad owns a record label, and it wouldn't be the first time he'd hook us up. The room was tiny but Charlie decorated it with posters of all my favorite bands: the New Pornographers, Vampire Weekend, M83. There was a row of chocolate-frosted cupcakes lined up on a table in the shape of L+C. There was a bed in the corner with a huge fluffy blue blanket and a bottle of champagne resting on the table next to it.

"It's your eighteenth," he told me softly. "I thought you deserved something special."

I turned from him, grabbed one of the cupcakes, and took a huge bite.

"Thanks for the cupcakes," I told him, trying hard to make my voice sound cool and aloof. "Not sure what you think is going to happen on that bed, though."

"I know exactly what's going to happen," he said. Then he lifted me up before I could stop him, and I got cupcake frosting all over my shirt, and he carried me over to the bed and dumped me down on top of a mountain of pillows. He grabbed the cupcake from my hands and ate the rest, licking his fingers. Then he was over me, and I was tasting

chocolate frosting on his tongue and wondering how the hell I got so lucky with Charlie Price. From the beginning, he picked me, not the other way around. After we first met, he never let me go. I'm still wondering exactly why — why me — every single day.

3

Aubrey

I COULD LEAVE NOW. IT WOULDN'T BE HARD; when the fairy-elf slumped down to the ground, her frame no longer obscured the exit button. But the way she reacted right now, going from tough girl to helpless in less than five seconds — it scares me. *I can't feel bad for her. I can't.* I feel bad about so many things that I think I'll never feel okay again.

I push the button. I hear the lock click. I tug at the handle and it yields to my grasp. But my feet are rooted. I feel myself turn back. I watch myself kneel next to her.

"Are you okay?" I ask. She's let her cigarette slip from between her fingers to the ground, where it burns the edge of a blade of grass. She doesn't answer but her eyes droop closed, and I panic. She's so pale, so thin.

I put my hand on her shoulder. I don't even remember her name.

"Hey," I say. "Are you all right?" For all I know, she has anxiety attacks or a weak heart or something. She nods slowly.

"I just need a second," she mutters. "But don't go anywhere. Please."

"Okay," I say. But I can see a few other mourners congregating in the foyer. Soon they'll wonder what we're doing.

"Actually," I say, "let's get out of here."

"Wouldn't want to cause a scene," she says, not bothering to look up.

"*Parisians* don't like scenes," I agree, and she laughs a little, even though it's not funny. I hold out my hand and she accepts it. The bones of her fingers feel frail as I pull her to her feet. We step through the door—which I can barely open, it's so heavy—and onto Rue de Buci. It's my first time in Paris since I was little, and everything is substantial and impressive, from the towering wooden doors to the thick metal posts that line the sidewalks.

I feel faint with Charlie's betrayal, even though I shouldn't. I have no right to be; and I don't know how Charlie can still surprise me. I glance at this girl's face and all I can see is a slideshow of him and her: kissing her, laughing with her, scooping her up in a big hug, balancing his muscular frame on top of her fragile one. My imagined idea of the two of them together is happier than the reality of him with me ever was. I turn without a word and set off toward the metro. I need to get away; that's the only thing in my head. Technically, I can't feel like a victim without also being a hypocrite. But that's the funny thing about feelings—they don't make any sense, they just *are*.

"Wait!" she calls after me. I hear her running to catch up, but I cross the street just as the light's changing. I look back to see her dodging traffic and feel my mouth fall open.

"Are you insane?" I ask when she catches up to me. "What's *wrong* with you?"

"Listen," she says, out of breath. "I'm guessing you're not heading to the funeral luncheon, right? Let's go sit at a café for a bit."

"I don't want to sit anywhere with you."

"I'm not the one who screwed you over," she points out. Appar-

THREE // AUBREY   19

ently she's gotten over her wilting damsel moment. "He obviously treated both of us like crap. Don't you want to know anything?" Her breath emerges in loud gasps that seem disproportionate to her stature. "I, personally, want to know what other bullshit Charlie fed us."

"Okay," I say after a moment's hesitation. "But I can't stay long."

"I know a place this way," she says, gesturing westward with her chin. The cobblestone street is packed with people and lined with shops of every kind: boulangeries with mille-feuilles and precariously stacked pastel macarons in their wide window displays; ice cream carts with miniature red and blue awnings; corner cafés with cheerful wicker chairs outside, front-facing so customers can people-watch; and flower shops boasting bouquets in every hue imaginable. There are a million options.

"There's a tea salon right here." I catch sight of a little Invader tag, just one example of the street art I've been seeing all over Paris since I arrived — something I'd love to photograph any other time — above the salon's awning. Charlie's other girlfriend looks at me like I'm crazy.

"I don't want tea," she says. "I need a drink."

I have a funny feeling that this girl and I would have been friends under different circumstances.

She leads me into a café: outside it has the same furniture as the rest of the cafés lining the street; but inside there are just a few red leather booths and some wooden tables. It feels like we could be anywhere in the world . . . *except* Paris, where aesthetics are celebrated and nearly everything is elaborately decorated.

"*Bonjour, mesdemoiselles,*" says the waiter. I merely smile and nod, but the fairy-elf breaks out in flawless French:

"*Bonjour, monsieur. Une table pour deux, s'il vous plaît?*"

"How do you know French?" I ask once we're seated. She shrugs, fiddling with a beautiful gold ring with a blue stone — real sapphire, if I had to guess. She twists it above her knuckle as she talks, alternately biting her thumbnail.

"I've done a lot of traveling. Plus I spent most of high school in Europe. Took French and Spanish and Portuguese and Latin in school. Anyway. I'm Lena. What's your name?"

"Aubrey," I tell her. It's funny that we went this long without exchanging names. *Lena.* I've definitely never heard the name before, coming from Charlie. She laughs, but it's a little flat.

"*You're* Aubrey?" she says, incredulous. "Jesus."

"What?"

"So you're the 'good family friend,'" she says, using air quotes.

"Is that really what he said?"

"Oh yes."

"I've never even met his parents."

That gives her some satisfaction, I can tell. "You know, I was always suspicious of you. I never met you and I've met everyone else, and yet he insisted you were this good friend from childhood, a neighbor or something from Paris. Jesus, he *was* full of shit, wasn't he?" It's almost too much to process. My whole body hurts, like I've just finished working out. I've felt guilty for so long about the wedge that had started to drive itself between me and Charlie. And now to realize maybe I should have been angry, too . . . that all the blame shouldn't have been on me . . . I'm surprised by how much it hurts. "You're dating a jazz musician, you know."

"What?" I'm completely confused now. Charlie was hopeless with music. He couldn't even sight read when I played the piano.

"Not true? Doesn't surprise me. That's just what Charlie told me. Apparently you're dating a jazz musician and the sex is—"

"STOP," I say, louder than I mean to. She stops, her jaw dropping open. A few people glance our way. "I'm sorry," I say, quieter now. "That's just—I can't believe he'd make something like that up. About me. His *family friend*."

"Tell me," she continues drily. "What about *my* fake identity? Let me guess: I used to be his babysitter? I'm banging a tattoo artist?"

"No," I tell her, shaking my head. "I've never heard of you. He never mentioned your name." The second I say it, I regret it.

"Fuck you," she says clearly, just as the waiter is bringing us our menus. Her face has gone white. She pushes her chair back, moving as if to leave.

"Lena! Stop." My voice is high and nervous. I feel terrible; I didn't mean to hurt her. I find myself reaching for her arm—we're reversing roles now; it's me after her. "I'm sorry—" I catch myself. I don't want to talk to this girl, because I don't know what I might say. Still, I know how bad she's feeling, because I'm feeling just as bad. It makes me want to be careful with her. I find myself holding her gaze. I try to let her know that way that I really *am* sorry—for both of us. The whole situation is like some nightmare I can't pull myself out of. She sighs and lets herself sink back into her seat.

"Goddammit," she says. "Fucking Charlie. I dated him for *three years*. I *never* cheated on him. I could have," she says. "But I never would have done that." I swallow hard against my guilt. The waiter is back to take our order. He's dressed in black with a white apron, and he holds his pad aloft, pen poised and ready. "Whiskey on the rocks," she tells him in English now; I guess her "flawless French" is only situational. "*Un double, s'il vous plaît. Elle prend un verre de vin blanc,*" she says, clearly ordering wine for me. "Do you want anything to eat?" she asks me. I shake my head. To my surprise, she orders herself a croque-monsieur.

We sit in silence for a minute and then the waiter's back with a glass of white wine for me and her whiskey and a sandwich slathered in cheese. I watch Lena take an enormous bite of her sandwich, then another and another—like she hasn't eaten in months. I've always been the opposite: when I'm sad, I can't eat at all.

"I just can't believe he never mentioned me," she says again between bites, and I realize all of a sudden what a blow that would be.

"I'm sorry," I say. "He probably just knew I'd get paranoid. I'm not an easy person to date." I'm mostly being nice, but there's some truth in it; I've always been quick to jealousy. I heard somewhere once that the ones who are most jealous are the ones who have something to hide.

"That asshole," she says, her voice low. "Charlie could be a real jerk sometimes, but I never, ever would have thought he was capable of this."

I clench my jaw. The Charlie I fell for was sweet and thoughtful, almost to a fault. He was always a gentleman . . . until he wasn't anymore. Just before he disappeared, I'd started to blame the darkness in our relationship on myself—on naiveté. On never really getting to know him the way a person should know someone she wants to love.

"Oh, he didn't show you that side of him?" She lets out a bitter laugh, mistaking my silence for disagreement. "Lucky you. Listen, Aubrey," she says then, leaning toward me. There's a dangerous spark in her eyes. "Don't you want to know who Charlie really was? Think about it. You and I could probably talk all day about his lies. But what else was he lying about that we don't even know? Charlie's dead," she says. I catch a glimmer of doubt in her eyes. Her voice rises in pitch, sounding false. "I'm fucking angry. I want to know everything. Every single lie he ever told."

"What are you saying?" I feel sorry for her; it's clear that she loves him despite everything, that maybe she's even holding on to the hope that he's alive. It's a desperate hope—even a crazy one. She's probably been driven over the edge by grief.

"I'm saying it's obvious Charlie was full of crap. And I want to know what else he was hiding." I listen as she fills the space between us with her stories: the time Charlie surprised her with chocolate cake (my favorite), thinking it was *her* favorite, even though she likes vanilla; the time he'd called her from a New York area code (he'd been meeting me) when he was supposed to be in London; the time he showed up with a toolish yellow polo shirt in his bag ("toolish" according to Lena—I'd always liked that shirt) and blamed it on his then roommate, Liam.

Two hours and several lattes later, we're still comparing notes. Lena's question—*What else was Charlie hiding?*—has opened a Pandora's box.

"Has it occurred to you that there might be more going on here?" I lean forward, resting my elbows on the table. "I mean, what if we're only part of the story? What if there's another girl, or a few?"

Lena laughs, but it has an empty ring to it. "Yeah, I mean, I just don't think Charlie was *that* smooth," she says. "Think how hard it probably was just juggling the two of us."

"I know what you're saying, but think about it," I say carefully. Lena doesn't seem to realize how manipulative he could be, and I'm not going to tell her. "We might have *no idea* who he really was. Also—" I stop myself abruptly. I don't want her to know anything about my last couple of months with Charlie.

"Yeah?" She looks suspicious. "Spit it out, Aubrey. What are you holding back?"

"It's nothing," I say, shaking my head. But it's not nothing. Charlie had something that belonged to me when he disappeared. If I'm lucky, it was inside the plane with him. But if it resurfaces . . .

"What's wrong?"

I drag my gaze to her face. She's looking at me strangely. "You look terrible. What is it?" I clamp my mouth shut. I feel faint. If what Charlie stole from me is ever found, my life will be over. For the millionth time, I wonder if it would have been easier to tell someone, but when I consider it, I can barely breathe. "Aubrey. What aren't you telling me?"

I lie before I can stop myself, fumbling for words. "He just said something weird to me the last time we talked. I don't even really know what he meant by it," I try. "He said, 'Aubrey, there's something I really need to tell you.' And I freaked out a little, because I thought he was cheating on me. So maybe that was it." I laugh awkwardly. I've never been good at lying, and I haven't gotten any better since I started doing it all the time. "He was probably just going to tell me he had another girlfriend." Out of habit, I reach for my sketchpad, catching myself before I can retrieve it from my bag. I withdraw my hand and struggle to breathe more normally.

"Then what?" Lena's tone is impatient. I think fast.

"He goes, 'It's nothing to worry too much about—it's just something I've been needing to tell you for a long time, since I got back from visiting my parents in London.' Remember, they were there for a few months, living in a hotel while his dad was leading some kind of training program?" Lena nods, motioning for me to continue. "Then I asked him what it was, and he just told me to stop asking questions, that I'd know in a couple of weeks." There's a lot I'm not telling Lena. But it's nothing she needs to know. Charlie is dead now. And maybe it's for the best. Charlie's death is an awful thing. Still, I'm not the grief-stricken girlfriend I'm pretending to be.

"We should go." Lena's voice breaks into my thoughts. It's strained and louder than before. A few people are looking our way again. "We should go to England and figure out what he was up to. We can blow apart his lies. Surely there's a lot you know that I don't, and same thing the other way around."

I pause before answering—I'm not sure what she's asking me to agree to. "Go where? What exactly are you suggesting?" I'm not comfortable forming the "we" of it.

"You should come back to London with me," she says slowly. "I, for one, want to know who else Charlie was fucking. We can go to all the places where he hung out. What was he doing when he went back there? Seeing friends? We can drop in on them, ask some questions. I knew him when he was in high school there. I know all of his friends there—they'll talk to me." She looks truly excited for the first time since we arrived at the café, and I wonder again whether she thinks she's going to track a living, breathing Charlie down and confront him herself. "We find out what he was hiding," she goes on. "School doesn't start back up for me till the last week of August. It's probably the same for you, right?"

I nod in response to her question. It's tempting . . . but not for the reasons Lena's mentioning. I only care a little about what Charlie was hiding. I'll be happy to put him in my past, to move on from this and have a normal life again. But I *do* need to know whether my secret—a secret no one in the world knew except Charlie—is safe. Only when I find and destroy the journal will I truly be able to move forward without fear.

It's horrible the way his death brings me a small measure of comfort. It makes me wonder who I've become. There was a time when I thought I might love Charlie. When I met him I thought, *Here is someone I could be close to.* I used to wonder what he might mean to me someday. I never would have thought that one day I'd face his death and feel only emptiness and relief.

Lena interrupts my train of thought. "What if . . . ?" she trails off, refusing to meet my eyes. "What I'm about to say is totally crazy," she qualifies. "But I can't stop thinking it." I press my lips together and wait. "What if he faked his death? What if he's alive?"

I stare back at her, incredulous. "Do you know what you're saying?" I ask. "Staged his death and, what, somehow caused a plane to explode in midair? What about the jacket they found with his blood on it?"

She clamps her mouth shut and her cheeks turn red.

"Listen, Lena," I say in a softer tone. "I get that it's hard to let him go. It isn't like I haven't hoped the same thing." I've actually hoped for the opposite, but Lena can't know that. "Of course, I hoped it more so when I didn't know the truth about *you*," I amend. She lets out a bitter laugh and I flush. "But what you're saying is nuts," I force myself to finish.

Lena's eyes darken. Am I the only one concealing something?

"You're right," she says finally. "He's dead. But this thing you say he was going to confess to you and never did. I want to know for sure what he meant. Are you in?"

"No," I tell her, my heart pounding. "I can't go with you." Part of me wants to. I know I'll never feel truly safe until I have my journal back. Another kind of girl might take Lena up on her offer—follow her boyfriend's ghost to London like some sort of female crusader team. But I can't do it. I don't have the money, for one. And I came to the memorial service for closure. I thought I wanted it. But all this trip has done is thrust me into a spiral of panic and guilt.

"Why don't you just dig around online?" I ask. "Email his friends, try to figure it out that way?"

Lena shakes her head. "No way," she says. "It's too easy to lie in emails. People feel more accountable when they're faced with a real human."

Lena didn't strike me as particularly strategic; she seemed wild and careless. But of course she's smart. So was Charlie. So am I.

"I'm not coming," I tell her. "I don't want to know anything else." Normality is what I've been craving ever since my conversation with Charlie in the hotel that day, months ago. Since before that, really. Since the incident that set it off. I want my old life back.

Lena nods, but she looks disappointed. She digs through her bag, brings out a scrap of paper and a pen, and scribbles something on it. She throws down a few euros on the table and takes a final sip of her latte. Then she pushes the scrap of paper in my direction.

"In case you change your mind," she tells me. "I'm due to head back to London on the eight a.m. Eurostar from Gare du Nord tomorrow morning anyway. That's my train number and my mobile number and that's my address in the city."

Then she walks out of the restaurant without looking back. Maybe she can get away with jetting all over Europe, but for me the stakes are higher. I'm not the type to just whisk off to London, throwing down cash and taking risks. I have a family that worries when I'm not around. I barely even got clearance to come to Paris. I crumple up the paper and shove it in my back pocket, willing myself to throw it away.

4

Lena

TRUTHFULLY, AUBREY'S KIND OF LAME. I don't know what Charlie saw in her. She's pretty, sure. Hotter than me, if I'm honest. But she's got a stick up her ass like I can't believe. I can't believe Charlie cheated on *me* with *her*. She was probably awful in bed with their boring, responsible, condom sex. I wonder if Charlie really lost his virginity to me, the way he said. At least if he was telling the truth, I have that on her.

The thought of her in bed with him . . . It's a thought I'll probably never be able to get rid of.

I take the metro at Odéon and make my way back toward the 10th, where the streets come alive in the vibrant Canal Saint-Martin neighborhood, with its picturesque bridges arching above wide waterways. It's usually my favorite part of Paris, but today the sight of the canal's tree-lined banks and iron footbridges does nothing to lift my mood. I'm crashing in the neighborhood with an old friend from boarding school. When my parents heard I was coming here and not staying with my aunt and uncle, they flipped. But my aunt's worried eyes and my uncle's hacking cough and the way my cousin Elodie hangs on me would have sent me into a rage spiral.

Carey's asleep when I walk in. It doesn't surprise me. Carey's a stoner type, inherited family money and all that. He's into the party scene over here, which isn't all that different from the London scene: all-night raves fueled by E and Special K. Then he comes down from it and lies around smoking pot until he has his energy back up. Carey doesn't even work. He's just a useless, lazy bum. And he can afford to be. He's sprawled out on the leather sofa in only his boxers, his skinny white legs draped over the sofa arm. A trail of drool is trickling from one side of his mouth. Truthfully, I'm always waiting a little anxiously for the day when I get the call that Carey's in the hospital or in prison. I kick him once, hard. He grunts a little but doesn't move. I've been counting on Carey for distraction, but he's as useless as always.

It hits me in a wave so forceful that I crumple to the ground next to the sofa, feeling the harsh, splintered wood of the floor snag and rip my tights. *Charlie is gone.* His hands, weaving through mine. The way he whispered in my ear just before moving to kiss my neck. The muscles of his back under my fingers. His arms wrapped around me on a cold day, the scruff of his facial hair against my cheek, tickling. Making me laugh. Wrapping me into his coat with him in the park, and pulling me down into the snow. His lips on mine as he hovers above me. His nickname for me. All of it, gone. Ripped away. And I didn't even know he'd been ripping it away slowly all this time. All the times he said he'd meet me and he didn't, all the phone calls I waited for that never came, the distance: physical and emotional and always brutal.

Charlie's gone, but he could still be alive. Aubrey thought I was crazy when I said it; but she doesn't know what I know. And I'm not ready to tell her . . . yet. Not when I don't trust her. I don't realize how loudly I'm crying until I feel Carey's hand on my head, pushing my hair back. He scoots down from the couch and settles next to me on the floor, guiding me into his shoulder.

"You can snot on me if you like," he says. I look at his bloodshot eyes and laugh over my tears and curl up into his side. He pushes me forward and arranges a pillow behind my back. I nestle my head on his shoulder and begin to fade. Without Carey, I'd never have lasted as long as I did with Charlie. Without him I'd have cracked long ago. This is what I'm thinking as I drift off.

I wake up in Carey's bed at four a.m. He's gone—probably back out at whatever party he's managed to sniff out. It's actually perfect timing because my train leaves for London at eight, and without coffee I'm hopeless, and I have lots to pack. I take a quick shower in his bathroom, then dig an old towel out of the dirty clothes bin, trying hard to ignore its musty smell. The maid must be due to come any day; Carey never does his own laundry. I scrawl a quick note to him on the corner of a receipt: *Thanks, babe. Cookies on the counter.* I made my favorite for him yesterday morning before the funeral. Baking is more of a way to calm my nerves than any kind of hospitable gesture, but he won't know that. I made white chocolate macadamia. Charlie was allergic to macadamias.

I know part of what I'm feeling for Charlie is grief. I've lost this love I thought I had, but apparently never did. Grief isn't what's driving me to London, though. It's anger. If Charlie's alive, he needs to pay for what he's done to me. If only Aubrey were there, it would be that much sweeter, making him face both of us at once. But either way, I'll confront him. I'll make him tell me to my face that he was cheating on me. I'll find out what the fuck he was lying about besides Aubrey. He doesn't get to be a coward and leave this mess for us to deal with. He owes me more than that.

At six o'clock, I throw my duffel over my shoulder and make my way out the door, pulling it shut behind me. I stop in quickly at the boulangerie on the corner. When I open the door to the shop, I'm assaulted by a fresh, yeasty smell, left over from the morning's baking. I buy a café and an almond croissant, my favorite when I'm in Paris. The croissant is still warm when I bite into it, but as with the canals, it's hard to take joy in the simple Parisian pleasures I usually treasure. Then I take off in the direction of Gare du Nord. I haven't thought much more about what I'll do when I get back to London. I haven't thought about much at all since Aubrey and I parted.

I was hoping Aubrey would show up before I left. I gave her my cell phone number and Carey's address, and I'd be lying if I said I didn't wait an extra ten minutes before leaving for the station or check my phone obsessively for unfamiliar numbers.

I know I can track down Charlie's skeletons without Aubrey's help. But beyond the satisfaction of seeing his face when he sees both of us together—if we find him and force him to own up—something Aubrey said yesterday hit me hard. *Charlie never mentioned you.* So if he didn't mention me—the girl he spent three years of his life with, including one year when we were practically inseparable—what did he talk about? Who was he? I only know Charlie as an extension of myself, and I need to find out who the hell this other Charlie was. Because apparently I've had no fucking idea. I saw one angle, the one he chose to show me. Now I need the rest. And she holds the key to at least another cache of something important. I can interview his friends, his teachers, all I want. But I'll only be able to detect the lies that conflict with *my* Charlie. I'll never be able to tell about all the rest, not without her help.

Charlie always liked to have the last word.

But not anymore, not in this.

I pass through the crowds quickly, stopping only to validate my ticket. Gare du Nord has an impressive arched and pillared exterior, but the inside is an ugly place, a great big mix of travelers and beggars and shopkeepers. There's a little stall selling "Manhattan hotdogs" for five euros each. There are train times and destinations digitally projected onto a large screen that hovers in front of me and at least a dozen tracks with trains waiting to depart. I find my train to London St Pancras Station on the board and work my way over to track 6, nearly stumbling over a baby stroller. "*Pardon*," I say to the baby's mother, but she fixes me with a stiff glare. I'm heading to car 15 when I feel a hand on my wrist. Fingernails dig hard, piercing my skin. I jump and swivel. Everything I've been feeling this weekend bubbles to the surface.

"Christ!" I yell at Aubrey, causing several other travelers to turn our way. "You can't just grab me like that." I'm breathing hard, stooping over my knees. Somehow the encounter has shaken me up in a big way.

"I'm sorry," she says. "Seriously, I just wanted to get your attention."

"Well, you did," I tell her in a hard voice. "Congrats on that. What are you doing here?"

She responds by waving her ticket in my face. I squint at the small type, doubting her up to the moment I see confirmation of a single journey to London St Pancras.

"You changed your mind?"

"I want to know what else Charlie was hiding," she says. Her voice is cold. My eyes meet hers. She's unwavering—calmer and more confident than yesterday. "Here's the deal," she continues. "I have, like, a few hundred dollars. That's it. I can't come for long. So we'd better make this worth it. And—" Her voice cracks. She shakes her head like she doesn't want to say more.

"What?" I challenge.

"He had something of mine. My journal. I want it back."

Now it's my turn to nod, just as the last bell rings to signal the train's departure. If some stupid journal is what's bringing her with me, then fine. "Okay, then. I guess I'll see you in London."

"See you in London," she agrees. Her mouth is drawn in a cool line, and with a night's sleep, some of her sharp, cold beauty is back. Then she turns, and we both part for our separate cars.

I've almost reached mine when I turn to watch her recede into the crowd. The thing I can't figure out—the thing this whole crazy idea I had depends on—is whether I can trust her.

Because I know she can't trust me.

5

Aubrey

"List of . . . sofas you've spilled wine on. Go."

I sigh, twirling a bit of loose fringe between my thumb and forefinger. I'm lying on a beach towel that's covering my shady hostel mattress, sketching characters on my little pad of paper as we talk. Mercifully, my notebook doesn't seem to interest Lena—she hasn't asked to see it, even though she's pried into every other aspect of my life.

We sprang for a single-sex quad, which amounts to two sets of bunk beds in a closet-size room with a single light bulb and a narrow shower stall in a corner. Luckily it's just us in the room. We each chose a top bunk on opposite sides of the room. There's a shared toilet in the hallway. The light bulb flickers a little and its chain sways in the breeze that comes through the open window—we're trying to air out the putrid, musty smell that's probably coming from the mattresses. I don't want to speculate on its cause.

By now I know that Lena's lists are mostly for her benefit—so she can tell stories about herself—but I try to play along. I don't know why we're not staying with one of the supposed million friends she has here in London, where she was headed anyway, where she has family and all that. When I agreed to come out here, I'd assumed she'd thought it through. I assumed she had someplace for me to stay. Now I see that was pure stupidity on my part.

"I've never spilled wine on any sofas," I tell her. I pull the edges of my beach towel around me, but it's futile. I'll never be warm. "First of all, I'm technically not supposed to be drinking when I'm in the U.S. It's not like I sit around sipping wine with my friends all day. I mean, I'm eighteen. Secondly, when I do manage to procure booze, it's usually guys who get it, and it's usually beer." Lena already knows I've done much less, seen much less, than she has. She wishes I've felt much less; at least when it comes to Charlie. I know she wants to believe that she and Charlie were more special than we were; and they probably were. But she doesn't know that.

"Procure," she mocks. I try not to blush. "You're so cute, Aubrey," she says in a condescending tone. Maybe it's because she looks elfin and wide-eyed that she can get away with so much. Or maybe it's that people like me don't hold her accountable.

"How about you?"

"There was my best friend's sofa, twice," she says, propping herself up on one elbow. "Nothing a Tide pen can't correct. Then my parents' sofa, which was kind of a problem because it was crazy expensive. You should have seen the way my mom's eyes bugged out when she saw it . . . and then I poured a bunch of baking soda over it because I thought I had read somewhere that it would absorb the stain, but it actually made it worse. Then there was the leather sofa in the rental apartment I—"

"Lena." I break in while I can still control my tone. "Can we talk about something that matters? Like why we're here?" I was hoping to keep my voice neutral, but she bristles.

"I was just trying to lighten the mood. If we're going to be friends, we can't just dwell on the reason we're here all the time. Talk about depressing."

"I don't want to be your friend," I tell her. "I'm not here for that."

"Well," she continues, in a falsely cheerful tone. "Thanks for being clear."

"I'm sorry," I say. "It's not that I wouldn't want to be your friend otherwise. You're great. I — I can see why Charlie cared about you. I only meant that I want to figure out what was going on with Charlie," I say. "What he wanted to tell me that day. And I want to find my journal."

"Okay. Thanks for the compliments, I guess, but seriously, spare me. He clearly wanted to tell you about *me,* that day you had that conversation. It must have been the big secret. Maybe he tried to tell you and got scared, so this was the big way of doing it. Disappear. Vamoose. Gone in a puff. Laugh from afar when ex-girlfriends collide. Sounds about right for Charlie."

"That sounds nothing like Charlie," I tell her, my voice uncharacteristically hard. "You've got to stop saying stuff like this. He didn't have the guts to stage something so elaborate."

"Holy hell, Aubrey," Lena says, lying back on her cot. "I think you have some anger management issues. You seem all nice, and then you say the craziest stuff."

I press my lips together and turn over on my side. It's only night one. If I'm going to make this work with Lena for even another day, I've got to fake things a little. It'll be no good if she's already sensing the truth.

"Anyway," Lena goes on, her voice softer now — almost like she's afraid of what she's about to say. "Charlie used to talk to me about disappearing all the time. He used to fantasize about it."

"What are you talking about?" My words are clipped, my jaw tense.

"He never said anything to you?" I shake my head, even though Lena can't see it.

"He talked a lot about how he'd disappear if he could. Start over, leave everything behind. And I'd always be like, 'You do that anyway. You move around, you get to make new friends and try new schools. It's always a new beginning for you.' Because it was; that was kind of his thing. The exhilaration he'd feel every time he moved or went somewhere new. I used to think it was sexy. I used to think he liked adventure. But later I got it. He just liked running away."

"You really think he could be alive," I say. It's not a question; I can tell what she thinks from the conviction in her tone.

"I do. I think he did this shitty thing to us and told us in his own way, and disappeared. How did you find out he was missing, Aubrey?"

"There was a news blast. An email with headlines. 'Oxford University student missing since Sunday,' or something like that. Then I Googled around."

"Ever think he wanted you to know? Did you get that news blast regularly? Charlie was a freaking genius with computers. He could have pushed it into your inbox."

I pause, thinking. Yeah, I had signed up for Oxford's student paper, the *Cherwell,* but only after Charlie had encouraged me to. *To expand your cultural horizons and learn more about Oxford,* he'd said. I'd liked it because it made me feel closer to his world. "It's possible," I admit. "But not likely. He's *dead,* Lena. They found his jacket."

"Yeah," she says. "And that's the only thing they found. But I'm just saying . . . maybe he brought us together for a reason."

"Are you here looking for answers or looking for him?"

"It doesn't matter," she says, her words cold. "Him, I guess. If I'm completely honest. And when I find him, I'm going to tear him apart. You and me both, Aubrey. I'm not letting him get away with this. I'm not going to be some joke to him, wherever he is." I'm surprised by the heat now in her voice.

"He's dead," I try again. *He's dead, he's dead, he's dead.* I repeat it until I realize how desperately I want it to be true. I *need* it to be true.

"But maybe not."

"He has to be!" I shout it this time. There's a silence so long and deep that I think it'll never end. I've done it. I've given myself away.

"I'm angry too," she says finally. "Just a different kind of angry."

Only then can I breathe a sigh of relief. She doesn't know my secret. How could she? But soon maybe she'll figure it out, if I'm not careful.

"New list," she says into the silence, her voice falsely bright. "Ten things you hated about Charlie." When I don't answer right away, she says, "Go." I rack my brain, thinking of things that are safe to say.

"I hated how he always walked on the outside of the sidewalk," I start. "And took the side of the bed closest to the door. I hated how he always tried to be chivalrous."

Lena is silent for a minute. "Go on."

"I hated how he brushed his teeth."

Lena laughs a little, lightening the atmosphere. "I know what you mean. That weird gargling noise."

"I hated that he always said he wanted a soda, and bought himself a soda and took two sips and threw it away, instead of just drinking a couple sips of my soda. I always offered. I hated that he looked at me weird when I laughed too loudly. I hate that he knew how to hack, and thought it was hilarious to spam my email account with fake messages from unfunny names like 'Hank E. Panky.' I hated that he didn't see street art on the sidewalks even when it was right in front of his face. I hated that every fight we had, he wanted to hold me immediately after to make it all better. I hated that at restaurants, if there was even a tiny speck of an olive, he'd make them take the whole plate back." I'm building steam. I'm on a roll. I have this heady euphoric feeling, the same feeling I get when I hit mile six when I'm running. Like I can keep on going and going, an object in motion staying in motion.

"Wait." Lena cuts me off. "What are you talking about? He loves olives."

"Charlie *hates* olives more than anything," I correct her. He wouldn't even let me keep them in his mini fridge. And I love them. I eat them with egg salad, PB&J, you name it.

"No, no, no," Lena says, sitting bolt upright in bed. "You're wrong. You're thinking of someone else. He adores them. He literally used to bring them into bed and eat them in front of me. It was gross. He wouldn't brush his teeth afterward and his breath reeked. That was the one time I wouldn't have minded the gargling."

"You're sure they were olives? And not, like, figs?" I'm trying to ignore the icky feeling *bring them into bed* thrusts at me. My parents are so strict that Charlie and I only got overnight time during the nights I stole with him here and there in random cities in between lies I told.

"Jesus. I know the difference between an olive and a fig."

I look, expecting to find her face twisted in scorn, but instead she looks worried. Her blond brows are wrinkled up so tight that they're joined in the middle. She kind of looks . . . I squint.

"Are you about to cry?" I ask.

"No!" she says in the unmistakable tone of a person about to cry. "You're just wrong. Your whole list was wrong. And I don't want to sit here and listen to it. It's like you're trying to manipulate me. Are you trying to mess with me? Why would you want me to think I don't know my own boyfriend? I was with him for three years." Now she's definitely crying. "God, I don't want him to be dead," she says quietly when her tears begin to subside. "It's too hard."

"Lena," I start. Her feelings for him — her desperation for him to be alive — make her look like a drowning girl. I'm not here on this trip to find Charlie, like she is. I'm here to find what he stole from me.

"Forget it," she says, sniffling. "Let's go to sleep." The way she says it, there's no choice. So I lean over and pull on the grimy string attached to the single light bulb that hangs from the cracked, splotchy ceiling. I lie awake for an hour. I keep thinking about the olives thing. I had been serious about it. That really was one of the things I hated most. It was embarrassing, and weird, and psychological. The Charlie I knew — this is the important thing to clarify — *the one I knew* hated olives. He couldn't stand the sight of them. He was forever digging them out of things and putting them on the side of my plate. Lena's Charlie, from the sound of it, loved olives. She had no reason to lie about that and I don't think she's a good enough actress for her tears to have been a show. So who was the real Charlie?

Until right now, I didn't realize that maybe Charlie gave us each a different version of himself. What does it mean? Was Lena's Charlie the real one, because it's easier to deny oneself pleasures than to force displeasure? Or if Charlie tailored himself to what he thought we'd each want, why had he always scoffed at my preference for graphic novels over classic literature and my interest in maybe one day attending school for illustration? What was he hoping to achieve? That was the last thought I remember having before I drifted off, pulling the towel edges around me as far as they'd reach.

My watch reads one o'clock when Lena shakes me awake; and for a second, I'm confused, because it's still dark as night out. Then I realize: it *is* night. There's movement from behind Lena, and a guy in a black hoodie moves toward me, his head barely clearing the top bunk, so I see only eyes and a tuft of brown hair peeking from beneath the hood. I scream. Lena clamps her hand over my mouth.

"Get up," she whispers. "We're going out."

"Out where?" I don't want to go out. I don't trust this person; I can only see his eyes, but usually all you need are the eyes in order to trust. I can't read them, no matter how hard I try.

"Xander knows this club," she says. "It's getting started right now."

"Seriously? Now? It's one a.m.!" I'm saying this but I'm thinking, *So this is Xander.* Charlie mentioned him, said he was one of his good friends from the London days, back when he was a sophomore and junior in high school. I'm wondering if he's as good a guy as Adam—if he can be trusted like I instinctively knew Adam could, when I first met him. And I'm also thinking, *How did Lena know how to find him?* She's full of secrets, I'm just beginning to learn, and it doesn't sit well with me. I didn't even know Lena knew about Xander before now, though I should have guessed it. Of course she did—London was where she first met Charlie. She knows all about his life here.

"Is she coming or what?" Xander says to Lena.

"Relax," she tells him. Then to me: "Aub, Charlie partied at Fabric all the time. Xander's a lead; but so are all the others who hang out there. There are tons of people there who knew him." She's right. It's a lead, and obviously the kind we'd need to explore in the middle of the night.

"You should have prepped me," I tell her as I climb down from the bunk. By the time my feet hit the cold tile floor, I can see she's already dressed, almost like she first planned on going without me —and I wouldn't put it past her. I'm going to have to be a lot more wary of this girl. She's wearing a black miniskirt so short it barely covers her butt, with a loose, plain white tank top that has armholes so wide you can see half her rib cage—and her Day-Glo pink bra underneath.

"Z," she says, tugging Xander's hoodie. "Go get the bike. We'll meet you out front in five."

"Z?" I ask, as I pull on my jeans. "Isn't Xander spelled with an *x*?"

"Duh," says Lena. "It's phonetic. Are you always such a nerd? Oh. You can't wear that." She's looking at my outfit like I'm wearing something straight out of *Little House on the Prairie*. "I knew I'd have to be the prepared one," she says with a sigh, and I can't help smiling as she rummages through her brown canvas duffel. "Here." She whisks her arm through the air, and a slinky gold thing traces a path from her hand to my lap.

"So I'll wear it with my jeans."

"It's a dress. Just don't wear a thong." She winks and hands me a pair of high, strappy shoes. "What shoe size are you?"

"Eight." I'm still eyeing the dress warily. "I literally won't be able to lift my arms," I say.

"Eight's perfect! Me too. Maybe Charlie has a thing for average-sized feet." Her joke hurls me back into the present, into the dreary little hostel and into the reason we're even here. Sometimes when I'm not paying attention, I find myself liking Lena a little. I think about what Charlie must have loved about her, and wonder if I could care about her too. But when I catch myself thinking that way, it feels like I'm betraying myself.

"Are you sure we're going to find something at Fabric?" I ask her.

"No," she says. "But it's the first place I thought to look. And Xander can get us in. He's always had a thing for me."

"That's funny," I say. "Because I knew about Xander. But I thought he was this totally geeked-out gamer. I didn't realize he was such a clubgoer."

"Holy shit," Lena says. "Did Charlie tell you he was a gamer? No. No way. Charlie probably never played a video game in his life, and Xander's his club buddy, weed hookup, you know. That guy." My heart's pounding and I'm about to protest that actually, Charlie wasn't the clubber type. He was super into philosophy, and claimed to have a soft spot for video games, both of which made him kind of a nerd. He told me he'd smoked weed once and hated it because it made him paranoid. But she's already pulling me out the door. I do my best to tug the gold slinky thing farther down my thighs — then give up when I realize it's just not possible.

I think of Charlie's eyes as we walk to the corner where Xander's waiting. "Thanks for giving us a ride," I remember to tell him, and he nods back. Charlie's eyes were blue, a pretty blue. Not bright like mine but paler, practically gray. They were always wide and direct but even when I first met him, I had the strange feeling that I couldn't see beyond them into his soul. And then later, he started talking about how he didn't believe in the soul's existence.

It's occurring to me belatedly that it's all relevant, all tied up in this terrible nightmare; but then we're squeezing in behind Xander and speeding off on his BMW motorcycle past the formidable, towering lions that guard Trafalgar Square—*how much money does this guy have? He's only, like, nineteen*—and I'm hating, hating, hating Charlie even more than ever, for the awful ways he's lied to me and because he thought he had me pegged. He was so sure the guy he presented me—the "safe" one who played video games and read philosophy and hung out with fellow nerds—was someone I could love.

6

Charlie

YOU LOOK AT HER AND ALL YOU SEE are her huge blue angel eyes. But you already have an angel. Sometimes she's blond, sometimes a redhead, always wild. *Lena,* you remind yourself. You have to remind yourself of her name a lot lately, like if you don't say it aloud it'll disappear into the U.K. or Boston—at boarding school or into her family's palatial house—along with her face and body and the way she laughs. If you don't say her name every now and then, she'll cease to exist. She'll become one of the stories you make up for the guys, a hot lay and a tongue ring and *bang.* Your stories always pack it, whether they're real or not.

This one isn't wild like Lena. She's guarded, vulnerable. You've got a sixth sense about people. They always say it: the teachers, the therapists, even your mom when she talks around that cigarette. Your dad doesn't say it because—where is he? Bangalore, Abu Dhabi, Shihezi . . . and you're in London, Paris, Bombay, wherever the closest and best international boarding school is. And your dad's off being a diplomat and making other families but not necessarily taking care of them, and your mom's just smoking that cigarette, telling you you've got a sixth sense.

"Let me help you," you tell the girl, just as a sweaty guy wearing a wife-beater that doesn't cover his gut bumps hard into her shoulder. All these people, these commuters—they walk around her like they're a creek and she's a rock in the middle of it. She looks at you with hesitation, so you flash her the charming smile that's seen results. She's got two suitcases and for the whole thirty seconds you've been watching her, she's been yanking them up the subway stairs. The wheels of one suitcase catch on an old, wadded-up napkin and drag it up with her. Drag, lift, bump. Drag, lift, bump. It's dumb because there are, like, thirty stairs and at this rate it'll take her thirty minutes and then people will really get pissed. As she leans to the left to leverage her weight, her shoulder brushes against the grimy, tiled walls. New York City subway stations aren't places where you want to touch anything, not even the things specifically meant for touching, like wooden benches and elevator buttons.

"Okay," she says a little reluctantly, and she hands you the bigger one.

"You sure you've got the little one?" You want to be certain she knows you're a gentleman, the kind of guy who gives a shit. She smiles and nods and heaves the smaller load the rest of the way without much trouble. You walk behind her so you can check out her ass.

Lena, Lena, Lena, you remind yourself, biting your cheek hard, like it's some kind of mortal sin to check out another girl. (*It is.*)

Then you get it. It sweeps across you, this tidal wave of revelation:

If you *don't* say Lena's name, she's imaginary. When you're *not with her,* does she exist? She may as well not, except in your imagination. The brain, Adam always said, likes to play tricks.

All this right now could be an illusion. Lena could be a fantasy, Aubrey could be 110-degree heat making watermarks on asphalt. You get me.

You're nineteen when you meet Aubrey. She's seventeen; it's the summer after her junior year. You're getting a few extra college credits at NYU. She's moving a bunch of stuff out of a boyfriend's dorm room.

A whole existence passes between the bottom of the 6 train landing (at Bleecker) and the top. When you emerge into daylight, there's an intersection with a gas station and the thrum of steady SoHo traffic sweeping across Lafayette. You decide to kiss her, just not right then. You bide your time.

"What do you have in here?" you ask her. You're a little out of breath and trying not to sound like it. She brushes her short, wavy black hair out of her eyes. It's glossy, like the fabric of your dad's ties. Silk. Her eyes are blue and her skin is so pale you can make out the veins beneath her lids. Her lips are red and chapped. She bites the bottom one.

"Clothes, books, some shoes," she says. She reaches for the handle but you act like you don't see. Now that you've got her, you're not letting her walk away.

"Visiting the city?" (You don't know yet that she's moving her shit out of her boyfriend's place.)

"Wouldn't that be nicer than reality," she says back. You like her right away because she says what's on her mind. She's wearing a white T-shirt that's just a little see-through. You can make out the sunburn on her chest and the faint gray of her bra. Her shirt's tucked into a black skirt with a tight waistband. The black skirt is long, all the way to her calves, like she's Amish or Hasidic. But then she's wearing these cute little red shoes on her feet and you know she's just weird in the broader sense. Her left hand has four gold rings on it. She sees you staring and puts it in her pocket. Then she sighs a little, and you have to stop yourself from moving closer to breathe her air.

"Look, I'm obviously not wanting to talk about it," she says.

"I don't know about that. Otherwise you would have left already. But it's cool. I understand." Beads of sweat appear on her lip and she blinks. "My apartment's just there." You beckon vaguely in the direction of Prince Street. "If you want some water."

"The bodega's just there," she goes. She waves in the opposite direction, toward a green-and-white-striped awning down the block off Houston, where the quieter streets wind away from the chaos of Broadway-Lafayette house boutiques and cafés and stores. Sassy.

"But my water doesn't cost four dollars."

"You're not some creep, are you?"

"Nope. Just a guy with free water who has a quick break in between Comparative Lit and Nichomachean Ethics," you say. You know that'll get her, the school thing. You know it'll make you sound safe. (*Because you're not.*) You shake your head hard.

"You okay?" she wants to know.

"Let's go," you say. "Where else do you have to be?"

"I was going to get a cab," she says. "To nowhere. I'm moving my stuff out of my boyfriend's dorm. I was living with him all summer. We just broke up."

"You have nowhere to go?"

"I have nowhere to go. Nowhere to be, either."

"Good thing I found you, then." You grab the other suitcase and start walking. You don't look back because you can feel her behind you. You feel like, *This is it. This is the new reality.* And a surge of ecstasy goes through you, just because it's even possible to create a new reality in the space of a set of stairs.

Turns out Aubrey's parents have no idea she was living with the boyfriend. He's a freshman at NYU and she normally lives in Illinois, but she got an unpaid internship in New York City to be with him. She's about to start her senior year in high school. The ex-boyfriend was from high school, a year ahead. He threw her cell phone at the wall when he broke up with her, approximately forty-seven minutes before you offered to help with her bags. Her parents think she's been living at her friend Rae's, but she can't even go there because Rae has a boyfriend, a little sister in town, and a dog Aubrey's allergic to.

She tells you all this while you're sitting in your studio. (*You have an East Village studio because your parents still wipe your ass for you.*) You keep your studio blank, like a canvas, aside from some furniture that was there when you moved in. You do it on purpose because who knows who you'll feel like being when you wake up? Say you wake up to a poster of the Knicks and you just fucking hate the New York Knicks that day? So you keep it all blank, zen. Plus you're in town for, like, six weeks. It's just not enough time to commit.

"You can stay in my bed and I can stay on my blowup mattress," you tell her. "Till you get a place." You're not going to kiss her yet. She's not that kind of girl. You want to be the kind of guy that's right for her kind of girl.

"No way," she says. "I don't do spontaneity." She means it, you can tell. She pokes her pinky through the handle of the yellow coffee mug you've given her, filled to the brim with iced coffee, the

Stumptown brand they sell in glass bottles at the bodega. She pokes her finger in, she pokes it out. You wonder if she's teasing you. (*She's not; you're just being an asshole.*) You want to kiss her. Her eyelashes are so long, they rest against her cheeks even when she's just looking down. She's thinking.

"I think I'll probably just go home," she says. "The internship was at Condé Nast, and I wasn't getting paid anyway. It was just a front for getting out here. It's not like I want to get into publishing. I was only out here for Kevin."

"Well then," you say. She's not wholly at ease and won't be until she's convinced you're a good guy. "Why don't you at least use my wifi"—you say it "wee-fee," because that's how they say it in Paris and you forget; she smiles, and it's an accidental mark in your favor —"for booking flights or whatever? And you can borrow my cell to call your parents. Seriously. Take your time." Without waiting for her reply, you stand up from the table and grab a book from the shelf that was already there and stocked when you moved in. *The Unbearable Lightness of Being.* It's the right book; you know it by the way her eyes light up. You knew she'd be a book girl, a Kundera girl. You've known other girls like her. Still, she doesn't say anything. She's not giving in so easily.

An hour goes by and she types on your computer and breathes into your phone and you pretend to read *The Unbearable Lightness of Being.* Finally when you're so bored and hungry you think you're going out of your mind—images of cheese naan and chicken korma are playing dodge ball through your head—she gets up from the table and sits near you on the foldout futon you're using as a bed. Just perches on the edge like she doesn't want to get too close. Clasps her hands in her lap, even.

"Thank you," she says in a sweet, quiet voice. She still can't look you in the eye.

"It's no big deal," you say.

"No, really." She lifts her head and you see her wet, shiny eyes. "I didn't know what I was going to do. I didn't have any plan. I wish I could take you out to dinner or something. My flight doesn't leave until nine. But I'm flat broke. I'm so embarrassed."

"So I'll take you out to dinner," you tell her. "My parents still give me an allowance. You can thank me next time." She wiggles an eyebrow at you.

"When's next time?" she wants to know, all disbelieving.

"When you visit me. Now that we're dating." You crack a cocky, mischievous grin so she knows you're messing with her and not crazy (*you are crazy*); and in that second you know you've got her. Then you two go out for the best Indian food you've had outside of Bombay. Halfway through the meal, your phone lights up. It says, *Lena.* And for a second you're shocked because you really believed, for the space of maybe an hour, that you had made Lena up. Digital technology says you didn't.

Guilt rolls over you. It's so strong it activates your gag reflex. But then you put everything back in order in your brain. Lena on one side—she's not in front of you, so she must be a fantasy—and Aubrey on the other. Aubrey's in front of you, so she's real. (*At least for right now.*) You don't know what'll happen when she gets on that plane tonight and disappears. All of a sudden you're deeply afraid. You put down your fork and watch the piece of chicken you speared slide back into its creamy, almond-flavored sauce.

7

Lena

THE CLUB'S BUMPING; IT'S HARD FOR ME not to wiggle my hips like I'm here just to party. Rushmore and Cid Rim are tag teaming, spinning a good mix. I feel that old familiar thrill when I take Z's arm and he leads us downstairs, through the hidden entrance, past all the girls waiting and glaring. We're prettier, more powerful, we *know someone*. It never gets old. I just want to dance, dance, dance, and the feeling's shooting through every part of my body, until I'm filled up with sensation.

But that's not why we're here. One look at Aubrey reminds me of that. The girl is practically a depressant in and of herself, like I could roll her up into a little white pill and pop her and pass out. I need her anyway—I need her for answers, I need her for unraveling this messy Charlie nest.

She looks like she's never been to a club in her life, and for a second I pity her a little. Aubrey's sheltered like no one I've met before. More sheltered than that girl Rachel from Iowa City, who came out to summer enrichment and couldn't hack it. She went home on the earliest flight, her face all screwed up in a snotty red mess, when they caught us smoking weed. It was her first time. We all laughed and she cried, and then she was gone, and the rest of us stuck it out all summer and got our precollege credits. Aubrey, though, she makes *me* cry. I'd never tell her this but sometimes when I look her way, it's all I can do to fight against the tears welling up behind my eyelids. I don't even know why. It's messed up.

Z's my favorite of the guys Charlie partied with. He's sweet and caring—a total nice boy, totally googly-eyed over me—except that he's a pothead and basically houses a pharmacy in the apartment he shares with his brother in the East End. Not that that makes him any different from every other guy I know. The different part is *sweet* and *caring*. Z, he looked out for Charlie. Anytime something went down with Cash or Spencer, Z had Charlie's back. That's why I knew he'd be the first one I'd talk to in London. If someone here knows what Charlie was doing before he went off the grid, it's Z. And if Z knows, he'll tell me.

I need to find out what really went down before it chokes me. Like with Aubrey—that's why I wanted her with me. She knows the most besides me, even if she knows nothing about the day he disappeared. If she and I put our heads together, we'll figure out what he was up to. I've been thinking, if everyone who knew Charlie got together and sewed up our ideas into one big piece of fabric, the fabric would turn into this totally massive, useful quilt with me and Aubrey as the stitches. That's why we're here. I pull out a cigarette and take a deep drag, my smoke mingling with everyone else's in this thick-aired and pulsating room. Figuring out Charlie means living Charlie, inhabiting Charlie, *being Charlie*.

In method acting, that's what we did. And that's what I'm doing now as I shrug off my leather and check it in with the sequined, red-lipped girl. Z grabs my wrist and yanks me in, he's in a party mood too and I wonder if he's already moved on to something harder than weed, before I think to look back for Bree. That's what I'm calling her; I decide it right now. It makes her sound a little less wet noodle, a little more chill.

"Hey, hey." I skip back to where she's standing by the coat-check girl. "Let's do this!" I have to scream over the *thrum thrum* of the bass. It's in my blood and up my throat and pouring out my mouth. "Come on." Through the strobe her eyes are dark, inscrutable. She gets like that, like a switch turns off when she's not nervous. I've known her for two days, and I already know that.

"What are we doing here?" It's a hiss: *whatarewedoinghere.* All one word. *Hissss.* I'd only be half surprised if her tongue were forked.

"Um, feeling out Z," I tell her. "May as well start with him."

"Right," she says all incredulously. "Just as long as you're not here to party."

"Don't you get it?" I lean forward like I'm gonna tell her some kind of massive secret. I laugh when she cringes but my heart sinks; I can't lose her. "*We're being Charlie.* That's how we figure it out."

"Oh, so *that's* how we find him." I know it's a taunt.

"Right," I counter. "Unless you have better ideas." Aubrey presses her lips together in a disapproving little squeeze that I can almost picture on a fifty-year-old version of her, like I know right then what her mom looks like, and I sure as hell don't want to meet her. Aubrey's pretty, but *man is she tough.* Charlie must've wanted a challenge.

"You guys coming or what?" Z's back. I open my mouth but Bree pipes up.

"We're coming." She squares her shoulders and walks off toward the dance floor, straight ahead. There's a bar to our right and a smoking room just behind it, even though everyone's smoking on the dance floor anyway. I inhale the gray haze deeply as Aubrey coughs and brings a palm to her mouth. I catch the glance of the bartender and we lock eyes. He smiles and gives me a wink —he saw Aubrey's coughing fit too. The door to the smoking room pushes open, and I make out a couple of blob-shaped heads, their features indiscernible through the haze of thick fog.

Aubrey's awkward but oddly unselfconscious on the dance floor. It's all I can do not to laugh outright as she writhes and flails in that gold dress of mine, her short black hair bouncing around her face and neck—her movements are not at all in sync with the music. Everything happens in slow mo: We're in the middle of the floor and some trance music comes on. People are sweating to my left and right and it's packed; but still she finds a way to wiggle her hips all over the place and wave her hands over her head. In another setting it might look like a sacrificial tribal dance. She's in her own trance-world, like all it took was putting one foot on the dance floor to fall all the way down the rabbit hole and into the music. Her misplaced confidence might be endearing if she were anyone else.

We stay like this for a little bit, Bree moving in her world, me just doing my thing while Z moves in my orbit. At one point I notice a guy stumble into Aubrey, crushing her foot. If it were me, I would have shoved him off with a few choice words; but Bree just smiles this sweet little smile and laughs it off, then closes her eyes and lets herself get wrapped back up in the music. I'm not a great dancer, but Bree's horrific. And yet . . . it almost makes her cute, the way she throws her entire self into it. After I get done being totally shocked,

I grab Z and move back toward the bar. Bree's fine there, having more fun than she wants to admit. I can't help the fiery feeling moving through me. She acts like such a wide-eyed green thing, but there she is, letting herself forget why we're here and having a good time. I don't know why I feel deceived.

"I have to ask you some stuff," I tell Z. "When's the last time you talked to Charlie?" I try not to act like this isn't the whole point of being here.

"Charlie?" Z's brow furrows. He lifts one hand for the bartender, like he's been doing it all his life. He's twenty, though, so he's been doing it for at least two years—one of the major perks of being back in Europe. "I don't know, three or four months ago? Yeah, we met up in Mumbai. I was there with my family. He was nostalgic, I guess, asked if he could come crash with me. Why? You're not still with him, are you?"

"What's that supposed to mean?" It's obvious he doesn't know what's happened to Charlie, and he thought me calling him meant I was done with my relationship. And here I thought they were such good friends; that's what Charlie always said.

"Forget it," he says. "What's up, Lena?" He hands me an Amstel Light and grabs one for himself, slipping a wad of bills toward the bartender without bothering to count.

"I need to know what you meant by that," I shout over the deep thrum of the music. "Charlie's gone. That's why I'm here."

"Gone?" Z's mouth drops open, his forehead squinches.

"Dead," I affirm, drawing a line across my throat. Okay, so maybe it's callous. But it's also like, we're in a club. I'm trying to keep it light; and it's not like I believe Charlie *is* dead. If I cry, Z's not gonna talk to me; he's going to get all nurturing and pity-party on me in an unsubtle effort to get on my good side. And then I've lost.

"Jesus. How did it happen?"

"He crashed in his dad's plane," I say, steering him away from the bar. "There was an explosion. He was alone." I catch a glimpse of Aubrey. She's not dancing anymore; she's looking around for me, and that lost puppy look's back. I almost ignore it but I feel guilty, so instead I hold a finger up to Z to let him know I'll be back in a sec.

"Hey!' I grab her and she turns to me, looking pissed. Her eyes move to my beer and then she looks even more pissed. "Look," I say. "I'm making headway with Z. Why don't you ask around about Charlie? These dudes are always hanging out here." I jab the air around us, pointing out guys in hoodies, guys in wife-beaters, guys holding cigarettes, short guys, paunchy guys. "So make use of it," I continue. "Some of them probably hung with Charlie at one time or another. This was his favorite bar. He loved coming here, meeting new people. Just give me ten minutes."

"Okay. Just don't leave without me." Her voice is anxious. She's hands down the most high-strung girl I've ever met.

"Obviously." As much as I need her, it's feeling like she's the brick tied to my ankle right now.

I glance over at Z, who's been chilling in the corner drinking his beer, but he looks a little dazed. For a second I wonder why we're doing this; if deep down I don't want just to confront Charlie and make him pay, but also to touch him and see him. But how could I feel anything for Charlie, given what he did to me and Aubrey? It makes me feel sick inside. The really healthy thing would be to write him off altogether and let the past be the past. But what he did doesn't erase those years, those good memories. The times I loved him and felt him love me back. Those are what I'm mourning right now. They're why I need answers. But I wonder: *Am I looking for Charlie to find answers, or am I just looking for him?* The thought causes another wave of shame to burn through me; he was a jerk who treated me and Aubrey like crap, and now I can't accept that he's gone.

"Continue," Z says to me when I catch up with him.

"He's presumed dead, but they never found his body," I tell him when I plop down next to him on one of the benches that line the room where the bar is, just off the dance floor. "Just his bloody jacket."

"Everyone thinks he's dead," he says.

"Yeah."

"The cops, his family. Everyone but you."

I flush. "It sounds crazy. But I have reasons to believe it. Real, tangible reasons."

"What reasons?" Z's eyes are intense.

I look down at my clasped hands. I've been digging my thumbnail into my palm so hard, it's begun to draw blood. I gasp and move my hand to the side so Z can't see.

"I can't tell you the reasons," I say, my voice thick with desperation. I want him to believe me, but I can't trust what I know with Z or Aubrey or anyone else.

Z nods, but his eyes are clouded with an unmistakable pity. The ease of our conversation is gone. Z transitions to a couple of other, more boring topics that I don't really listen to, and I'm still feeling the weight of his compassion. He goes on about an email Charlie sent him. A poster they stole while they were at University of the Arts London's classical studies program for teens.

Then all of a sudden he whirls around like he's just figuring something out. "What do you really need?" Z turns his gaze, leveling me. "This isn't just a passing-through-town thing, is it, Lena? And who is that girl you dragged here with you? No offense, but it doesn't exactly seem like you two are friends."

"That's Aubrey," I tell him, sighing. For some reason I feel like, *No no no, play your cards close to your chest.* "I seriously am just passing through. Seeing family and all that. My parents are in Marseille now but I've got my aunt and uncle here. I just wanted to get away from France after the memorial service. Thought it could be good." That's half true, anyway. "I mean, yeah, sure, there's this element of maybe someone knows exactly what happened the day he vanished and the events leading up to it. Can you blame me?" I let my eyes well up because the tears are coming. They come at super unexpected moments, like this one when I'm only being half sincere. This is one of the few times the tears have worked in my favor.

"Well, I don't know," Z says. "I'm sorry. I don't know anything about it. But can I just be honest? I never thought he was good enough for you." My heart freezes a little because everyone loved Charlie. Everyone.

"No?"

"I'm probably just jealous," he says. Then he leans forward, close, and this Z who always seemed so nice, so *benign*, seems like some other Z with hostile motives. I move away slightly and am about to toss my beer in his face to wake him up when I feel Aubrey's hand on my shoulder.

"He's got nothing," I tell her, ignoring the disappointment in her eyes. "But I'm still optimistic. There are other—"

"I didn't say I've got nothing," Z interrupts. "There's that stupid journal he lost. When I saw him a few months ago in our hotel room, it was all he could talk about. He was obsessed. It got pretty annoying."

"Okay," I say. "What makes you think his journal was important?"

"Just the way he wouldn't stop talking about it afterward," Z said.

"When was this?" Aubrey asked sharply. "Where were you?" Her face is gray. She looks sick. I try to shoot her a question with my eyes, but she ignores me.

"It was a few months ago. Mumbai."

"Mumbai." Aubrey looks even more confused. "Why were you guys there?" She turns to me. "Did you know about this before?"

"Nope," I say. "But I wasn't exactly his keeper. Charlie traveled all the time." It had been one of the ways we were most compatible, actually. We got each other's desire to take off without a moment's notice—were always surprise calling each other from exotic locales.

As we talk, Z is scrolling through pictures on his iPhone. When he stops at the one he wants, he hands Aubrey the phone. I intercept it before I can think. The picture of Charlie sends a shock I'm not prepared for through my entire body. In it, Charlie and Z's arms are slung around each other and they're smiling broadly into the camera. They're sitting on the edge of a bed, the fancy kind, complete with tall wooden bedposts. Charlie's messenger bag is lying open on the floor next to them, a couple of books spilling out. The sight of his face—his smile—hits me with overwhelming force. Aubrey eyes the photo, furrowing her brow intently. I watch her face turn from gray to white. But just as quickly, she turns to Z, her mouth set in a grim line.

"The journal he lost," she says. "Was it this?" She taps the screen with one finger. The book she's indicating is fairly non-descript. Simple, brown, nothing special about it.

"I think so," Z says distractedly.

"It's hard to see here. Do you remember what it looked like?"

"Brown leather, a front flap. Leather tie that wrapped all around, I think. He was always writing in it. I figured just notes about the trip. Why . . . ?"

"Where did you lose it?" Aubrey's strung tight, her cheeks sucked in and her slim frame rigid.

"Taj Hotel," he says. "Colaba. In Mumbai. That was the night before we visited Adam at his place in Andheri. Why?" Instead of responding, Aubrey's eyes widen, and she brings a fist to her mouth. I watch her gnaw on her nails, one after the other.

"Will you relax?" I ask. "What is wrong with you?"

"I'm not—" But she can't continue, she's freaking out so bad. Worse than that, her whole body is trembling. I stand up and then Z stands up, moving a couple of paces away from us.

"Look, Lena," he says. "This is messed up. I'm out of here."

"Just wait a sec," I plead. I still feel like there's something I'm not getting from him.

"Nah," he says. "Whatever this is, I don't want it. I'm sorry about Charlie." Then he's off, *nice guy–turned–every guy*, I can't help thinking.

I turn on her, furious. "That was our best shot!"

"Really?" she says, starting to lose it. "You getting cozy with some guy was our best shot? You totally ditched me. This isn't my scene.

I've never traveled abroad. I'm not comfortable wandering around a Euro club on my own. Do you know how stupid I felt?" Her head is in her hands, and she's turning around in this little circle.

So that's it. She's mad that I left her alone. Embarrassed, maybe. "Calm down," I start. "I'm sorry. We still—"

"Do you even *know* how hard it was for me to pull this off? For me to be here at all?" she asks. I have no idea what she means. I have no idea what she gave up.

"Just come here," I tell her. "Let's go into the bathroom."

"No." She jerks away from me. "I'm tired of listening to you, tired of following you." I'm about to make a joke about how it's been less than three days, but I bite it back. Instead I draw in a long breath.

"So let's go outside," I say. "You can tell me all about it out there."

Aubrey pushes past me. She doesn't bother to grab either of our coats from the coat check, but mine's leather so I have to. I watch her weave through the line that's still forming on the stairs, other teenagers waiting to get in—it's only two o'clock—and I shove in past the coat-check people. I slap a five on the counter and hand the girl my ticket.

Let her still be outside. My leather jacket is seeming less and less worth it. It only takes about a minute, though, before I'm shooting out the double doors and gasping deep, cold air. I see her right away, hunched into herself, my dress hiked all the way up her thighs where she squats against the cold brick wall.

"I wasn't flirting with him," I tell her, sliding down next to her. "I really was trying to dig. I can't help that he turned it around. Or that he sucks. Or that my club idea turned up empty. I say yes a lot," I explain. "Sometimes to my detriment."

"My parents don't know I'm here," Aubrey says quietly. She breathes once, twice, like she might give herself over to panic if she doesn't focus hard on those breaths.

"Mine don't either." I keep my voice light, bubbly. "Mine don't care what I do as long as I check in every few weeks."

"Mine care, Lena." Aubrey turns her eyes on me. "You have no idea. They count on me. I've never done something like this in my life. You think I can just run off?" She laughs but it's hollow. "Your club idea didn't come up empty," she says. I open my mouth to ask what she means, but she holds up her hand. "Just wait a second. We've got something here, but you're taking it so lightly, like it's some kind of joke or adventure. I need to be able to trust you. I don't have money, I don't have time, my parents are probably freaking out. I was supposed to be home already."

"Why haven't you told them?" I keep my voice quiet, even.

"Because they'd be out here in a second to bring me home." I look at Aubrey. Her face is serious.

"I'm sorry," I tell her.

"Why did you ask me to come along?" she wants to know. "I know why you're doing this. Anyone could see you're hoping he's still alive, that 'body missing' means he's out there somewhere. But my own reasons are totally different. So what does it matter if we're together?"

I can't look at her. I'm afraid my eyes will betray my secret—the real reason I think Charlie's alive. So I avoid the question. "I don't have some grand plan. I'm telling you. I thought Z could help. All he really said to me before you walked up was that Charlie was weird in Bombay, which doesn't do us a hell of a lot of good."

"Wait." Aubrey cuts me off. "How was he weird in Mumbai?

What did Xander say about it?" She looks so interested that I feel guilty breaking her heart all over again.

"Just, whatever," I say. "That he was moody. He was curt and distracted and sometimes he said the same thing twice or contradicted himself. But Z thought it was just stress from school and all." Aubrey stares at me, thinking.

"So we're talking about just a few months ago," she confirms.

"Yep, after exam season at Oxford."

"And before that . . . what was his moving history? We met just before he started his first year there, the summer beforehand in New York."

I sigh, wrinkling my forehead. Charlie's life was hard to keep track of, even when he and I were talking every day. He forgot to tell me he was moving to India at all, and then *bam,* all of a sudden he calls from Mumbai. "He spent most of his time in the U.K.," I say, thinking back. "But when he was a kid, he lived in Paris. Let me think." I rack my brain, piecing together everything Charlie ever told me about his personal history. "Okay, yeah, he was in Paris pretty much exclusively until he finished middle school. Then he spent his freshman year in Bangkok. Then I guess that didn't work out, so his mom moved him to London for his sophomore and junior years. That's where I met him, the summer before his junior year."

"I guess summer's when he had the most game," Aubrey says, and I laugh. The comment is unexpected coming from her, especially because she sounds so sincere about it. "So then what?" she prods. "Senior year in Mumbai?"

I nod slowly. "Yeah . . . and you know the rest. New York for the summer just before he started Oxford." I pause, thinking hard. "I guess he did start acting pretty weird toward the end of the school year," I offer. I'd never thought much of it—had just assumed Oxford's exam season was heinous.

"What's weirdest is that he never told either of us he was going on the trip to Mumbai," Aubrey points out. I flush, but she's right.

"I mean, his parents were fighting a lot then. Maybe that's why?" My heart thuds a little.

Then I shrug, trying not to read too much into it. "Like I said, he traveled all the time. It wasn't a big deal to him."

"The journal in that photo," Aubrey breaks in. She's looking at the ground, the stoplights, anything but my face. "It's my journal. The one I've been looking for. My dad gave it to me for my birthday and . . . it's the same one. I'm sure of it. If he lost it there, it might still be there. Z didn't say he went back for it. Only that he talked about it." Her eyes are trained on mine, and we're thinking the same thing.

"Bombay is far away," I say. "And expensive to get to."

"I need that journal, Lena. I have to have it. We need to go there right away."

I'm surprised by the force of her words. Bombay is a big trip. I'd considered it, but for it to be our next stop is a big deal. "I'd thought maybe we'd continue in London, or go back to Paris, depending on what we find here."

"Z said Charlie was always writing in the journal," Aubrey reminds me. "And he mentioned Adam. Maybe Adam knows something. Maybe something in the journal will give us insight into what he was thinking. Why continue in London when we know we have a lead in Mumbai?"

It's a long shot. I know it, and I know she knows it. But this journal seems to mean so much to her. And really, she's right. While tenuous, this is the best lead we got from Z. If Charlie was writing in that journal just a few months ago . . . it could definitely shed some light on what he was thinking.

"Please." I can tell by the way she says it that she's not used to asking for things. "I need this."

"Okay," I tell her. "Bombay it is. I'm on board." In an instant she's moving to her feet, the gold fabric of her dress—*my* dress—catching on the jagged bricks at her back. She pulls me into a hug, and I feel the force of her gratitude. It makes me happy, doing this for her. I can't explain it, but I want her to be happy.

"My parents are going to be just thrilled," she says wryly, smiling.

"I thought you don't do stuff like this," I tease. "Who knew you'd be the one pushing for another continent?"

"Maybe I'm discovering my secret jet-setting identity," she says. "And," she adds, trying to sound brave, "it's not like I don't have a credit card for emergencies. This probably qualifies. But don't we need visas or something?"

I almost laugh at how worried she looks under the bravado, but I bite my lip. "Pssh. All it takes is a quick trip to the American embassy. NBD. And don't worry," I add just in case. "I'm footing the bill." *Shit, I guess I am*, I think as I say it. She doesn't say anything, just looks at me. "Trust fund," I explain. "I only stay in hostels because I want it to last forever. Plus I like an authentic experience."

She shakes her head. "That's too much," she says. "I can't accept it."

"I can't go unless you accept it," I threaten. She stares at me for a long moment, disbelieving. Then she throws her arms around me again.

"Thank you," she whispers. "No one's ever—"

"Get ahold of yourself," I interrupt, easing out from under her embrace. "Or the offer's off the table." Still, I'm glad to have been able to do something good. I don't want to like Aubrey; but there's something about her vulnerability and openness that I'm drawn to.

"Is this crazy?" she wants to know. She kicks off her shoes and holds them in one hand, her feet bare against the pavement.

"Yes," I tell her. "It is absolutely insane. It is definitely crazy, even for me." I didn't know she had it in her, but I'm happy she does. Aubrey's surprising; you think you have her pegged, and then . . . this. I swing an arm around her. She wouldn't have let me touch her earlier tonight, but this time she leans close like we're old friends, and we move in the direction of the gross, crappy hostel.

In reality, I suggested staying there for Aubrey — because I knew she didn't have a lot of money. I didn't want to insult her by offering to foot the bill, or put pressure on her to spend more than she has. I never would have stayed in that hellhole otherwise. But there's no way I'm doing that in Bombay, where *hostel* means "roach-and-rat-infested room with a hole in the ground in place of a toilet." In Bombay we'll do it my way, with my money. As we walk, I'm hoping the magic that's settled around us — satanic or otherwise — conjures up some answers fast, before she changes her mind, or worse: figures out what I'm hiding.

8

Aubrey

I CAN'T EVEN IMAGINE HOW MUCH THE Air India flights cost Lena. Fifteen hundred dollars each? Two thousand? For not the first time, it strikes me how generous she's being. How coming out here—simply because I felt it was important—was a big leap of faith on her part. She had no reason to be so kind to me, and yet she was. I wonder if we'll find my journal. I wonder if Adam will have any information that could help us. I wonder, even, what it might have been like to date someone like Adam—someone intelligent and kind, with integrity—rather than Charlie. If I had, I wouldn't be on a plane to India right now—or at least not for the reason I am.

I chomp on a stick of cinnamon-flavored gum the whole time, while Lena alternates between reading *Us Weekly*s and humming along to Bollywood films. Four hours in, her tray table is littered with discarded wine bottles and cans of Diet Coke. The fact that Lena is this wealthy—enough so to drop thousands on our flights out here without batting an eye or even clearing it with her parents first—is awe-inspiring. But she wears it casually, and she never boasts. The way she's done everything she could to make me comfortable and not indebted—even the small things, like sharing her snacks and helping me fill out my customs form—demonstrates her generosity. I like Lena, and I can't help but see why Charlie fell for her. I've never met someone so uninhibited, exciting, and open to emotions.

They're all qualities I admire. I've always had trouble making friends; I'm the only girl in my family, and it's never been easy for me to relate to other girls my own age. I've always been a little shy, never comfortable enough in my own skin to seamlessly fit into a group. Lena is the type people want to be around. They gravitate toward her naturally—even the taxi driver, who engaged her in conversation on our way to the airport; and the flight attendant, who gave her an extra bag of cookies for free. Lena has all the qualities I've always wanted. Sitting next to her on the plane like this, I can almost pretend like we're sisters. It's not a bad feeling; but the truth of it is, we're worlds apart.

Lena must know Charlie so much better than I do. After all, they met in London a year or so before his parents moved him to Mumbai to finish high school there. They spent time together—presumably days on end and lots of nights too. I, on the other hand, met Charlie in a subway station just before leaving New York for good. Our relationship has always been long-distance. We're from different backgrounds in every possible way.

She has money like he did; she's traveled the world like he had; she knew him for two years longer than I. She has the advantage. More than that, though, she's self-assured. Even I'm not immune to her fearlessness. It inspires jealousy and admiration all at once. I know I shouldn't care. Mostly, I don't. If by some wild chance Lena's right that he's alive and we do find him, I'll make him wish he'd been dead all along.

And maybe we'll also find out that he's a spy for the CIA, or something, and needed to vanish to take care of some top-secret mission. And needed to have two girlfriends for some highly classified government project.

Right.

I don't know why I can't just tell him to go to hell, within the confines of my mind. Why I can't let go of my fear over the journal and accept this whole incident as a second chance that I desperately needed. I've been wanting to escape Charlie's pull for way longer than the past two weeks; I was planning on telling him a heck of a lot more than just *Go to hell* before he disappeared. I'd planned to confront him, tell him I was through with everything no matter what the consequences. So I can't understand this attachment I'm feeling, now that he's gone. I guess I just have to get my journal, and maybe also get confirmation of his death, for closure. It's true that not knowing what happened the day he died— and not having a body to prove he's gone— is driving me a little crazy.

Now Lena and I are hanging out in a bustling open-air café in Colaba, a neighborhood in South Mumbai, waiting until our hotel opens up. It's called Café Leopold, and it has all kinds of American comfort foods mixed in with traditional Indian fare. I order jalapeño cheesy bread. Lena's in the bathroom now, washing her hands. The air is hot and oppressive; it's over ninety degrees, with only a few fans to cool the customers. The tables around ours are packed with sweating bodies, and shouted commands ring out from the kitchen in the back. The chaos of it makes me dizzy; I've never felt at the mercy of a place until now. Mumbai conveys this sense that anything could happen at any time: I have to be on high alert. But I'm feeling like my life has started to spiral out of control, and I no longer have any idea what I want out of it. I'm just along for the twister.

The thing is, it's exciting. It's the first time I've ever leapt before I looked, and especially with a girl my age, someone whom I find myself liking more and more. Of course, I'm nervous about what we'll find. I'm also nervous about how my parents will be when I go home to Illinois. I start college in less than two weeks. When I checked my email using the airport wifi—in Heathrow, not Mumbai; it's becoming obvious that Internet's going to be spotty in Mumbai, at best—I had this chipper email from my future roommate at Georgetown:

> Hey Aubrey! So psyched to be your roomie next year! I saw on your profile that you're into art, that's totally cool! I'm a dancer, and I was on the state championship cheer squad too this year! I'm going to try out for the pom squad for sure! Write back so we can coordinate stuff to bring. I've got a huge comfy beanbag chair and some plastic stacking shelves we can use to keep food on!
> Talk soon, can't WAIT! xoxoxo

I didn't respond because, well, I just don't think I can match that level of chipper right now; and anyway, I feel like I'm a million miles from college and all the stuff I'm supposed to be excited about. And I'm excited about the wrong stuff: like being in this noisy café with its bullet holes in the windows and inching closer and closer to—*what? Disaster?* Thinking about what will unfold if we do find out what happened to Charlie is like anticipating a tsunami, but I've never not been a masochist. The relief of having my journal back will be worth it anyway, no matter what happens. That's what I have to keep reminding myself. That's what I told myself when I dashed off a two-line email to my parents, letting them know I'm not in Europe anymore.

"God," Lena says, pulling out her chair and squeezing in carefully, because it's only an inch from the person behind her. "Look at all these lame tourist outfits." A bunch of bangles slip back from her wrist to her forearm as she motions around us; and for the first time, I see the teeny-tiny, jagged image of a sheep tattooed across her wrist, no wider than my thumbnail.

"You kind of fit right in," I say without thinking. Lena glowers. But it's true—when she's not wearing slutty dresses, she seems to favor loose, baggy, printed pants and these oversize tanks that show off whatever Day-Glo bra she has on. The others here are wearing basically the same thing except for the Day-Glo part, and lots of people are tattooed or pierced. "I meant it as a compliment!" I backtrack. "But it *is* a little weird how everyone's dressed the way you think tourists in India will be dressed." We both know I am trying to win her back. I like Lena, though. More and more. Part of the reason I like her is because she's so open with me, despite that she could easily have seen me as an adversary. She's the one who wanted me to come along to London. She might have been angry that Charlie took me into his life, but she never blamed me or made me feel bad about it. She's also never made me feel judged. Even when she teases me for being nerdy, she's almost affectionate about it. With her I feel less afraid. I feel myself emerging from my shell.

"I wonder if they also grew their dreadlocks specifically for the occasion," I say, keeping my expression serious. Lena rolls her eyes.

"Maybe some of them are legit," she allows. "By the way, did you know this is the café that was hit during that big terrorist attack a few years ago? The same one that targeted the Taj Hotel."

"Gee, that makes me feel super safe. Thanks for bringing me here."

"They never hit the same spot twice, Bree. This is basically the safest spot in Bombay." I recoil at her use of "Bree." I can't help it.

"Don't call me that," I snap. I feel bad one second later. She didn't know. She couldn't have.

She lifts one eyebrow. "Jet-lagged or just bitchy?" she asks. I sigh. Maybe I am jet-lagged. But it's more than that. Charlie was the only one who ever called me Bree, until now. It's odd, the way they both chose the exact same nickname. I don't want to think about everything it implies about them, the way they think, the way they think of me . . .

"I'm a little tired," I admit. "But shouldn't we get going on this? Look into Charlie's contacts out here and stuff?"

"Whatever. I'm tired too. Just another hour before we can check in."

"Not *whatever*," I tell her. "I have school in less than two weeks," I remind her. "I have to be back for orientation in one. We don't have tons of time."

"I have school too," she tells me. "But you can't rush this process."

It's ironic, coming from her. I lean back in my chair, eyeing her. She seems so *unconcerned*. It's almost like she already knows what's going to happen. "Why are you so calm?" I ask.

"Just genetically blessed with an even temperament, I guess."

"Stop." I lean forward, resting my arms on the table. She's avoiding my gaze, and I don't like what that might mean. "What's your deal?"

"My deal is that I'm tired, and I want to check into our hotel, and I want to sleep for, like, nine hours before I start thinking about this. Okay? Just chill, Aubrey. You're not going to figure anything out unless you take a few steps back." She takes a sip of her mango lassi. "Just try to enjoy Bombay while we're here."

"It's annoying how you call it Bombay. It's Mumbai."

"No one calls it 'Mumbai.'" She rolls her eyes, showing her scorn for my lack of knowledge. "That's just for official paperwork. Conversationally it's still 'Bombay,' even among Indians. I've been here enough to know." That piques my interest. *Glittering eyes,* I think, watching hers light up. Whenever Lena talks about travel, her eyes glitter. It reminds me of the Roald Dahl quote, "*Watch with glittering eyes the whole world around you.*"

I tell her as much, and she laughs, rolling her eyes.

I blush, embarrassed. "Why *have* you been here so much?" I ask, quickly changing the subject.

"My parents," she says. "They brought us here two summers running for three weeks each time. Typical rich-parents thing to do: expose us to a third-world country so we won't be ruined forever."

"Too bad it didn't work," I comment.

Lena lifts an eyebrow. "My, my," she says. "Who knew you had such bite?"

"Why the sheep?" I ask, tapping her wrist. I'm eager to change the subject again. It feels like we've been bickering constantly this whole time, and I don't want that. Lena blushes and shoves the bangles back down her arm, so they cover her wrist.

"Lamb," she corrects. Then, "I don't know. I just felt like it."

"You just felt like it?" I say, doubtful. "Come on, what's the story?" She's clearly embarrassed, and I can't help but feel even more curious. It takes a lot to shake her up.

"I actually don't know," she admits. "I kind of wonder that a lot.

It's not really me, is it? I mean, I always thought if I got a tattoo I'd get something like 'Rock on,' or whatever. Not that, but you know. Maybe something from an album cover." She pauses. "But Little Lamb was Charlie's nickname for me. I was out one night, had a little too much to drink, woke up in the morning, and it was there." She finishes with a shrug. "I guess I was feeling sentimental that night."

"Wow." I'm impressed. Or maybe shocked. "Wasn't someone with you? A friend or something? Or like, wasn't there a receipt? Are tattoo artists even *allowed* to do that when you're drunk?"

"No receipt." She bites her lip. "Charlie was with me. He didn't remember it either."

"Really." There's this awkward pause. My heart's pounding. My head's back with Charlie, filtering through all the nights, wondering if this happened before or after we met, and when did Charlie get so into drinking? He was never a partier with me. I clench my jaw, hard, to prevent myself from asking. I don't want to ask. I'm not sure I can handle it on three hours of sleep. Lena's still staring at the table. She takes a long, slow sip of her lassi and avoids my eyes. *Later,* I think. For some reason, pity worms its way into my heart. Later, after we've gotten some sleep, I'll ask her all these questions.

But then she looks up, stares me straight in the eyes.

"Six months ago," she says. "You want to know. It happened six months ago."

An hour later we're rolling our bags into the Taj Mahal Palace Hotel. I can't imagine how much this little aspect of our trip is costing, but Lena says in Mumbai—correction, Bombay—you don't do hostels and there's nothing in between, so it's perfectly okay with her that we stay here and not just inquire after my journal like I'd planned.

"A few nights won't kill us," she says, and I try not to worry about how bad it is to owe people favors. I make a mental note to call my parents as soon as we have access to a phone, since my cell doesn't work out here. I try not to think about what they'll say—or the hurt they'll feel—when I explain the most recent turn of events. The days when I turned to them with everything are starting to seem like a distant memory.

"I could have stayed somewhere else, you know," I say. I'm looking up the wide spiral staircase at the arched ceilings above. The "old" Taj, they told us when we checked in. This is the wing that wasn't damaged by the fires in 2011. It feels like a real palace, which is exactly how it's supposed to feel.

"You could have," she says, yawning, "but that would be stupid. I'd have paid for this room anyway. I might as well share it." Again, my chest expands a little. She's always acting accidentally bighearted, like none of it's any big deal.

A quick trip to the front desk turns up nothing, and I have to work hard to conceal my disappointment. "Nothing, ma'am," is all the concierge tells me when I ask if someone left a leather journal in one of the rooms a few months back. "Are you sure?" Lena presses. "You're not just, you know, not saying? Because it was my friend's journal." She jerks her thumb in my direction and glares, then slides a twenty-dollar bill in the man's direction. He promises to check with a manager but returns empty-handed. He doesn't return the twenty.

"No worries," she says. "We have lots of other stuff we can do here. I just have to think back to who Charlie was friends with out here, and we can Google them or look them up on Facebook or something. And if he had your diary or whatever when he was here, then we've narrowed your search for it, at least. He wasn't that many other places in the months since."

She's right, and the realization heartens me. But there's another reason I forced the issue of going to Bombay, as I'm trying hard to call it now. Something I can't tell her and probably can't do anything with anyway. I wish it were just the journal; but my willingness to be here is more than that. Here, I'm closer to the thing that ultimately ruined me and Charlie. I'm closer to all the reasons we fell apart. I can't tell Lena, so I follow her silently up a set of wide, winding stairs toward our room.

It's luxurious. The beds are covered in gold bedspreads with elaborately embroidered red patterns. An arched alcove leads to a balcony with an intricately patterned iron guardrail, overlooking the Gateway of India. A silver tea set rests on a broad wooden console, and a crystal chandelier hangs overhead. It's a stark contrast to the grimy chaos and slums we drove through to get here. Lena's happy, I can tell. " 'I came in like a wrecking ball,' " she sings under her breath, as she surveys the room. I barely stop myself from rolling my eyes at the truth of it.

"We'll start tomorrow," Lena tells me, her voice half muffled from where she's flopped her thin frame across one of the queen-size beds. "This is just too good."

"So — is this where you stayed when your parents were teaching you lessons about the less privileged?"

"Fuck you, Aubrey."

I grin. "I'm getting in the shower." I'm halfway through the bathroom door before I turn back. I've been so guarded with her, but I can't ignore how generous she's being.

"Thank you. Really." I hesitate. I've never been very good at opening up. "You're being very generous."

Lena waves me off with one hand, her eyes already dropping shut. "Don't mention it." I can't help smiling at that. So cool, so casual—but all her real emotions are there, just under the surface, just behind her words. Maybe we're not so different after all.

My fingers are itching for a pencil—I'd love to work this room into a comic—but instead I slip into the bathroom and close the door gently behind me. I'd stick around and press her for more information about the city, or maybe strike out on my own, but Bombay is intimidating—I've never seen anything like it. The cars practically careen into each other, always swerving at the last second. A slum stretches for at least a mile beyond the hotel; our view from the sixth floor overlooks it and the Arabian Sea beyond. From the bathroom, I can see some children jumping among heaps of trash and others squatting to poop near the side of the road. When we were outside, peddlers hawked stacks of lychees and bananas from wooden carts. Women thrust their babies at us, motioning for pictures. This was all in the trip from the airport to the hotel; I'm exhausted just from having absorbed it. I'm not ready to brave the city alone. Plus, I'm pretty sleepy too.

That's what I'm thinking as I step in the shower. But all of it is a cover for what's *really* occupying my mind. I've always been good at that—thinking loose, easy thoughts to cover up the hulking ones that lie in wait. This time, it's about Adam. Adam, Charlie's old roommate from Bombay. The one who met up with us once when Charlie and I connected in D.C., just eight or nine months ago. Adam took a year off after high school and stayed in Bombay to work for an NGO. He's still here. I sent him a Facebook message before we left, and Lena and I talked about meeting up with him tomorrow. It's the plan. If something weird was going on with Charlie in Bombay, Adam would be the one to know.

I ignore the pounding in my heart as his face flashes through my memory. Blond hair, a rugged build — he was captain of the cricket team at the American School in Bombay — tanned skin from hours in the Indian sun. I scrub my hair harder, digging my nails into my scalp until it hurts.

We were in D.C. because Charlie's dad was there for work, and Charlie was on break from college for the holidays, and I was on Thanksgiving break from high school, and could drive there easily from Chicago. I told my parents I was staying with his family; but in reality, we had his uncle's empty bachelor pad in Georgetown all to ourselves for five days . . . except for the two nights Adam stayed there too.

Adam. Three shots of tequila. Charlie passing out early, my head on his shoulder. I was about to turn eighteen. There are wrappers all around us from the cupcakes we've been devouring; we each had at least three. Adam's on the foldout couch and I'm with Charlie in the master bed, but Charlie's snoring loudly, so I go out to the kitchen for some water.

I scrub, I rinse. I transfer the pain of remembering into my body, my head. I turn the heat up until it's scalding, burning all of the germs and mistakes away. Finally, when I start to feel lightheaded, I switch the nozzle off and step onto the thick, lush white area rug that partially covers the gray marble floor of the bathroom.

I reach for a towel and notice flecks of red under my fingernails. Blood. My scalp is tender from where I scratched too hard. I know what I'm going to do even before I reach for my pants, which lie rumpled on the floor, and pull out the piece of paper that's folded up in the back pocket. There's an address scrawled on the back, hastily jotted down from my Facebook account just yesterday.

Lena is sound asleep by the time I get out of the shower, so it's no trouble to sneak off. The taxi driver tells me, in halting English, that normally it takes two hours to get from Colaba to Andheri, even with the Sea Link. That before the Sea Link, it would have taken four hours in rush hour traffic. But today we're lucky, he says. It's a Hindu holiday and there are no cars on the roads—only people, crowds of them, many walking hand in hand or with arms slung over one another's shoulders. It's an expression of affection between boys and other boys, men and other men, women and women— but never men and women mixed. Friends are showing each other the closeness they can't show the opposite sex in this strange country where arranged marriages still happen all the time.

But after we get off the Sea Link and pull into a neighborhood the driver calls Bandra, the atmosphere changes. The stalls along the dusty streets display a mix of old and new. The clothing gets a little more stylish, and couples cuddle up along the sea. My driver is like a tour guide. We drive along the busy Bandra streets just as the sun begins to sink. Every time we pause, women with babies or small children pound on the taxi windows for handouts. I don't have any rupees yet, but I slip a few American coins through a cracked window, along with an apple and a bag of chips that I had in my purse, and they go nuts.

There are bakeries and outdoor clothing stalls and men with sewing machines setting up shop on the side of the road. There's a hair salon with a sign that reads CURL UP AND DYE. There's a tiny ice cream shop advertising something called *kulfi*. Cows walk in the streets and laze on the sidewalks. Horns never stop honking; and on the backs of trucks there are signs that read HORN OK PLEASE. I can see why Adam never wants to leave: in this short drive, the sights and sounds are enough to infuse my tired body with energy that could last a decade.

Charlie hated Bombay; that much I remember. He hated the smells, the homeless people, the pollution, the sick and deformed animals and people. He hated having to sterilize vegetables and brush his teeth with bottled water. You'd have thought Charlie would have been used to that—he moved around all his life—but he was much more of a Europe/North America kind of guy.

I can feel my pulse racing as we turn onto a busier highway. I remember this road from our trip from the airport earlier today. Adam lives in Andheri, right by the airport, on the northern end of Bombay, where the slums stretch for miles and aren't punctuated by the bungalows or restaurants that dot Bandra, or the British-style cafés of South Bombay.

"Linking Road," says the driver in his melodic, carefully syllabled way.

I've seen the pictures Adam's posted on Facebook and Instagram. Since graduation, he's been working for an NGO set up to aid educational programs within the slums. In some of his photos, he holds little Indian babies who are screaming and reaching for their mothers standing just out of the frame. In others he beams over mountains of chicken-studded rice, mystifying sauces in simple silver tureens waiting by his elbow. My favorite photo, though, is one of a goat wearing a T-shirt next to a stall that displays Bollywood posters. There's a cart holding piles of lychees just barely in the shot and a sign offering the services of a bonesetter in the background.

I've seen Adam's house, too: a low-lying slum house — not the worst kind, sheltered by a tin roof or a tarp, but the "nicer" cement-block kind — with the words HOME SWEET HOME painted next to the door. Behind the house rises the Holy Spirit Hospital. Even before I reached out to him on Facebook, I knew Adam lived in the neighborhood of Andheri. But as of yesterday, I have his whole address:

Opposite Merwans bakery
Near Andheri East Metro station, SV road
Andheri East, Mumbai, Maharashtra

"Is this how you get your mail?" I typed at him. And he answered with "Yep. ☺"

Adam's not expecting me and Lena until tomorrow, and by now it's nearly seven p.m. I'm standing there in front of the salmon-colored house, having paid a total of ten dollars for my ninety-minute taxi ride, when I realize how insane I'm being. I swivel back toward the taxi, but it's too late; it's already halfway down the street.

I take a step away from the house. People are everywhere; the house is so small, I could probably reach around and hug it. Instead I turn, hating myself for doing something so stupid — for coming here all by myself with no real idea where I am or how to get back.

Then the curtain that functions as a door swishes, and I hear his voice.

"Aubrey," he says. It's all it takes. I turn, moving toward him like I'm on a leash. Women with baskets on their heads eye me curiously, but I ignore them, pretend there's no heat flaming in my cheeks at all, and focus only on Adam. He steps inside the shack and I follow and he closes the curtain behind us. It's all black and we're the only ones inside. "Aubrey," he says again, but he whispers it this time, like it's a prayer.

Then he's on me, pushing me against the wall, his mouth on mine as I wrap my legs around his waist and he hoists me up, pinning me there, working his tongue inside my mouth and his mouth on my neck and finally, when he lets me down, his hands in my hair.

None of this was ever about Charlie, I realize, as my hands intertwine with Adam's and press against his back and work their way over the muscles of his chest. The minute Lena and I hopped on our first plane—the minute there was Bombay—Charlie ceased to exist. Adam fills all the emptiness inside me that Charlie created.

It's dark when I slide my room key into the lock and push open the door to the suite. Lena's breathing is rhythmic; she only stirs a little as the lock clicks into place behind me. I feel an ache in my chest. She misses Charlie in a way I never will, because my heart's with someone else. I want so badly to erase her pain. I pull the blankets over her exposed shoulders, and she turns in her sleep. Then I slip off my shoes and slide under the covers without bothering to change. It's too risky to wash the scent of Adam's cologne and sweat off me; Lena will wake up and want to know what I'm doing at three in the morning. She doesn't deserve another betrayal. I'm caught off-guard by how much this secret hurts.

9

Charlie

You breathe in, out, steady. you've got it under control, everything's controlled. You're fine. Your little lamb's back in New Hamp-
shire at her liberal arts college, just an hour from her cozy family in
Boston. And Aubrey's in her senior year of high school in whatever
little Illinois town she's from—you can never remember the name
of it; it's somewhere just outside Chicago—and you're back in uni
in Oxford, far away from both of them, which is how you like it
these days.

You laugh because it's only been three months with Aubrey and
you like it best when they're both far, far away—but you also like to
hang on to them, like that rope that connects you to them. It's better than having some girl at uni, always buzzing around. For the first
year or so with Lena, she was like that . . . buzzing, always on you,
always chirping about something and needing something, and those
summers away from her were the best. But you love her, you really
do. She's your lamb; Aubrey's your loris. You love them both, and
that's the problem. Sometimes the love just seeps in and takes over
and you forget who you are, and that's when it gets overwhelming.

That's why you needed those summers away, and that's why you're better off with them both out of the U.K.

It's been just over two years with Lena. There are the talks: Can you make it through college? Can you spend the summer together? Can she visit over winter break—her parents will pay for it. And every time you have to study up. Read it over (the book) to remember the basics: her habits (twirls hair, clicks teeth when thinking); her favorites (chocolate peanut butter ice cream and shrimp tempura rolls); the memories (Burning Man last summer, fishing in the Catskills the summer before that); everything down to the colors of her fingernail polish and what she smells like. If you get one detail off, you lose the game.

Keeping them straight is harder than you figured. Sometimes they merge into one indistinguishable personality. You have to keep it straight, and it throws you—it's not just who *they* are but who *you* are with each of them. Everything down to the clothes and how you do your hair. Sometimes it makes you angry. Sometimes you're so angry you feel like it's crawling out of your insides on top of your skin, visible to everybody. But they smile, they laugh at your jokes, each one lays her head on your shoulder, and you know: you're the only one who feels your anger.

It was fun at first. Aubrey, irresistible Aubrey. You had no choice —you had to be with her. She's deeper, more intense than Lena, like a dark, swirly vortex. Inscrutable. Mysterious. Addictive. A challenge. The calm before the storm, the eye of the tornado. You could be somebody different with her.

Now it's harder. There are phone calls or at least emails, to the extent that you can get away with it (*two different girls, two different yous*). There are endless details to remember. And all the time you're not with them or texting them or talking to them or emailing them or finding excuses not to do any of those things, you're recording it in the book. To keep it all straight.

That was why you stopped talking to Adam, and Phil, and Henry, and Z, and Alex. You kept blending your two selves into one and they were getting confused. You were making mistakes, creating holes. You couldn't keep your selves straight and sometimes you couldn't decide and sometimes you were someone totally different, unrecognizable. It was a fresh start. That's why Liam had to go, and Adam before him. It's why you live alone now in this big, empty dorm room. Just you and your two girlfriends and your book. Your favorite pages from the book are at the beginning, when things were simple, when the lists were easy and strictly factual:

LENA

» The only time Lena drinks soda is on planes
» Likes mint-flavored floss and cigarettes
» Adds butter to her coffee
» Wears FlowerBomb perfume
» Hates the color orange
» Hates gummy candies/anything with gelatin
» Had pony when little named Beans
» Childhood friend named Bettina, now in rehab
» Closer to mom

AUBREY

» Pours whole milk on her ice cream
» Wears Vanilla Mist body spray

» Has neg. thoughts on "using the Lord's name in
  vain," especially around her parents
» Good at Ping-Pong, checkers
» Childhood best friend named Karen
» Closer to dad
» Says "pop" instead of "soda"
» Allergic to pine nuts, walnuts

Then things got more complicated—less fact-based and more emotional. Then you stopped letting Lena visit. Now you meet somewhere off campus. Once she surprised you and you blamed all the evidence on Liam. You said, "Liam hasn't moved out yet," but in reality that's not why there was a book of selected Keats poems on your desk. (*Research.*) You said the Van Halen CDs were Liam's older cousin's.

You've started dreaming about it at night. Lena's face with Aubrey's black hair. Aubrey twirling Lena's silver boxing glove pendant over one red-painted index finger. Lena with ballet slippers, dancing to Tchaikovsky until her movements become jerkier and jerkier and she's on puppet strings tugged by you, and then you switch and she and Aubrey are the ones tugging the strings and you're the one doing the dance and they're both laughing.

Your grades are slipping, not that it matters. They don't flunk people out, especially not you. They need your family's donations; everyone knows that. There's a freaking building on campus named after your grandfather.

Sometimes you open the book and flip back, way back to the early days, when you first started it, after the move to Bangkok after middle school. It started as a list.

BANGKOK CHARLIE LIKES:

```
banana nut bread
hammocks
collecting rocks
jazz music
curse words (in any language)
```

Then a year or two later:

LONDON CHARLIE LIKES:

```
kangaroos
roller coasters
molten chocolate cake
comic books
```

Then there started to be differences. Conflicting information. You began to get confused.

PARIS CHARLIE HATES:

```
music (all except soul)
marsupials
fucked-up shit
self-help books
```

It was no big deal. Your interests change all the time. That's what happens when you travel—you see some stuff, you try a lot of stuff. That's what happens to everyone. "We can't keep your interests straight, Charlie," your parents say on the rare occasions when you're home from boarding school and your dad's back for a holiday or whatever. But they laugh, like it's some big joke or quirky personality trait.

Problem is, your interests change *all the time*. And Aubrey, she demands something different: she wants your interests to stay the same, when you're with her. When you first met her, you shared strawberry milkshakes. You saw her again, and your interest in strawberry milkshakes had disappeared. They made you want to vomit. But you said it and her brow furrowed and her mouth turned down and you said, *Just kidding*. And you drank the goddamn strawberry milkshake. Everything had to stay the same. You'd hoped she was different, that she'd be amenable to change. She's not.

Lena wasn't either. Imagine having to pretend for three years with Lena. Just imagine what it would be like, trying to pretend you like basketball for two years running, or that you're into sports at *all* anymore after a couple months' fascination. Lena never got it. You hoped she'd accept you the way you are—the you that's changing and interested in lots of different things—but she never did. So you had to be a consistent person, to please her.

That was why Aubrey was exciting at first. She was a change. You could be a different thing with her. Then she got stale too. It was easy when you were younger, always moving, always picking up people and later discarding them when you left, always able to slip on another cloak without anyone knowing the difference. Now it's harder. And you're angry.

But you love them, you really do.

Sometimes you love Aubrey so much you want to smother her. Really smother her. Wrap her all up in you until she can't breathe anymore. Until she has to breathe your air, with your lungs. You love Lena so much, it's like aliens take over your brain when you're focused on her. Sometimes you're thinking about it so much, missing her so much, that you forget to eat or drink anything for entire days. Your vision clouds and you get weak, and you remember.

You hate those cloaks you slip on for them, but they keep you strong. You read the book, you study, you impersonate. It's what works. It keeps you feeling good. It's these other times, these times away from them, when all of it sets in: the post-adrenaline crash, the exhaustion, the panic from the couple of times you almost slipped up. Then the rage boils up.

But you love them. That's all you need.

Sometimes, though, it feels like a kind of death. *Lambs to the slaughter.* It's a phrase that's lodged itself in your mind. It's ugly, that phrase. When you start thinking that way, you get shaky. It becomes hard to focus. What gives your brain relief? Pot. You only openly smoke pot around Lena. (Aubrey doesn't like it.) And even then only occasionally. Here, in the privacy of your dorm room, it's all the time. *Focus.* It helps you focus on how much you love them, your little lamb, the gentle one—and your loris, the one full of poison. And how angry you are that you're making mistakes.

10

Lena

It's obvious something's up the second we sit down in Kala Ghoda Café. We do this awkward dance where first Adam moves toward Aubrey's side of the table at the same time I do, and then he doubles back and lingers at the chair across from her before settling into the one across from me. Like it's about something bigger than just which chair to plant his ass in. Kala Ghoda Café is little and mostly empty—it's just across the street from Trishna's, the seafood place famous for its garlic king crab, but somehow it escapes the crush. I thought of it because I knew it would be quiet—it's where my mom and I used to go to read *Vogue India* and eat carrot cake and avoid my dad's obsession with organized tours. Plus it's beautiful, with its whitewashed walls and lofted ceilings and black-and-white photographs decorating the walls. But as we sit down I realize it's too quiet, as in everyone's-gonna-hear-everything-we-say quiet.

Adam's good-looking, I notice right off. Not my type, but sexy enough in his athletic way. He's not the I-moved-to-India-and-became-a-hippie type. He's wearing a faded blue T-shirt with the state of Texas outlined in white, cargo shorts, and brown leather flip-flops. The boy might as well be wearing a sign that says

AMERICAN. I never met Adam during the year he and Charlie lived together. I heard about him, but what I'm seeing surprises me. Adam's tan and muscular, with short blond hair. And he's *loud.* Charlie was friends with everyone . . . but this guy's so not Charlie, to the point that I'm wondering if Charlie kept me from meeting him on purpose. Aubrey's met him before—a fun fact that makes me seethe.

"So you guys met, what, once?" My question's as innocent as it gets, but Aubrey's head jerks up and her knee bangs the table. I raise an eyebrow. "Jesus, Bree. Nervous much?" I'm needling her on purpose, and I can't even figure out my motives. I *like* Aubrey. She's the closest thing I have to a friend in all of this. I don't know what's prompting me to hurt her.

"Right," she says fast, looking at the table. "In D.C. Around my birthday."

"So that was . . ." I raise one eyebrow again, partly because I can do that and it's awesome, partly because I'm still foggy on the time-line here.

"Your birthday's in December, yeah?" Adam breaks in. "The third, right?" Aubrey's head snaps up again, and she stares at him, then nods really fast.

"Yeah," she says. "But we were in D.C. the weekend before, Thanksgiving break. The twenty-ninth. For Charlie's birthday."

"I know," Adam says easily, and Aubrey blushes. I glance from him to her. *What's going on here?* If I didn't already know that Aubrey has the biggest stick up her butt ever, I'd think she and Adam have a thing. But that's impossible.

"We only met the one time," Aubrey clarifies.

"Right," I say in my most patient voice. "Because we just covered that particular base." Adam's eyes dart from me to her and back again, looking confused.

"I know," I tell him. "It's totally weird. Charlie had two girlfriends at once. Take it all in while you can."

"So what can I help you guys with?" he finally asks, shifting in his chair. I've made him uncomfortable. I'm good at that.

"As you may or may not know," I tell him, "Charlie's missing, presumed dead."

"Of course I know."

"Well then, *of course* we want to know anything you can tell us about Charlie in Bombay. Think hard. Maybe we can start with who he was around you."

"Who he was?" Adam screws up his eyebrows. "What are you talking about?"

"Charlie was lying to us," Aubrey explains. "About more than the fact that there is an *us*. He lied about random things. Stupid things. The way he liked to dress, his favorite foods, books he read. We just want to get a sense of how his personality was with you."

"And then we want to find him and castrate him," I add. Adam raises an eyebrow and Aubrey blushes. Then Adam opens his mouth.

"I don't have much to say," he says with a shrug. "We only knew each other for about a year. Less than a year. Charlie always kept to himself. It was hard on him, I think. He came into high school during senior year. Most of us had been here the whole time. Girls liked him, I guess. I mean, he had kind of a reputation for getting around . . ." Adam blinks, and he gives Aubrey and me a stricken look. "He liked attention. Maybe a little too much. He was that guy, the new guy. Plus he was funny; he knew how to tell a joke. Right—maybe I'd better stop talking."

I feel cold all over. Adam's giving Aubrey this puppy-dog look, all worried, and he puts a hand on her wrist. But Aubrey wasn't even dating Charlie then—I was. Something here's not right.

"It's fine," I say to Adam. "I don't know why any of this is coming as a shock, after what we've already figured out." Adam doesn't bother looking in my direction. "So when did you two start hooking up?" I fire the question at Aubrey. It's a gamble, but I have this gut feeling about it. I've always been good at reading people—except for Charlie, I guess. Bree's face pales and Adam jumps in.

"What's your deal? You this hostile to everyone?"

"Just to people who are hiding Charlie's secrets," I tell him. "How long did you know Charlie had two girlfriends? How'd you manage to keep that one from Aubrey, even after you met her? Is it such a stretch that you might have hooked up with Aubrey too? Maybe felt like Charlie didn't deserve her?" Adam's expression is priceless: open-mouthed, even disgusted. I find that all of a sudden, I can't contain my rage. I grab the water bottle I keep stowed in my bag and pull off the top, chugging it until my throat loosens. I blink hard.

"Chill, Lena," Aubrey says, her voice sharp, stronger than expected. Aubrey almost never lashes out like this, not lately. "Adam's here to help."

"I didn't know Charlie had two girlfriends," Adam says, his voice softer now. "I thought he was just this single, ladies' man type, not a world-class douche. I'm really sorry. I didn't know Charlie all that well after he left Bombay. We only met up that one time in D.C., but even that was kind of random. He called me up out of nowhere that weekend, and I had nothing else going on. Like I said, when he was here he was new. And he was gone all the time on weekends, so—"

"Gone where?" Aubrey's the one with the confused look now. "Did he really visit you that much, Lena?"

"No." My face burns. I can't tell if I'm angry or embarrassed. "No, I only saw Charlie three times when he was in Bombay. Because it was so far." Three lousy times. It was a miserable year. When he went away to college, it got better. But for so long, I thought Charlie wasn't in love with me anymore.

"He went to Kerala a couple of times," Adam tells us. "Maybe more. He knew a guy who owned one of those tourist boats. The kind that take people out for a hundred bucks, float around the backwaters for a night. He said this guy, Anand, could hook us up —a boat, weed, booze—"Adam pauses, looking slightly uncomfortable. "I think he wanted to be friends with my crew. I think that's why he offered, but we never took him up on it. I don't know who he went with when he went." All of a sudden I'm embarrassed for Charlie, for us. My body burns with it. My eyes meet Aubrey's, and then hers flicker down to the tabletop again; but from the way she reaches for her coffee and just barely sips it, her cheeks heating red, I can tell she's embarrassed too.

"God," I mutter. The whole thing has taken on this absurd quality, and part of me wonders if I want to go on. What do I have to gain from this chase? Another look at Aubrey and something tells me not to stop. "So. Do you still have the information? About the guy with the boat?"

Adam looks up, surprised. Then he nods. "Somewhere," he tells me. "In my email, probably."

I look to Aubrey for help, but she's silent. *What, Aubrey, not so certain he's dead anymore?* "Don't you want to find out for sure if he's alive, Aubrey? Or is it more convenient for you to keep on blindly believing he's dead?" I know what drives me to say it, even though part of me hates myself for hurting her. I know my motive and so does she, and she feels the full weight of my words as she shoves back from the table and runs outside, her chair clattering to the floor behind her as she goes. Adam shoots me a furious look and runs after her, confirming everything I already suspect. I've hurt her, something I've thought recently I couldn't do. But she's betrayed me. I was starting to think we were becoming friends. I was beginning to trust her. I watch them as they stand outside, Aubrey crying and him wrapping his arms around her. I'm not done. That was just a bite. There's a lot more in me.

11

Aubrey

CHARLIE COULD HAVE SLEPT WITH ME, but he didn't. He knew I wasn't ready, so he waited for me, and it never wound up happening. It's something I'm both grateful for and regret. Early on, Charlie said all the right things, did all the right things. It was something he was especially good at.

The Jefferson Hotel in Montreal was lovely. It was in Mile End, a trendy neighborhood—walkable—its streets lined with shops and cafés. It was only my third time out of the country, the first being France with my parents when I was little, and the second Niagara Falls just last year, which hardly counts for anything. My parents thought Charlie and I were on a trip with Charlie's parents; they also thought Charlie's parents were just as much a unit as they were —strong and steady and loving. Not the kind who'd rent us a private suite in a five-star hotel for the express purpose of our private vacation.

Charlie's parents, they didn't think like any of the adults I knew in Illinois.

It made me nervous. But they were cosmopolitan, cultured. They treated Charlie like an equal. "They trust me," he said over and over when I said, gaping at the lobby—which resembled an old gentlemen's club from another era—"Are you *sure* this is okay?"

"If it's not okay, Bree, it's too late now," he told me, slinging an arm around my shoulders. I remember leaning into him, responding in such a natural way to his touch. His wool felt pea coat tickled my cheek; it was cold in Montreal—a chilly autumn, just a few months after we met. It all felt so grown-up—like we were playing house. But I wanted to assimilate well to this world; I figured it was no better or worse than the one I came from, just different. I wanted to understand it, to be a part of it. To maybe decide whether to belong to it.

I wasn't sure, having met Charlie, whether I could ever go back to the way things were, when I was just a suburban girl in Illinois. *That's what happens when you meet someone different,* I thought to myself as I stood there, taking in the grandeur of the hotel. *Your world opens up just a little.* I felt scared then, because I was certain I'd never stop craving that expansion, bit by bit, relationship by relationship, person by person.

The thought made me cold; I didn't know where it had come from. I hugged Charlie tighter, waiting for him to complete check-in. There was a staircase to my left, stretching upward in the tradition of the kind of European elegance I'd seen in books. It was wide and sprawling and covered in thick carpet in a shade of dark green. On its underside, facing out into the room, were row upon row of books. They weren't just for show. I wandered over and ran a finger over the titles as Charlie got everything organized. They were mostly classics: hardbound, with the kinds of spines that have visible stitches. The kind I was used to finding in my grandparents' house when I was a kid.

A young family took up a large portion of the room. Two blond children were playing with a chessboard while their parents discussed something quietly in nearby leather chairs. Their mom was also blond—and glamorous, in a tweed blazer with elbow patches and brown leather riding boots. Their dad was sturdy and handsome, like maybe he played one of those highbrow sports like polo. The little girls spoke with British accents, and their suitcases were made of pink leather.

In Illinois, my parents were probably just sitting down to dinner. Maybe they were smiling at each other across my mom's famous turkey tetrazzini casserole, saying things like "I hope Aubrey knows what she's getting herself into," and "You like this boy, don't you, Mac?" and "As well as any other boy her age, I guess, though they're all a pretty sorry bunch. This one doesn't follow *any* sports teams, not even college football. He's not my kinda guy; but I'm not the one dating him," and "I just want her to be safe. Did you hear her say he isn't any kind of religion at all?" In my imagination, their smiles faded and their brows creased and they leaned toward each other over the vinyl floral tablecloth, spooning turkey and noodles and mushroom sauce into their mouths as they lapsed into a worried silence.

Charlie tugged on my sleeve as I stared at those books, bringing me back to the present. I clasped his hand tightly, letting the warmth of his palm seep into me. I remember thinking: *I have to stop being this way. I need to start believing this stuff is real,* because sometimes it all felt like I was playing a part in a story. Stuff like this only ever happens in novels.

"Here," Charlie said, handing me a glass of sparkling wine. "This is for us. Complimentary at check-in. We can take it up to our room."

"Don't they—?"

"Shh! No. They think we're of age. I *am* of age." He winked a lit-tle devilishly and pulled me toward the elevator bank. We ascended three stories, four, five, and then we were there. The hotel on this level was carpeted in red, its halls narrow. There were photographs on the walls: women on horseback, men leaning on croquet mallets in front of mansions. I felt my fear creeping into my throat as we drew closer.

Then Charlie opened the door and the suite spread out in front of us: a long leather couch and two pale blue crushed-velvet chairs that almost looked as if they'd been vacuumed, since their texture was mottled with uniform streaks from changes in the fabric. There was a little bar to our left; a vase full of white hydrangeas rested on its granite surface. A bowl of truffles lay in the center of a long glass coffee table, and a large wall-mount TV oversaw the whole thing. It took my breath away; and yet I was having trouble entering.

Charlie took my hand and pulled me forward. "The best part isn't here," he said softly. He swung me around, fast, and I laughed awkwardly. Then his arms were around me from behind, and he was walking me forward, one foot in front of the next. "It's here," he whispered, pausing at the threshold of the bedroom.

The bed was beautiful: king-size and covered in a fluffy down comforter. It did nothing to distill the panic that worked its way into my throat. I breathed in sharply and Charlie must have taken it for awe, because he began kissing my neck, my cheek, moving to-ward my lips. "I knew you'd love Montreal," he told me. "I've been wanting to take you here since I met you."

I was okay dipping a toe into Charlie's world, but I wasn't okay with this. It suddenly became obvious: Of *course* Charlie expected this. Of *course* this was a given. I should have realized it the second he suggested a whole weekend away. He had made all of these assumptions, and all of a sudden I was furious with him for not asking me and with myself for not anticipating the situation.

"I'm not going to sleep with you," I said, whirling to face him. "I can't sleep with you. I've never slept with anyone and I'm not ready. I'm sorry. I know that's why you brought me here, and I should have known, and I should have told you sooner, but I was stupid, and I'm sorry." I stopped, breathing hard. Charlie stared back at me, his face a caricature. "I'm sorry," I repeated. After the last apology he seemed to snap him back to himself, like some internal rubber band.

"Hey," he said. "Why would you apologize? You should never apologize for something like that. Hey, come here." He started to lead me toward the bed, then caught himself and changed direction, pulling me to the long leather couch in the main room. "Sit." He patted a spot next to him. Then he drew me into him, pulling my head to his shoulder, and I promptly started to cry.

"Hey, shhh. Aubrey, listen to me. *I'm* sorry. I didn't realize any of that. I should have talked to you first. I don't expect that. Really. I'd be happy holding hands all night if that's what you wanted."

"Holding hands." I laughed. "Yeah, right."

"Holding hands is way underrated," he said. "It's actually way better than all that other stuff." I raised my eyebrows at him, but he managed to look sincere. "I'm totally serious," he continued. "You know why?" I shook my head, and he touched the tips of my fingers with those of his opposite hand, the one that wasn't already resting on my shoulder. A tingle worked its way up my spine. "It's better," he said, his voice low, "because it means more. You don't hold hands with just any girl." Then he wrapped his fingers through mine all the way and pulled me into his chest, and I nearly stopped breathing.

"Sometimes I forget you're a little older, I forget you've done things," I started.

"None of it matters. It's all new with you. It's all a first with you."

"You're so melodramatic," I told him, masking how I really felt: hopeful. I wanted him to mean it.

He pulled away and looked me in the eye. "Have you ever been here?" he asked, tapping his heart with one palm. "That's kind of how it works."

Charlie and I didn't stay in that hotel. He said he got it all wrong, kept repeating that with a funny scowl on his face. "I've got it all wrong," he kept saying. "I thought you'd like the books, the atmosphere . . ."

"I did! I do!" I kept insisting.

But he said, "No, no, I screwed it up. It's not something you want. I should have seen that. We're not staying." He was upset with himself the whole way out of the hotel, until we ordered a rental car and climbed inside it with our bags and began to drive.

"What about the money?" I asked. The hotel must have been a few hundred dollars at least.

"Money doesn't matter," Charlie said. "You being happy matters." Sometimes it was like Charlie read the manual on stuff boyfriends should say, or maybe wrote it. So we drove from Montreal all the way along the Saint Lawrence River until we reached Quebec City. Along the way we stopped in a park and lay in the grass and wrapped our coats around us until there was just a tent of coats and us and some geese squawking in the background. "A coat taco," Charlie said. "We're the filling." And I laughed and thought about how perfect it all was, sans grandeur, because in this way I could be myself: I could bring a little of me into his world instead of leaving myself behind.

When we got to Quebec City, we stopped in a roadside dive and ate poutine until we felt sick, our fingers coated in cheese and gravy. Then we found a cute little place to stay, a mom-and-pop B&B that didn't even ask us for ID, and we were so tired from the day that we curled up atop the mattress and fell asleep with all our clothes on, his arms wrapped around me.

The next day we got under the covers, and some of our clothes came off. We didn't sleep together, but everything we did do was on my terms. "There've been a couple of times that I'm with you," he whispered, "and it's like, there's no air in the room." I smiled. That time, I didn't tease him. Our heads were nearly touching on the pillow. He moved forward, closing up those last inches, and placed his lips on my forehead. I woke up happy that morning and stayed happy all through the rest of that perfect weekend. It was one of a handful of times we really got away, just the two of us, for an entire weekend. Each time it took all kinds of finagling on my part—lots of lying to my parents. Back then, I thought it was worth it.

So many mornings, I woke up happy that Charlie was in my life. Then one morning, I stopped waking up happy.

I haven't been in many long-term relationships—only two—but here's what I think: For a while, you wake up happy. Then other things happen, small things—misunderstandings like the one in the hotel. And they accumulate, and one day you wake up with a weight on your chest, one that takes all day to shake. And that's when you know: happiness with that person is only fleeting. That person, that thing—it feels for a while like it might be right, until you realize it isn't, not quite.

I tell Adam to leave, even though it's the last thing in the world that I want.

"Are you sure you're okay?" he wants to know. "I don't like her, Aubrey." He glances back through the warped glass windows of the café where Lena sits, her blond hair draped around her shoulders, concealing her face. The expression Adam gives me when he faces me again is protective. This whole time, Adam has made me feel cared about in small ways. It was something Charlie never did. It's given me so much comfort as everything around me has started to fall apart.

"You don't like her because she wasn't afraid to call us out," I remind him. "You don't really know her. She's my friend . . ." I trail off, my cheeks burning. It's just so weird to talk about Charlie with Adam, after everything. It was true what we told Lena; we only saw each other that one time. I only cheated that one time. But all the letters, phone calls, flirty texts, over the next eight months . . . those counted for something. It was unconscionable. And yet, I cared about them both. I didn't exactly let myself fall for Adam; I always felt like it happened despite everything, like I didn't have a choice.

"So I guess people can tell," he says, smiling a little, but it doesn't reach his eyes. "I guess we have some sort of invisible yet obvious bond, huh?"

"It seems like it." I reach out to him, burying my head in his chest and wrapping my arms around his back. I pull him to me in a tight hug.

"Aubrey." He rests his chin on my head. "I'm just so sad for you."

"I'm sad for both of us. Charlie, too. And Lena. We're just a huge, sad mess." I don't have to say why I'm sad for both of us; he knows. We can't be together, not yet, and not this way. Probably not ever. We never talked about it until last night.

"Last night can't happen again," he says, more like it's a question.

"You know it can't."

"And you're sure you want me to go?"

"I don't even know how much longer we'll be in Bombay, Adam. Knowing Lena, she'll want to hop the next plane to Kerala. Track Charlie down there."

"What do *you* want?" The question is simple. Too simple. His heart beats against his chest in a way that's so normal I can't stand it. A simple thing, a heartbeat, to make sense of the mess this summer has become. Two months ago, Charlie was still here. I'd never been to Asia at all. I didn't know Lena. I only knew what I thought was the truth — my truth, Charlie's truth — never mind all the dark layers beneath it.

"I don't know what I want." What I don't tell him, but what I'm thinking, is how it's not about wanting at all: I *need* to know what happened to Charlie, to determine whether my secret is safe. My stomach turns when I think about what Lena would do if she found out that Adam is the lesser of my evils. My palms are sweating, and I'm struggling to figure out the best way to answer Adam's question. "I think I need to stick this out, figure out as much as I can about what was going on with Charlie. I can't explain it. I can't *not* chase this now that we've started." Adam pulls back from me a little, tilting my chin up so I'm forced to look into his huge green eyes.

"I'm not going to see you again, am I?"

"I think you'll do okay without me," I tell him. What I don't tell him is that he's far better off this way.

"You were way too good for Charlie," he says. His eyes pull down at the corners, and I look away to avoid tearing up again.

"You didn't really know him." It's weak, unconvincing.

"Neither did you." He hugs me again, drawing me into his chest, and all I want is to hit pause at this moment so I can stay in it forever. All year, I tried to put Adam out of my mind. I have him now, and we can't be together. It seems so unfair. Underneath that there's the same pulsing guilt I've felt since I met him. Miserable, relentless, unforgiving. So many times, I tried to choose. Then Charlie stripped me of the choice altogether.

The door to the café swings open and Adam and I break apart. Lena strides toward me, ignoring Adam.

"I paid." Her voice is cold. "But you already knew that. Or at least expected it. Am I right?"

I reel, feeling as if I've been slapped. But how could she not be angry?

"Bye, Adam," Lena says. "Be sure to send Aubrey that info. The guy with the houseboat. I'm sure you two will be talking anyway." Adam's eyes dart to me and I nod, urging him away with my eyes. His presence will only fuel her fire. And we've already said our goodbyes.

"I'll email you," he tells me. Then he shoves his hands in his pockets and walks back the way we came, disappearing into the throngs of people that line Mahatma Gandhi Road. Clouds of dust rise up behind him until a chai wallah's cart obscures him altogether.

"You disgust me," Lena says, her voice thick with venom. Her eyes are a monstrous black color, and I'm so shocked by the strength of her anger and what it looks like, her hair floating around her small frame like a false halo, that for a second I can't speak.

"You dragged me out here—took advantage of me—just to sleep with some guy?" Her voice is accusing, unforgiving. "You act like you're in this with me, like you really need this—journal or whatever—like you're my *friend*. And really you just want a free ticket to see your new boyfriend. You're as sick as Charlie." She's nearly yelling now and I'm backing away, and the few people who are leaving Trishna's stare. We're these two white girls, behaving in the worst possible, most American way.

"Aubrey," Lena continues, "I want to kill you this instant." I know by now that she's melodramatic, but somehow this time I don't doubt her.

"Lena, let's—"

"Shut up." Her voice slices through my words like a razor. "I just want to know one thing from you. Did he know?"

"Did who know?" I'm nervous. My palms are clamming up.

"Cut the bullshit, Aubrey. When did you tell Charlie you were cheating on him?"

Relief floods my entire body. She's still only talking about that. For a second, I thought she meant something else. "It only happened once," I say.

"When did he find out? Tell me, Aubrey. TELL ME." There's a crowd gathering now: a little boy leading a cow ten times his size, a well-dressed middle-class woman in a pink and orange patterned kurta, three men eating from the kinds of tin trays they have at roadside food stalls. I just want to get out of there as fast as possible.

"I tried to tell him a few times," I say quietly. "It just never worked. He never wanted to listen. I finally told him three months ago. When he was visiting me at my parents' place in Illinois."

"Your parents met him." Her voice is dull, flat.

"Of course. They never would have let me visit him those other times if they hadn't."

"What was the date?"

"Why?"

"You don't have the right to ask questions right now. Just tell me the date."

"I guess it would have been . . . May nineteenth. Yeah. That's right, because he was in town that weekend for my high school graduation, and I told him the night before he left. He had to fly straight back to school to finish the year out." Lena sucks in a breath, and her already pale skin turns an eerie shade of blue-white. "What? What is it? Lena. Tell me."

"I don't have to tell you anything," she says, then whirls on one heel and heads back down the crowded, filth-strewn roads in the direction of the hotel. Once again, Lena's in charge. It's all I can do to keep her in my line of vision as she moves, weaving her way expertly among cows and goats and peddlers and beggars. I'm afraid, suddenly. I'm afraid because I'm wholly dependent on her. She's my ticket home, my way through and away from this messy city.

Also, I realize for the first time: I'm in this. I'm so far in it that I honestly can't envision returning to my other life, the safe and supported one back in Illinois, where everything was predictable and ordinary. Maybe meeting Charlie a year ago set this chain of events in motion, but Lena's infused it with purpose.

I have this weird feeling, pain twisting in my stomach and squeezing my heart. Lena feels betrayed. Like I used her for a free ride.

Adam was on my mind when I suggested Bombay. But I would never have pushed her to go all the way out here—or taken advantage of her kindness—if Z hadn't mentioned the journal. If I hadn't seen it for myself in the photo. I never would have come just for Adam. I *need* her to know that.

I run after her, following her yellow shirt through the crowd, bolts of adrenaline and fear shooting through me. I can't tell when Lena became important to me, but she has. I breathe a sigh of relief when I see her turning onto Colaba Causeway, still in the direction of our hotel. She's so impulsive, she could have gone anywhere. I follow her up to the room and let myself in with my key before she can change keys or figure out a way to lock me out. She curls up on her queen-size bed and turns away from me toward the wall, humming softly to herself like she does sometimes when she's not talking. I sit on the edge of my bed next to her. I want to hug her but I don't feel it's my right. Her legs are folded up behind her, and her curls spread out over the white bed cover, just faintly yellow against its silken embroidery. Sun streams in through the window, casting a beam over her. She looks ethereal in its light. In a few hours the sky will turn orange, yellow, pink, and purple with another breathtaking sunset. I know, because that's how it was last night; and nothing seems to happen in India without Technicolor.

"Talk to me." My voice is unabashedly pleading. "Please. Lena, I'm sorry. I didn't come out here for Adam. But I should have told you anyway."

"You should have," she agrees. Then she's silent.

"I'm sorry," I say again. "I truly am. I don't know what I was thinking. I was just . . . afraid to trust you. I didn't know you yet. But now I see how wrong I was."

She doesn't tell me off. She doesn't move. I sit there for an hour before I give up and turn on the TV, flipping on a Bollywood dance channel because I hope it'll pique her interest. She barely shifts position. She's so quiet and so still that she could be sleeping, but I can tell by the sound of her breathing that she's not.

Two hours later I order room service. The waiter brings up butter chicken and palak paneer for me and shrimp korma for Lena, along with two portions of cheese naan; and still she doesn't move. She hasn't eaten all day. I wonder what she's thinking about. I feel like a sentry, standing guard. I feel like I'm too obsessed. But this is my new reality. My hands are clammy, I'm anxious, I'm wildly afraid she'll leave. I'm acutely aware of the strength of my feelings for her. We're like that for the whole rest of the night: Me watching, waiting. Lena thinking, rejecting.

12

Lena

I TELL PEOPLE THAT I MET CHARLIE at a summer enrichment program in London. Which is mostly true. But Charlie wasn't in the Talent Identification program sponsored by Duke, the one masquerading as a résumé booster that was, for me, just an excuse to jet-set like I always have every summer, thus getting me out of my parents' hair and freeing them up to go wherever they want: a safari in Botswana, a treehouse village in Provence, et cetera. I love that my parents are in love and want alone time. I do.

What people don't know about having parents who are madly in love is that it makes it harder to fall in love yourself—the bar's set way too high. I was never expecting to fall in love with Charlie. I never expected to fall in love with anyone the way my parents are in love. Their love is like the fucking white whale. No one else has it. No one in our world, anyway. But there it was, the night I met Charlie. Maybe we Whitneys are blessed, maybe we're cursed. No one knows for certain, but it sure feels like a curse right now.

What people also don't know is that Charlie, though a frequent patron of many other summer enrichment programs, was just kind of bumming around London that summer. I met him while I was in the program, but he was selling a bunch of old vinyls online. That's why I don't mention it a lot—because Charlie and I technically met online. And that's still vaguely embarrassing if you're under the age of twenty-three. He posted the vinyls on Craigslist and put a link to the ad (labeled "Moving Sale") on the campus online message boards, and I answered it, and that was that.

Well, not exactly.

I showed up at Charlie's place around eight thirty on a Sunday night. I had classes the next day at seven a.m. and had just moved all my stuff into my summer dorm room with this girl, a violinist named Alice Choi, who barely looked up from her book when I came in. It was going to be a super fun summer.

I got to Charlie's and knocked on the door and it immediately opened because two shirtless dudes wearing black jeans and carrying a bookshelf walked out. They let the door slam shut behind them before I could grab it, so I had to knock again. This time a girl—tall and blond and big-boned—answered.

"I'm here for the records," I told her. My hair was red then and my fingernails were gray and chipped.

"Charlie's back there." The girl motioned with her head down a long hallway, so I walked past a bathroom and a tiny bedroom with exposed brick walls, barely big enough to fit a twin bed in it. It was more like a glorified closet. I remember thinking how I'd never live there, not in a million years and (I thought later) not for a million Charlies. That's where Charlie and I differed. He was adaptive; I had standards. He had access to money but could take it or leave it. Not me, no way.

I saw Charlie a second later. He was standing in a little room that served as both a kitchen and a living room, talking to some old guys about a lamp. "I mean, I liked the look of it," he said. "I'm not really familiar with antiques, so I don't know if it's worth anything." His eyes flickered over to me.

"I'm Lena," I said. "I emailed you about the vinyls."

"Right."

It sounds stupid, so I never bothered telling anybody this, but in that one little flicker of the eyes was everything: our whole relationship, an infinite path I just had to let myself step onto. I could see everything laid out in front of me, mostly in shades of blue and ivory. Which is strange to think about now, because those are calming colors, and nothing about us was ever placid. I could envision our first kiss and all the things that would go along with it. It was certain—I didn't have to *do* anything. And I wanted to step onto that path. But I also wanted to make him work for it. I grabbed the carton of vinyls, which was super heavy, and tried not to strain too much under its weight. My red hair was pulled back in a messy bun and I was wearing this big baggy dress I'd found in a designer consignment shop, something supposedly fashionable that was probably more akin to an old lady's discarded muumuu. I knew how I looked (crappy) and I knew I didn't care and he didn't care and it didn't matter. It was all there in that one look: the inevitability of it.

Inevitable. It was the word for us. The word our relationship would rest and revolve on.

"Okay, well, thanks," I said. "Here's your forty pounds." I sounded like I didn't care, but inside, my heart was beating like crazy. I wasn't nervous, exactly, because I knew how it would all pan out. It was like someone said, "Here's how it's going to end; now enjoy the ride."

"These guys will be gone in a minute," he told me. "Stick around." I leaned against the windowsill with my crate of records at my feet. Charlie looked over at me, smiling a little under blue eyes, hooded lids. Everything about Charlie other than his eyes was dark: his hair, the way he moved. Everything he did seemed like it had some deeper message I was supposed to decode. But I wasn't intimidated. Charlie had met his match in me, and we both knew it. Charlie fiddled in the refrigerator and I stood there and then the guys were gone.

"So you like The National?" He nodded toward the stack of vinyls. The record on top featured a woman with her face split in two by a mirror. *Trouble Will Find Me* is one of my favorite albums.

"I do. Easily top five. Are you cleaning out the fridge?"

"I am. But I figure you're going to need help carrying those when I'm done."

"No need," I said. "I've got it covered. Not so sure about you, though."

"Oh?" Charlie poked his head out of the fridge. "Feel free to help me out, if you feel so inclined." I moved toward him and eyed the open refrigerator. It was full of moldy stuff.

"This is disgusting." I plucked a jar of fuzzy pesto sauce from the top shelf and dropped it into the open garbage bag that Charlie had dragged over. It was already half full with old ratty towels and crumpled bags of chips.

"Yeah, toss it. Toss it all."

"This?"

"No, I want that." Charlie grabbed the still-sealed brick of ched- dar cheese from my hand and rummaged in a drawer next to him. "Want some? I forgot to eat." I shook my head, and he ripped open the package and dug in.

"It's fun seeing the inside of your fridge," I inform him. "I've never known a guy our age who eats pickled herring."

"Roommate's," he told me. "This, however, is mine." He wrested a jar of hot peppers from my grasp.

"When do you guys move?"

"We have to be out by tomorrow morning. Wanna come to our packing party?"

"Is that code for a getting-rid-of-leftover-booze party?"

"Pretty much."

"Then yes. Just don't expect me to work at all. Why aren't you taking the vinyls?"

Charlie paused, straightening. "That's not about moving," he said. "That's about karma. Plus I knew I'd meet someone interesting if I listed them. Only certain types of people collect vinyls."

"I'm definitely interesting," I said, halfway out the door. "I'll tell you about it when I come back."

"Tell me now," he said. "Help me finish the fridge."

"Didn't I say I'm not here to work? Will you still be partying after midnight, or is that when you vanish?" (I actually said that. How could I have known?)

"We'll be partying all night, up on the roof. Come by whenever. Text me."

"I'll do better," I told him. I didn't know what I meant; I just said it, and it sounded good. Then I left. Most of what I said and did with Charlie was for dramatic impact, to play the game. Charlie was a guy who needed to be kept on his toes.

"Don't you want help?" he called after me. But I didn't answer.

Part of me didn't want to go back. It took a long time to take the records back to my dorm room. Then I had to have dinner with the program, and then there was the simple matter of sneaking out after our eleven p.m. curfew. I was only sixteen then, but I'd already had ample practice with sneaking out. That was the easy part. The hard part was, I was tired. I had class super early and Alice Choi had had a change of heart and wanted to bond all of a sudden. But I also knew that my fate hinged on going. So I pretended like I had to call my mom outside in the hallway, and I went. It took me thirty minutes to walk from my place in Islington back to Charlie's place in Knightsbridge. I didn't know how old Charlie was. He could have been anywhere from seventeen to twenty-two. At that point, I didn't know his last name. I just had a phone number and an anonymous Craigslist email address. All I knew was, if I went back, my life would change.

I got there and Charlie was carrying a shelving unit downstairs with one of his friends, a guy I'd find out later was named Peter. He was a short, skinny Asian guy who was too small to carry shelving units by himself. I walked right past them and upstairs to the roof. "Aren't you going to help us out?" Charlie asked. "I'm here for the party," I called back. I could feel his eyes on me the whole way, even after I was out of sight.

Here's a little secret: I effing hate showing up at parties alone. This was worse than usual because I didn't know anyone and it took Charlie forever to make his way up there. For an hour I talked to random people. But the good thing was, they'd all been there for, like, two or three hours and were drinking their faces off that whole time, so no one cared who I was or would remember anyway. The rooftop was beautiful. London spread out all around us, its lights ablaze. From a certain angle, it could have been any city, on any night. But it was London, and it was that particular night. It all meant something. I was only sixteen but with my new red hair I could pass for eighteen, and I was hovering on the precipice of something big.

Two vodka OJs later he was at my shoulder.

"Oh, hey," he said, breaking off mid-conversation with someone else, like he hadn't expected to see me there.

"Hi," I said.

And then we were talking, all in a group, and I was being the kind of charming I can be with the help of vodka; and he said something and I rolled my eyes and he said, "She just rolled her eyes at me!" and seemed to like it, and I said: "Well, what did you say? I'm sure you deserved it," and he said, "Let me show you the view from the other side of the roof," and we went over there and he kissed me, cutting me off in midsentence with his lips and his tongue. Just like I knew he would.

For much of the night, we walked around the city. We got pizza a few blocks down at a place called Merv's. We picked up his rental car at a parking garage, but first we stopped on the corner where there was this huge, cement egg-shaped chair. Charlie grabbed my hand and pulled me into the chair next to him and we kissed for an hour.

"I must be having fun," he told me when we finally stopped and my head was resting on his shoulder. "Because it's been an hour and fifteen minutes and I'm paying for this car by the hour."

"I must be having fun too," I said back, "because I have to get up at seven and it's already three." We went on like that for two more hours: kissing on the corners, in the car, against the exteriors of buildings, the grit of their filthy brick walls leaving trails on my shoulders and back. Charlie's hand on my waist with me in front of him. Later we packed the rest of his apartment into the car, we talked on and on about stuff I don't remember anymore, not that it matters other than in the sense that it kept us happy. Finally at five a.m. I got in a cab and headed back to my dorm room. "I'll call you tomorrow," he said. I knew he wouldn't, and he didn't. After all, he was leaving. But I also knew it wasn't the last I'd hear of Charlie.

The boat in Kerala is different from what I expected. So's Anand. He's older than we are, first of all — maybe in his midtwenties. And Aubrey, she's quaking in her prissy ballet flats. I plan to keep her quaking. She deserves it. I paid fifty dollars for the use of Anand's boat for eighteen hours. Around the time we were looking for a boat, the sun was high. The water looked clean and inviting, but the paths to the boats were mostly just mud with a few plywood boards thrown over it. We trudged up and down maybe seven of those paths, and it was all a show. I made this big deal out of checking out five of Anand's boats before settling on the one Anand himself is sailing, partly to torture Aubrey, but also because it would be too much of a giveaway to choose his right away, even though hundreds of tourists must come through here. I don't want Anand to know how we found him, that we know Charlie. We'll find out more if we're covert. I like the word *covert*. It makes me feel like we're protagonists in a spy movie.

Aubrey's looking for her stupid journal and I'm looking for Charlie. Still looking, still believing he's alive, even though it's been more than two weeks since his alleged death. Still thinking we'll find him, if only we search under the right rocks. Like he's a lost puppy. Am I crazy for thinking this way? Aubrey thinks I want answers; and I do, but I want them from Charlie. I'd feel bad for her if I weren't so angry with her; but anger has pretty much filled every fiber of my being, until I almost ooze it. I woke up furious this morning in our hotel. My whole body was coiled and so tense that my muscles were sore, almost like I'd spent all night working out.

It got me thinking about all the things that are put on for show. Charlie and me, for one. His heart was apparently half elsewhere. Aubrey and me . . . sometimes it feels like a screwed-up fledgling friendship with her. I've always been popular, moved around a lot, had groups of friends wherever I've gone. But I've never had just one friend who was *mine,* precisely for the reason that I do move around a lot. That's what it's started to feel like with Aubrey. Then I stop to think about how messed up it is, how much we've already lied to each other. And now, finding this boat, weaving more lies, and a true friendship—the kind I've always craved—feels impossible. Sometimes it feels like my whole life lately is one huge lying mess. Sometimes I wonder if I would have thrown my whole self into Charlie the way I did, if only I'd had closer friends.

I made this big deal about choosing the boat, but there was no choice to make. Let's be honest: The other available boats were just as dinky and rotted as this one. This one is just a little bigger. So when

Anand approached us with a deal and assured us he'd sail it himself ("top captain"), it was a no-brainer. Aubrey's impressed. But we
needed the boat that comes with Anand, that's all. It's wood-paneled
and thatch-roofed, and the bottom level has a wraparound deck. A
ladder near the bedroom leads to the upper deck, which is fully exposed to the sun. From where we stand on the lower deck, we can see
the water lapping up against the sides. It's fresh water, but probably
just as toxic as the sea, and the whole time we're standing out there
I'm thinking, *I'd love to push her in.* I shoot her a grin and make a little
shoving gesture with my hands, and she recoils. I'd never actually do
it. But she doesn't know that.

I try not to think about Charlie in Kerala, of the whole life he led
here that I was never a part of. Three years. Three fucking years. I
look at Aubrey's short dark hair lifting in the breeze as the boat sets
off and try not to think about her future with Adam, how she still
has the promise of someone waiting for her. I don't. Charlie was my
world . . . and then he destroyed it. Objectively I try to think about
what that does to a person. What it's probably done to me. I can't
see myself clearly enough to know for sure. I'm jealous of Aubrey's
hope, her innocence, the way she's leaning on me to make all the
decisions on this trip and can lean on Adam when she gets home.
The jealousy is so strong it nearly knocks me out. A wave of anger
and hatred makes me gasp, and she trains her bright blue eyes on
me, concern radiating from just under her knitted brow.

I should tell her the truth now. I can destroy her if I want to, right
now.

I can see it in her face: Adam is everywhere. She still has that
early-stage, just-in-love distracted glow. She's pushed Charlie out,
let this other guy claim a prominent space in her heart. I don't know

why it bothers me. It shouldn't, but it does. Maybe because I feel like I'm sliding back while she's pushing forward. Maybe because I'm protective of this person who deceived me.

Anand has retreated to the kitchen, where he's frying up the fresh fish we're having for dinner. Anand is handsome in a way I didn't expect: young, muscular. Tall with appealing features and chin scruff. He has a gentle smile, crinkly eyes, a friendly way. He exudes confidence and ease, like he knows exactly what to expect from the world. Like nothing's ever caught him off-guard.

I crack open one of the beers that Anand left for us on the picnic-style table and take a long pull, mostly to still my trembling hands. I have issues with what I'm about to do. Big ones. Moral ones. But my anger builds up under my skin, bleeding through my pores from the inside out. I know nothing will make it go away except revenge. I make my decision to tell Aubrey the truth right here, standing on deck while Anand works away at the fish, sliding a knife over their scales and gutting their putrid insides. I want to gut her the way he's gutting them. It's not rational. I want her to feel guilty about what she did to Charlie. I don't even believe he's dead; but I know she believes it, or she wants to. I can hurt her, so I decide I will. I want to do it right here, right now, while we're trapped on this boat and there's no way she can possibly escape.

"Look at this, Aubrey." I say it in a falsely cheerful voice. My pulse thrums at my temples. Aubrey looks up expectantly, responding to the kindness in my voice. She moves toward me to stand at the entrance of the little cabin that houses the bedroom and the bathroom. The just-setting sun frames her figure in the doorway. "It's so romantic!" I continue. "You and me, all curled up under mosquito netting. There's only one person I can think of whom I'd rather do this with." I turn to face her, pasting a huge grin on my face. "Can you think of anyone? Maybe our ex-boyfriend? The one whose heart you stole and skewered?" I fight to keep the grin on my face even though I'm quaking inside worse than Aubrey is quaking on her exterior. I imagine I must look manic, crazed. That mean, angry part of me wants Aubrey to be more than a little afraid. My heart accelerates and my hands turn cold.

"Lena," she tries for the millionth time in the past twelve hours. "I'm so sorry." But I can sense the weariness in her tone. Her explanations haven't helped, haven't done anything but piss me off further, even after a whole night of listening to her exhaustive pleading. I'm not letting her off. She seems like the kind of girl who gets off easily all the time—like all it takes is a sincere apology and a good-girl smile. Maybe Aubrey needs to learn that the world can be harsher than that. I glare at her and turn away, and this crazy surge of anger works its way up my chest and out through my temples. It's time to tell her.

"Oh my god," I hear her say. This is new; she actually sounds irritated. The smell of fried fish is in the air, the boat is coasting through an idyllic landscape, and the air between us is leaden with fury. "You do realize I didn't 'do' anything to *you*, right? So what, you always get this angry on Charlie's behalf?"

"Are you fucking kidding me?" The question is a threat, and the tension of the last couple of days is too much. My vision is cloudy and I'm shaking. I lower my voice to a hiss so Anand won't hear us from the kitchen. "Charlie would still be here if you hadn't set this whole thing in motion."

"We have no idea what happened with Charlie!" Aubrey replies in a strangled tone, her fists clenched at her sides. She takes a step toward me. My heart is pounding in my ears. "We don't know why his plane crashed. Why would you think it has anything to do with me?"

I'm so furious I can hardly see. "It has everything to do with you," I say, with venom. "Because if he's dead, it's your fault." There. There it is. I said it, but she looks nonplussed. She looks like she doesn't get what I'm saying. "Do you understand what I mean, Aubrey?" I'm the one moving forward now, and I back her against the thin wall that separates the sleeping cabin from the rest of the boat.

"I'm the only one left who thinks he might be alive. Why do you think the investigation closed like it did? Why do you think his parents threw together that memorial service so quickly? His entire family is sure he's dead," I say, relishing every hateful word as it pours from my mouth. "Because he left a suicide note." I pause, preparing myself to put the final nail in the coffin. "I found it. I showed his parents."

"No," she whispers, her blue eyes turning a ghostly shade of gray that fades almost entirely into her white orbs. I'm an inch or two away from her now, no more. I have just one more thing to say.

"It's the truest thing you've heard in weeks," I tell her, my voice low. "You're right, I'm probably crazy for thinking it's all a setup. But if you're right, for all you did to him, you may as well have killed him yourself. He wrote the note the night after you told him you cheated. It was dated May twentieth." I stop, waiting for the guilt and remorse to overcome her the way I've been fantasizing it will. Aubrey already believed Charlie was dead; this will merely illuminate her role in his death. She deserves to suffer. She should hurt for her betrayal, whether or not he actually *is* dead. For being the kind of person who would do what she did.

Aubrey's jaw moves mechanically like she's about to respond; I wait, but her eyes shift to a space behind me. Then they widen in fear. I turn to see what she's looking at, and my heart stops. I take a step backwards, and my shoulder collides against the wall. I'm right next to Aubrey now, both of us vulnerable.

I can't tear my eyes away from what scared her: the outline of Anand in the door frame of the bedroom, backlit by the setting sun. In one large palm he carries a plate loaded with the heads of the fish he's just finished cleaning. Their dead eyes gape. In the other hand he holds a large knife. It hasn't yet been cleaned. It drips blood and gristle onto the deck. Anand's demeanor has changed. His body is tense, powerful.

"You're friends of Charlie's," he says in an odd, flat tone. I look into Aubrey's eyes and see the terror that mirrors mine.

13

A Letter from Charlie

May 20th

Mom,

<u>Dear Mom</u>, I should have started. I should
have done a million things differently,
don't you think? And now it's too late to
go back. I should have offered you more
affection more often. Sorry, I'm so clumsy.
Soon, I'll be gone, and there won't be any
making up left to do. Why will I be gone?
Why me, Charlie, your only son? Don't think
this is about you, or Dad being gone all the
time, or anything else. You've always tried
your very hardest--if I've fallen short it's
been my own undoing. If you are reading this
now, please be assured that I am gone. You
need to let go now. If you're looking for

answers, all I can say is this: Life got a
little overwhelming. I bit off more than I
could chew, which you always warned me about,
didn't you? This time I did it, and I didn't
know how to fix it. It has ruined me.

Mom, did you ever know how much I love that
quote by Aleksandar Hemon? The one on the
inside cover of your book Let the Great World
Spin? I was flipping through your copy one
day just by accident, while you were making
dinner . . . maybe a few months ago when I
last visited you in Paris over school break.
Dad was away again, so it was just you and
me, but that was okay. I always liked those
weekends better, when it was just us. Anyway
I flipped through and I found this quote:
"All the lives I could live, all the people
I will never know, never will be, they are
everywhere. That is what the world is."

It's from The Lazarus Project, that quote.
When I read it, it hit me. I realized--
it's me. And it torments me, because I want
to live all the lives, know and be all the
people. I want the whole huge world to be
mine. That striving, that is why it had to
come to this. This time, all the people . . .

pushing each other around--it pushed me too
far.

And then, there's the betrayal. I've been
betrayed: my heart was bludgeoned with a
bat or popped with a pin or sliced with a
machete. It's what happens when you bite
off more than you can chew. It gets you
back, doesn't it? I don't know how you and
Dad do it, continue like you do--with Dad
one person when he's in Paris and someone
completely different when he's at "work."
When he's traveling, is it really work? Or
is his work just a cover for all the other
lives he's trying to lead? How do you survive
it? There's something I've been thinking
a lot about, Mom, since I read that quote.
If you try to live many lives and it gets
out of control, can you destroy just one
of them and let the others survive? Would
that simplify everything? It's dense. Tense.
There's another thing Hemon said: "Home is
where somebody notices when you are no longer
there." Did you know he said that? All the
places I've lived, I've never known which to
call home. Will you notice when I am gone,
when I was never much there in the first
place?

We'll find out soon enough--I just need a little more time. I wrote this early, before I've set everything in motion. Why? Because I wanted to write it at the moment of my decision when I can be the most honest. But death, it takes a long time to orchestrate. Today, on May 20th, I made my decision. I'm sorry to put you through this. Death is like that pair of empty shoes at 8:18. It gives me hope. That's why I chose 8:18. That's when everything will be complete.

Love,

Charlie

14

Aubrey

LENA SPEAKS FIRST. I HAVE TO GIVE HER CREDIT for that. I can barely stand, from the shock of what she's told me coupled with the fear I'm feeling.

Charlie killed himself.

My brain rejects it. If it's true, she's right that I'm partially to blame. So why, if she's known about this note all along, does she still want to believe he's alive? And yet everything about this trip has been surreal. None of it is anything I could have expected. Like this six-foot formidable giant waving a gory fillet knife at us. The image of my bed back in Western Springs fills my head: its white, curlicued frame; its yellow bedspread and fluffy, flower-patterned pillows. Ralph, our rescue mutt, curled on a sage green throw at the foot. I want to go back there and stay there forever. It was predictable. Comforting. Safe.

Nothing since the day I met Charlie has felt comforting, predictable, or safe. I used to love that surge of adrenaline—it was like nothing I'd felt before. Only now I'm stopping to wonder if it's healthy. It's taken a trip around the world and a stranger with a knife to give me pause. Certain psychotherapists would have a field day with this; I'd laugh if I weren't so scared.

"How do *you* know Charlie?" Lena demands, and at first I'm impressed. Her voice sounds confident and (to the untrained ear) diplomatic; and she's turned the conversation around, putting Anand on the defensive. "Let's all relax, shall we? There's no reason to get worked up before we even know if we're talking about the same Charlie." As she speaks, she takes a small step toward me and reaches for my hand. My first instinct is to recoil, but then she slips something inside my palm and carefully wraps my fingers around it. It's small and oblong and metal. A pocketknife. My eyes drag to hers, but she doesn't return my look. Anand is blocking the entrance to the bedroom — our only escape.

"No, I recognize you now." Anand's voice is low, each word coiled. "We've got the same Charlie, all right. I knew there was something familiar about you two. He had pictures of you both. Called you his girlfriend. 'Girlfriend,' singular, as though you look anything alike. Said he had this amazing girlfriend, this one girlfriend he loved, showed me pictures of two. Thought the guy had gone off the deep end at first, but I figured he'd just smoked a little too much hash. Charlie was my best customer." Anand lets out a guttural laugh.

"At least he only showed two pictures," Lena whispers out of the side of her mouth. "That's nice." I can tell she's trying to put me at ease, but I can't crack a smile.

"So where is he?" Anand demands, taking a step toward us. It forces us farther into the room. "Why are you here? You messing with me? You here to rob me like that little prick did? Or did you come to pay off his debts?"

"We don't know anything about his debts," Lena says slowly. "We came, actually, to ask you a few questions about Charlie."

"I got nothing to say unless you have money," Anand tells

us. "Why don't you just ask him whatever the hell you want to know?"

"Because Charlie's dead," I hear myself say in an unaccustomed, unwavering tone. Somehow saying it out loud makes it feel real. "He killed himself."

"No shit." Anand laughs again. He sets the plate of fish on a low-lying bench with a clatter and paces in front of the door frame, gripping his hair in his fists as his laughter grows louder and manic. Lena and I watch him, stunned. This guy is way off. "Shit, shit, shit," Anand mutters to himself as he spins. Then he's yelling "Shit" and "Motherfucker," moving around the bedroom and punching the walls, the furniture, anything he can reach. For the first time, the door is exposed.

I nudge Lena with my shoulder and motion with my chin toward the door. She's closer, so she begins inching out slowly. Anand is too caught in his rage to notice at first. We're nearly there when he refocuses and closes the gap between us in two strides.

"Do you know how much money he owes me?" Anand demands to know. "Over eighty thousand rupees." I gasp. Granted I don't know the exact conversion, but it sounds like a lot of money.

"That's only, like, thirteen hundred dollars," Lena informs me, seeing my face. "But Jesus, that's a hell of a lot of . . . what, hash?"

Anand nods, eyeing us closely. He's wearing a little smirk, and I realize Lena's fatal error. *Only thirteen hundred.* I don't know much about India, but I do know a little goes a long way. Even to most Americans, thirteen hundred bucks isn't paltry. Here it must be a fortune.

"Jesus." Lena is still reeling. "What is that, like, forty dollars per gram . . . Holy shit." She stops, her mouth open. "Three hundred grams?" she whispers. "Is that right? That can't be right. What, this is over a long span of time?"

"How well did you know your boyfriend, honey?" Anand says in this patronizing tone. "Not very well, I'm guessing. Since you're both here."

"Don't call me 'honey,'" Lena says, getting right up in his face. Anand glares back, and moves closer until he's just an inch or two away from her, but Lena doesn't falter. I feel my grip tighten around the pocketknife. Hoping I don't have to use it. Lena and Anand are locked in a stare-down. Something passes through Anand's eyes, and then his face softens and he backs off, holding his hands high in an indication of peace.

"Listen," he starts. "I think we got off on the wrong foot." I try to read his facial expression, staring hard into his murky brown eyes, but his face is impassive. All the hatred of a minute ago is gone, vanished or maybe pushed down just below his skin. "Come." He gestures toward the doorway. "Sit down and let's talk like civilized people."

Now that he is calm, his mode of expression is interesting; older-sounding, I think, than his twenty-some years. Maybe born of a more formal study of English than most Americans are used to. He directs us to the wooden table that's on the main deck just behind the bedroom cabin and still partially concealed in the shade of the upper level. We've missed most of the late-afternoon sun, but a blend of purples and pinks deco-rates the sky as the sun sets. Now that Anand is being nice to us, my breathing has slowed to what feels like a normal pace. Lena's back is still rigid, I note, as she selects a spot at the end of the bench and settles in across from Anand, who's come over wielding the tray he had set down on the bench just inside the bedroom. A couple of mosquitos buzz around, and I'm grateful I remembered to pick up bug spray in Mumbai; it's high deet and technically toxic, but it's better than risking malaria.

"Mind putting that someplace else?" Lena wrinkles her nose in the direction of the tray of fish. "No offense, but it's an eyesore." Her tone is guarded, and I can tell by the way her eyes pull down at the corners that she still doesn't trust Anand. I don't either . . . but it seems like he's at least backed down from attack mode. He gives her a nod and walks back toward the kitchen with the tray.

"I should fry up the rest anyway," he calls over his shoulder. "I hope you like whitefish and squid. I'm making some curry with the fish, and some paratha. Maybe it'll be easier to talk over dinner, once we've had more time to cool down." Lena stares after him with her lips pursed.

"He's up to something," she says, tapping her canvas shoe against the deck. She's not talking about Charlie, but somehow it triggers the memory of what she's just told me about Charlie's suicide note, and I'm overcome with a lightheaded, surreal feeling that I guess must be shock. I want to kill Lena for bringing me on this crazy journey, for keeping such an important secret. And I want to talk about Charlie, really talk about him for the first time since we've come here. There's got to be something we're missing. I open my mouth to say more, but Anand's back, carrying two frothy glasses of Kingfisher, which he places in front of us with a smile. Lena's smile in return is big and fake.

"Don't drink that," she whispers once he's walked away, humming under his breath. "He could have put something in it."

"You really think he would?"

"Never know." Her voice is matter-of-fact. "He's seriously pissed off. He could do anything."

"But he said—"

"Come here." Lena cuts me off and motions toward the narrow ladder that leads to the upper deck. She climbs the ladder and I follow her, taking a few tentative bounces on the first rung to make sure it's stable despite its rotted appearance. When I reach the top after her, and peer past her just-disappearing Toms, I have to stop myself from gasping. It's a beautiful open-air view from the top deck, and the water stretches ahead of us in a pattern of blue and gray. We're coasting by small stretches of land that punctuate the water. It seems impossible, but several of them hold equally small huts, maybe six feet wide at most. Outside one of them, an old woman hangs clothing on a line that's strung between two spindly trees.

"I can't believe people live there," says Lena, following my gaze from where she's plopped herself onto a patterned cushion at the front of the deck.

"Everything's different now," I find myself saying. I guess I'm offended by her conversational tone, by how easily she slips back into normalcy, especially after what happened with Anand. I'm still shaken from the scare, and now that we're alone, my rage comes tumbling out. I feel tears beginning to burn at the backs of my eyes, and there's a sense that I can't control what I might say next. "Don't you get what you just did to me? How could you have lied to me this whole time?"

"It almost doesn't matter what any of us did anymore," Lena says, her voice sharp. "So many things have gone wrong." She draws her knees up under her chin. "I'm sorry for telling you that way. I shouldn't have. But I couldn't keep it in any more after I saw you with Adam. It felt like . . . like you just carelessly used me to get to him. I know that what Charlie was doing to us both wasn't any better. But after being used by him, I can't stand that I let myself be used by you. Charlie was my life, and now he's gone, and I feel so lost. I thought you and I were becoming friends. I thought something good could have come from all this. But now I just feel stupid." Her voice is firm despite the intensity of her words.

"I'm sorry, Lena. I am. It was wrong. But I wasn't trying to use you. I didn't plan what happened with Adam. I hate that I hurt you. I want us to get past it." I pause, frustrated and confused. "But why didn't his parents tell anyone? And why, after this, are you still doubting that he's dead?"

"I was the one who found the letter," Lena starts. "About a week before his memorial service, just a few days after he disappeared. When I went to his parents' place. I went there to drop off food, see if they needed any help with anything, just . . . you know, just to be there. His parents were important to me. I didn't see them much, but when I did, they were so kind." Lena looks away, blinking back tears. My whole body is trembling as if there's nothing substantial holding it together. The world that looked so lovely not long ago is turning extra bright, then black, the edges of the boat blending together and collapsing in on themselves, as I process Lena's story.

"I went up to his room," she continues. "It was pretty bare, nothing on the walls, no decorations—like the way he kept all his other rooms, in the dorms, the apartments in the cities. It was almost like a hotel room. But there was this one drawer he always kept full of little items from his childhood. He didn't know I knew about it. Or at least, that's what I always thought. I used to look through it when he was in the shower or whatever. He had, like, a collector's edition of baseball cards. And some other junky things from when he was a kid: an *Archie* comic, a Christmas list. A note from a girl he liked in elementary school. A birthday card his parents gave him. And there on top of everything was something I'd never seen before." Lena is crying now; the tears are streaming down her cheeks and onto her collarbone, and she's wiping them away with both palms but not nearly fast enough.

"Tell me," I say. I'm not sure I want to hear, but I know I have to. There's no going back.

"There was this letter addressed to his mom. It was taped shut and it hadn't been there the last time I visited, so I guess I kind of knew what it was. There was a stamp on it, like he was planning on mailing it at some point and never did. I knew what it was, Aubrey." She looks up at me, her eyes less angry and more pleading. "I read it. It was a suicide note. I thought about hiding it."

"But you didn't."

Lena shakes her head, wiping her nose with the back of her wrist. "He wanted his mom to see it. That much was clear. She wasn't any saint, but she was devastated. She didn't want a scandal. You don't understand. The Prices thought Charlie was perfect. They were heartbroken. Their marriage was so screwed up. It was a disaster. His dad was gone all the time, his mom was depressed and drank too much. But they loved Charlie . . . at least his mom did. She funneled all her hope into him. I don't know how she's surviving. But at least it gave her closure. Even after they found the jacket with his blood on it . . . she was like me. She couldn't accept it. But this let her accept it. We organized the memorial service the next morning."

"Do you still have the note?"

Lena nods, leveling me with a hard gaze. "His mom was looking for it after the funeral. I didn't say a word. It's horrible, I know, but I couldn't give it back."

I'm silent. I don't want her to feel judged.

"There was something about it all that felt off," she goes on. "At first I couldn't quite figure it out. I kept thinking, maybe it's part of the act. The letter . . . parts of it were nonsensical. His mom chalked it up to the mental state he must have been in when he wrote it. Maybe he was panicked, or maybe he was high. But in the letter, he said everything would come together on eight-eighteen. That was the day he planned to follow through with it. But August eighteen is still a few days away. Part of me thinks he's still around, planning something for then. That the rest of it was just a grandiose diversion. I know it's nuts but it's my gut feeling. That's why I'm searching for him. I'm impulsive, Aubrey, but my feelings are so often right. Because why was it so cryptic? He didn't come right out and say, *This is what I'm going to do.* And a normal person doesn't commit suicide by crashing a plane. There are lots of easier ways to go. Sometimes I think I need to forget about it, accept he's dead like the rest of you. I've tried to make myself. I know it's the smart thing, the logical thing. But I just can't feel his death. It's not even that I want him alive. I know everything's ruined. I don't want him anymore. I know loving him wasn't real, because it wasn't real for him. But I keep thinking, *I'll look, and I'll find him, and I'll force him to take responsibility for something.* He just can't get away with this. I can let go of him, but not what he did to us."

"Why didn't you tell me? Why did you want to make this my fault? Even if I did set something in motion, would you have preferred to go on like we were, in the dark?" This last part triggers it: the tears, the frustration, even relief. And in their wake, guilt.

"I still feel as though telling Charlie about Adam was what set him off," Lena says after a minute of silence. "Even though I know that wasn't your intention."

All of a sudden I know: It doesn't matter that Charlie was doing the same thing to me that I did to him—a fact I didn't even know then. It doesn't matter that he made me unhappy a lot of the time, and that the relationship probably never should have happened in the first place. It doesn't matter how many excuses I made to do what I did that one night in D.C. with Adam—or the lies I told myself to explain away all the nights after Charlie found out my secret, when I stayed with him out of necessity.

They're just excuses for a series of awful events that I never, not in a million years, would have thought I'd be capable of. I lied, I cheated, and I played with fire. The reasons that led me to do these things are separate. And now, instead of feeling culpable, I feel overwhelmed by relief. Somewhere, deep down, I worried there was a chance he was alive. Now all I need is the journal to feel truly safe again.

I sink down next to Lena, feeling the full weight of these revelations. Not because of what it might have pushed Charlie to do, but because of what it's done to Lena and to me—my values, who I am as a person. I think of my parents, and who they raised me to be. I think of the way I've pulled away from them in recent months. When stuff like this happens and you make these choices, you can't go back to the way things were. You've changed yourself, and maybe you can never recover.

15

Lena

To her credit, she looks squashed. Nauseated. It makes me feel almost bad for telling her the way I have. *Almost.* She needed to hear it. Maybe it wasn't up to me to have hidden it, but what I said about Charlie's parents was true. They wanted to keep it quiet. They couldn't bear the scandal if it got out. I had wanted to respect that.

"Why did you hide it from me?" she repeats, staring at me with a glazed expression. "You never said. Why bother with all of this?" She swings her arm around, indicating the Keralan backwater landscape we're floating down. I almost laugh. It would be idyllic if it weren't so twisted. In another world, Aubrey and I would be best friends on some kind of Asian backpacking adventure. But instead we're in our shitty version of a haunted destination love triangle.

"I didn't know you yet," I say, avoiding her eyes. "His parents wanted to keep it hushed up. I also . . . I guess I wanted something for myself. Something you couldn't know about." I know I'm not answering the question, but I can't when I don't know the answer.

"But he's gone. I just don't understand how you can believe otherwise. This whole thing—it's just . . . it's so ridiculous." How much of this has been about a journal and how much has been about something else: proof of his death? And if that's the case, did she want to confirm his death or his life? Which would have made her happier?

"I'd like to remind you who's been paying for this 'ridiculous' pilgrimage," I tell her. I know right away it's the wrong thing to say.

Aubrey laughs once and shakes her head. "It's fine," she says. "You can stop paying, because I'm going to go. I'm not here to chase Charlie's ghost. Fuck the journal. This whole thing is making me crazy. I don't even care anymore, not enough to keep this up." She leans her head in her hands, laughs again, and starts muttering *"Oh god oh god oh god"* under her breath.

"What? Are you okay?" I'm a little concerned that I may have pushed her over the deep end. She lifts her head. Her face is blotchy and worn-looking; she could pass for much older than eighteen. But she's beautiful. It's a sneaky kind of beauty that hits you when you're not looking, and she's somehow prettier in her devastation. It reminds me of when I first saw her earlier in the week, at the funeral home—how she seemed sort of ghoulish but in a haunting, lovely way, like the doomed heroine in a Poe story.

"I'm not," she says. "But I just realized, I don't even necessarily know if what you're telling me is true. This could be just another lie, another manipulation. Maybe it's not true? You're clearly still in love with Charlie even after everything he did to us. Maybe you just realized I'm inconvenient, want me out of the picture, want to find him and claim him." I gape at her, my mouth open. What she's saying *is* crazy.

"Aubrey, if I were to find him again I wouldn't touch him with a ten-foot pole. I just think I deserve the truth of what my life has been for the last few years. If he's alive, I want to force him to answer some questions. Plus I want to expose him, see him pay for this."

"I don't know," she says. "This is an awful lot of trouble to go to for that. Sure there's not something else?" No. I can't claim to be sure. But I nod anyway. She laces her hands under her chin and frowns.

"Wait a second." I break in on her puzzlement. "For me this was about finding Charlie, getting some answers, eviscerating him. I *needed* that. But you're supposedly here looking for some stupid journal. I always figured there was more to it, that you were kind of in denial about looking for him, too. So what are *you* hiding? You've never told me what the deal is with the journal."

Her head jerks up. "It's personal," is all she says. Aubrey is handling the revelation of the suicide note oddly. She's crying, but she's laughing, and I'm about to ask her exactly what she *is* feeling when Anand shouts up the stairs, pulling me back into our present predicament: we're stuck on a boat with a potential felon.

"Food's ready," he calls out in this pleasant voice that, to my ears, rings insincere. I'm not thrilled with Adam at the moment; I feel like maybe he should have put Anand into context, told us he was more than just an innocent weed hookup, that kind of thing. And, like, why would he throw Aubrey into this situation if he supposedly likes her? I file that question in the back of my mind.

"Guess we've gotta play nicey-nicey with the chef," I say, making a mental note to come back to this journal of hers, which suddenly seems like a very odd reason for her to come along on this trip, if it's her real reason. I pull myself together as Aubrey struggles to mop her own face with the back of her hand. "How long till we can skip out of this place? It's almost nine, so I guess that gives us, like, twelve hours? Keep your wits about you, kid." I nudge Aubrey with my elbow, and to her credit, she cracks a grin. Part of me regrets having told her about Charlie's note, and part of me feels this huge sense of relief. It's sucked, carrying around that kind of secret.

I'm not shocked to find, upon reaching the bottom deck, that I'm starving. Emotion does that to me.

Anand has lit small lanterns all around the deck of the boat—a safe decision, I'm sure—and there are steaming platters lined up on the table, piled high with food. He's standing there with his creepy, placid grin; and yet somehow, it does nothing to ruin my appetite. It hits me that Aubrey and I haven't eaten all day, other than some mini tropical bananas at the hotel in Bombay this morning. I can't help but dig in with both hands—literally, since Anand has provided no silverware and seems to expect us to manhandle our food in the traditional way. I'm ravenous. It's been almost a day since I've eaten anything substantial. I use paratha to scoop the curry and biryani, ignoring the scowls Aubrey's shooting me from where she sits, arms crossed over her chest, her cheeks still a little mottled from crying. It doesn't occur to me until I'm full that eating Anand's food could have been a mistake.

"I feel bad about the way we started," offers Anand, wiping his mouth with a stained cloth napkin. "You seem like nice girls. Let me make amends."

"There's no need," Aubrey breaks in. "Anyone would have been upset in your position."

"Tell me, what is my 'position'?" he asks. I'm wondering the same thing, but I feel too exhausted to do much but watch them volley. Beneath us, the boat bobs against the shore where we've docked so Anand can eat. *We could run now,* I think. But where would we run to? My phone doesn't work all the way out here; I have no idea how far we are from Kerala or how to get there or even if there are people living nearby who could help us if we needed it. Beyond just that, it's pitch black out. I can't even see the neighboring huts from where we sit.

"I just mean, you had a bad experience with Charlie, and then we show up—" Aubrey catches herself and stops.

"Yes," Anand agrees, leaning forward, his eyes alight with something I can't identify. Everything about Anand now feels aggressive, I realize: his posture is tense and poised; his expression is blank but his eyes are sharp. "It's quite a coincidence, isn't it? What are the chances you'd show up—with no knowledge of the money your dead boyfriend owed me? Why would you choose my boat of all the possibilities? I think," he says softly, while Aubrey's cheeks begin to flush, "that there's something you two aren't telling me."

"We don't have any money for you," I assure him, the veins in my temples throbbing. "And we're not trying to take anything of yours. We didn't even know about you until a day ago. Charlie lied to us, just like he did to you. We're just out here to figure out the truth, same as you."

"I see," Anand says, breaking into a grin. "Okay then, I can tell you what I know. After all, you're paying guests. Speaking of which, is anything wrong with the food?" He directs this at Aubrey, who gives him a tight shake of her head. But her plate remains untouched. I glare at her until she meets my eyes, and she reluctantly twists off a piece of paratha. She uses the soft, chewy bread to mop up a tiny bit of curry sauce and tentatively brings the food to her mouth. Anand watches her in silence while she swallows.

"Trust is important," he tells us both. "It's something I value. You come here, you want me to open up to you about your Charlie, and yet you don't place any trust in me. Trust is symbiotic." He grins. "I learned that word from an American, a professor who stayed on my boat with his wife. You think I'm this bad guy, this drug dealer. You think, *How does Anand make his way, own five boats, and he's only twenty-three? Through drugs.* You're right about that, but I'm not a man without morals. There's a difference between a bad man and a smart man. I'm a smart man. Your Charlie, he was bad. Anyone could see it, just to look at him."

"The Charlie I knew wasn't bad," I observe. "At least not at first."

"People aren't born bad; they become that way," says Anand, and for the first time I'm impressed by the clarity of his thoughts. "It happens through a series of bad decisions . . . missteps over time. And a lack of balance. Me, I sell hashish. Finest quality. I have almost a hundred regular customers. Some people may say that's bad —but I have balance. I'm good to my wife, I run a good business, I'm kind to my neighbors. I don't deceive."

"You're married?" Aubrey wants to know. Her eyes dart to the empty space on Anand's finger where a ring should be.

He smiles broadly. "Married since two months ago. Why not? I found a beautiful woman and I love her, and our families approve. There's already a baby coming." At this, his face darkens slightly. "Which is why money's important now. But," he continues, "life is too short for anger. With Charlie, I will let bygones be bygones. I knew coming into it, with him, there was risk. Some people you can read. You can look into their eyes and know they're good, or you can tell right away that they're bad. It's the way they look over you when you talk, the way their mouth curls down in distaste at something you say or what you wear. They try to hide it, but it's there in every gesture.

"And then others, like Charlie, you can't read at all. Their eyes are blank. I knew it. I told him no when he first asked me for my services. But he was persistent, and he was willing to pay top dollar. So you see, it was my mistake."

"When did Charlie start coming to you?" Aubrey asks. Her dark hair is messy from a day in the sun and the humidity; it forms a rumpled nest around her pale skin, highlighting the dark circles that rim her eyes.

"A while ago," says Anand. "Maybe two years. He was recreational at first, purely into the enjoyment and used it to relax. A couple of grams here and there. When he started increasing the amount of his requests, I thought, *A little for friends, he's in high school, maybe there are parties.* Then he asked for more and I got mad, thinking he's dealing on the side, charging more than what I charge. We had a fight, and he swears it's just for him. All of it. That he doesn't know how much longer he'll be in Bombay and I've got the best hashish there is, so he's stockpiling. Never mind how he'll get it overseas — that's not my problem. The kid was always good on his payments. Always. Until his biggest order comes, and what does he do? Says, 'Give me a week, Anand. You know I'm good for it.' Then he's gone." Anand shakes his head. "Little fucker." The words sound silly coming with his south Indian accent, and I can't help laughing. I know it's a mistake the second I do. Anand's head whips around and he stares at me, eyes narrowed. I hold out one palm to assure him I don't mean anything.

"I'm sorry," I insist. "It's just . . . *'leetle fuck-ah.'*" It's probably

wildly inappropriate that I'm laughing, but I dissolve back into giggles anyway, and Aubrey joins me. Our eyes meet and we crack up,
leaning over the table and gasping for air. When I catch my breath
and have the courage to look up at Anand, I'm relieved to find that
he's smirking too.

"How did you meet him?" I ask once I've caught my breath.
"Were you lurking around the schoolyard, hoping to score some
new clients?" My tone is sarcastic. He doesn't catch on.

Anand shakes his head. "I tell you, I'm a standup guy," he insists.
"I met him through his half brother. Danc."

"Charlie doesn't have a brother."

"Not anymore," Anand clarifies. Aubrey and I glance at each
other in confusion.

"No," Aubrey says slowly. "Charlie was an only child." She
looks at me again and I nod in confirmation, though suddenly
I'm not so sure. But why would Charlie have kept something like
that hidden?

"I assure you, he had a brother," Anand says. "Kind of a black
sheep. His dad's son from a mistress. He lived with the family for a
while."

"It's not possible." My voice is hard, firm. "I've been to Charlie's
parents' house a million times. There were only pictures of Charlie.
No brother."

"The brother was disowned," Anand said. "He . . . chose his own
path, from what I understand."

"Meaning . . . ?" Aubrey demands, her face flushed.

"I never got the whole story," Anand says vaguely, pushing away
from the table. "Now, how about I fix us some chai? It's late. I'll
need to sleep soon."

"You said you'd tell us about Charlie," I call out to his retreating back. He pauses.

"Yes," he says without turning around. "I'm telling you all I know."

Before Aubrey and I can exchange anything more than looks of mutual disbelief, Anand has returned with three tin cups of chai along with a pitcher holding more. Chai is one of my favorite things about India—I can never get enough of the sweet, milky tea; and I grab for mine as if it were an old, familiar lifeline.

"From what I understand," Anand says, "Dane had some sort of fall from grace, and he and Charlie didn't talk much after that. They both moved around a lot, you know. They weren't always even in school on the same continent. Charlie stayed more often with their mother, Dane with their father. But they got back in touch, I know that." Anand goes on, but his words seem to merge into a soft, lulling drone. I look across the table at Aubrey. She's sipping her tea in this really relaxed manner, her shoulders slightly slumped.

"I'm so tired." I force out the words but they sound jumbled up, and Aubrey nods dreamily.

"Maybe you ought to get to bed," Anand suggests from somewhere far away. "We can continue our talk in the morning once you've had some rest. You girls have had a trying day." *Trying day.* It turns into *trying way, try to stay, hit the hay.* My eyelids begin to droop. I struggle to stand and find myself collapsing backwards into Anand's waiting arms. When did he stand up from the table? When did he move behind me?

"Aubrey?" I murmur. I try to lift my lids but they won't cooperate. Instead, I peer out from beneath their narrow slits, but I don't see Aubrey anywhere. I try to jerk my arm back, out of Anand's grip, but it's like I'm wading through water, or thick sludge. Nothing's working the way it should.

"Shhh," Anand whispers in my ear. His breath, hot against my skin, makes me recoil inwardly, but outwardly my limbs feel like wet clay. "It's okay," he tells me. "She already went to bed. Let me help you." I have no choice. I let Anand lead me back to the bedroom, where Aubrey is sprawled across the bed, face-down and fully clothed, snoring loudly. Anand eases me onto the bed next to her and again I make efforts to move my body away from him. His hands leave my shoulders. He moves toward the door and reaches for the light switch. I try to watch him, but I feel myself drifting from consciousness. Aubrey's snores intensify beside me.

"Sleep tight," Anand whispers, and the light goes out.

16

Aubrey

CHARLIE REACHES FOR THE SLIM FRONT pocket in my messenger bag; I slap his hand away. I've slapped his hand away from that very leather pocket half a dozen times now and each time he's retreated, a scowl darkening his handsome features. This time, he pushes further. "What are you hiding?" he asks, his voice low.

"Nothing." My face flushes. "Why is it so inconceivable to you that I might not be hiding something?" Still, my heart accelerates. I fight to steady my hands where they grip the magnetic clasp. My knuckles are white. I'm hiding far more than he suspects.

"You carry that thing with you all the time. You're hiding something. This breakup, it's . . . it's out of nowhere." Charlie's face is hard, his eyes dark. I expected him to break down when I told him about Adam. I wasn't expecting this denial.

"You know it's not," I whisper. I've given him so many reasons already, but still he's fighting it. I can't remember when I started waking up with a weight pressing on my chest. I don't know whether it was before Adam or after, but it's definitely not just about Adam. For months now, something about my relationship with Charlie hasn't felt right. But all of that has nothing to do with what's happening now — with what's inside my bag.

"You're hiding something." He clutches the bag where I do, his hand resting partially on mine and partially on the frayed leather folds. *"You pull it into bed with you. You don't let it go. There's something in there that matters. Fucking tell me, Aubrey. Tell me so I don't have to force it out of you."* My face flushes again; my head begins to ache. I think about what I'm supposed to tell him. I come up blank. What is in the bag? *For a second, I forget. For a second, I really don't know. It happens sometimes like that, when I get angry or scared: I black out. I have a hard time remembering the most important things.*

Then it floods back, and the pain of it makes me wince. My senses flood with the memory of what happened that night, three weeks ago: The wheels screeching, the smell of rubber on asphalt. The form of an old man, splayed and broken. Littered on the roadside like trash.

Reflexively, I move my hand to my brow. In that second he grabs my bag and yanks it toward him. Its contents spill across the floor: a lipstick, some receipts, a course catalogue for Georgetown. He rummages through the front pocket. The scene runs through my head on repeat:

Striking something large in the middle of the road—a deer, maybe. Dead already? It was just lying there.

The tires of my parents' car squealing as I swerve after the impact. Tears coating my cheeks. Blood clotting on my forehead from where it hit the dash.

Pulling over, clutching the handle of the door, poised to climb out. Squinting at the large, motionless lump. Hesitating. Paralyzed by fear. What if it wasn't a deer?

Roadkill. It was already dead, I told myself before I drove away.

Now Charlie pulls out a journal. The journal my dad bought me for my birthday. He flips it open and out spill stacks of newspaper clippings. He swears under his breath. I don't have to look over to know what he's reading. I've memorized the headlines: "Vagrant Struck by Hit-and-Run Driver." "Western Springs Hit-and-Run Motorist Remains Unidentified." "Homeless Man in Critical Condition After Hit-and-Run in Chicago Suburbs." *A dozen more. Now he flips the pages of the journal, poring over my scrawled confessions, his face turning white.*

"Aubrey," he says slowly, clenching a clipping in his fist. "What is this?" I shake my head, tears pooling in my eyes. I can't speak. I feel dread mingling with relief. Finally, someone knows what I've done. But what will he do with it? "You hit this man," he says, pulling my chin toward him—forcing me to meet his eyes. Mine are so clouded by tears that I can barely make out his features. I can't tell whether it's sympathy or something else that's contributing to the intensity in his voice. "That's a very bad thing," Charlie whispers, his hand still resting on my cheek. I feel chills sliding up the back of my neck. "You could get in so much trouble for what you did." I nod, and the room turns bright around me. My entire body is trembling now, as I anticipate his next words: I'm going to tell.

"I won't tell anyone," he says, folding me into an embrace. He holds my head firmly in place over his shoulder so I can barely move. My heart trumpets against his slower, more rhythmic pulse. He's incongruously calm. It doesn't feel right. My eyes flit around the room, settling on all the generic hotel room décor: a wooden lamp with a cream-colored shade; a speckled brown-and-blue carpet. A green satin runner on the opposite bed, meant to convey warmth. Ever since that first time in Montreal, we've spent our whole relationship in places like this. Every part of me is stiff. I wriggle my body, trying to pull away, but he only holds me closer.

"I forgive you," he says, and my heart clenches and my body turns cold. "I forgive you about Adam. It was only the distance making things

difficult for you. You've had so much on your mind. My poor little Aubrey." He leans his head into my hair and breathes into it. He caresses my back with one hand, and it's all I can do not to recoil.

"Charlie, I—" I struggle to pull back, to make him talk to me, because all of this is wrong. But he cuts me off.

"No need to say anything," he whispers, while his grip tightens on my arms. *"I love you and I forgive you."* He's squeezing so tightly I'm sure I'll have bruises. I realize I'm terrified. I wish I could grab the phone, run to the door; but just as in the car that night, I'm paralyzed.

"I forgive you for everything you did with Adam," he continues. *"I know what you did was just from the stress."*

"Charlie—" I start. He's not making sense. What happened with Adam came before the accident. I didn't mean for it to go further, to turn into something emotional. But it did. Charlie lifts a finger to my lips to silence me.

"You're devoted to me," he insists. *"I'll keep your secret. How could I not? How could I not protect my beautiful girlfriend? No one will ever find out, baby. Not as long as we're together."*

"You still want . . . to be with me?" I manage to ask. None of it makes sense: why he'd want me in his life after Adam, after this.

"Of course!" His eyes soften, and he leans in to kiss me everywhere: my cheeks, my throat, my collarbone. Every part of my body is screaming to pull away; his lips feel somehow violating. *"How could I not? Who would I be if I abandoned you at a time like this? No, Aubrey,"* he tells me. *"You haven't thought this through very clearly, have you? I'm not letting you get away so easily."* I can't explain why, but his words cause my body to seize up in terror.

Charlie stops kissing me, and reaches over to collect the newspaper clippings and my journal into a stack. My eyes follow the clippings, all *the words I've circled and notes I've taken in their margins. Some of them say, "I'm sorry." I'm not sure who I was apologizing to, but the stupidity of doing so is overwhelming. The journal contains worse. I needed an outlet. I've been so afraid to tell anyone. But now, I know that Charlie could turn these into a jail sentence if he wanted to. His eyes meet mine again and he smiles with compassion. In my state of unease, the warmth seems manufactured. This time, I can't help but shudder. His eyes narrow behind his smile as he slips the clippings and the journal under his arm. I move to stop him but he grabs my wrist and tightens his grip until I gasp with pain. Through the whole thing, his smile is unchanged. I'm bound to him now. I have no choice.*

I know something's wrong even before I open my eyes. They've been shut for a while now, even though I've been hovering between sleep and an awake state for five minutes, maybe ten. My head is heavy and aches from the memories that have been plaguing me all night —memories of that awful day. I experience a brief, gory image of fishhooks dragging down my eyelids, a snapshot in my brain. My whole body feels tired and sore. I feel Lena shifting around beside me, and I try to remember what's going on—Kerala, a boat, Anand, chai . . .

"Oh, shit," Lena says in a gravelly, sleep-clogged voice. "Shit, shit, shit. Aubrey. Get up." She elbows me hard and I pry my eyes open with effort. Things look blurred and my head pounds. I blink a few times and take in the room, eyeing it for signs of what's caus- ing Lena's distress. I don't panic at first; Lena still has her penchant for melodrama.

Then I see what remains of our possessions strewn across the bed. My green canvas messenger bag is lying open near where I lie;

crumpled bits of receipts, gum wrappers, and an open lipstick tube clutter the thin bedcover. Lena is on the floor, scrambling around under the bed. Her efforts grow more frantic by the second.

"Aubrey," she says. "My wallet's gone."

"What do you mean?" I ask. But I know exactly what she means. The abrupt switch from aggressive to saccharine. The false camaraderie. Us refusing the beers but accepting the tea, drinking from our cups only after we'd seen Anand drink from his; but accepting refills from the pot. Anand, I think now, didn't pour himself a second cup.

"Jesus," I whisper. "I think he drugged us."

"He *definitely* drugged us," Lena says, her words rushed and clipped. "Check your bag."

"Just try to stay calm," I say, in a level voice. But one glance tells me that many of my possessions — my earrings, my iPod, even some of my clothes — are gone too. "Do you think he's still here?" I stand up and move stiffly to the doorway, squinting into the bright sun. My head feels like it's being cracked open with a hammer. The boat's docked in the same location where we started yesterday, but the shore is oddly deserted; only a lone crewman is cleaning up the debris of a party a few boats down. From the look of it, everyone has vacated. The sun's high in the sky and I'd guess it's midafternoon. I wander the length of the vessel, picking up a Kingfisher bottle and dumping its contents over the side of the deck.

"Anand?" I call, heading toward the kitchen. My heart's slamming. I'm not sure whether I want to find him or not, but part of me is hoping this is some horrible coincidence. I reach the little galley kitchen and am half relieved to find it empty except for a trash bin that's overflowing with fish bones and some bootlegged DVDs that are scattered across the floor.

He's gone.

I go back to the bedroom to break the news to Lena. She's sitting on top of the thin mattress, her head buried in her hands. She's motionless.

"Aubrey—" she starts, dread in her voice.

"It's okay," I interrupt. "I do have a credit card for emergencies. It's probably enough for a flight back. And your parents will help with yours. They have to, right?" I laugh nervously. The truth is, my own parents are probably ready to disown me and would likely be happy to see me spend eternity in an Indian jail. They'd probably rather never see me again than welcome me home with an eight-hundred-dollar credit card bill and open arms. Because that's what a flight back home will cost. At least. I'll be babysitting for a year to pay it off.

My heart is working its way up into my throat, and I feel sick to my stomach. The thought of putting even more of a burden on my parents—and letting them see how awful I've been this whole time—is making me ill. They've been worrying about me; they're not oblivious to the way I've been hiding from them ever since the accident. Still, I can't tell them. I tried a few times. The thought of seeing their disappointment and hurt was too much. Now, though, I've made everything worse.

"It's not the money," Lena mutters. "It's worse." My heart goes still. I wait for her to continue. Her silence is scarier than anything we've faced yet. "It's the passports, Aubrey," Lena says, her voice dull. "They're gone too."

It takes me a few seconds to reply. Anxiety wraps itself around my vocal cords, making me feel like I might choke. "Both of them?" I ask.

"Unless you were keeping them somewhere other than your bag,"

Lena says. "Remember, you put them there after our flight two mornings ago? I already checked." It's true, I'd taken both passports that morning because I had the bigger bag and Lena had brought just a small clutch. She had wanted to keep the passports on one of us, though, rather than leave them in our luggage.

"No," I whisper, moving toward my bag. I check the front pocket, where the passports had been. "But there's a lock—"

"Broken." Lena lets out a humorless laugh. "Those locks aren't exactly built to withstand pickpockets." The lock was the reason that I had purchased the bag before my trip to Paris, but I'm not going to tell her that. I feel embarrassed, naive. And panicked.

"I'm sorry," I say, sinking to the floor in front of where she sits.

"It's not your fault," Lena tells me. "If anything, it's my fault. I'm the one who dragged us on this stupid trip. You never would have chased his ghost if I hadn't made you."

"You didn't make me." It's the most honest conversation we've had in a while, but it does little to calm my nerves. "What do we do?"

"I'm not sure. Go to the consulate? God, I don't even know where that would be around here. It would be one thing in Bombay . . . Oh god. I don't even have other ID to fly back there with. There's got to be an American consulate here, right?"

"I don't know. This is the first time I've ever really traveled. Maybe he's still around somewhere?"

"Right. He robbed us and then stuck around to see how we'd take it." Lena rolls her eyes and draws her long blond hair over one shoulder.

I stare down at the pile of things Anand left us: my library card, a Snoopy keychain, a little notebook that must be Lena's. Some receipts and a few American coins. The hotel key we never gave back to the Taj. The lipstick and some nose-blotting pads. Nothing of any use; thank goodness I had my emergency credit card in my jeans pocket yesterday—something I'd normally consider irresponsible but probably the thing that will save us. I'm thinking about this when I hear Lena call my name from the outside deck. I hadn't noticed when she left the cabin.

"Aubrey, come here! They're out here. The passports." I drop the pile of junk that I've been mindlessly sifting through and run to the deck to join her. I don't know how I missed it before. On the picnic table where we were sitting last night, there's the knife Anand used to gut the fish. It's pinning our passports to the table.

"Oh my god" is all I can say. It's so creepy. What was he hoping to prove? Lena yanks a few times on the handle but it doesn't budge —it's firmly wedged into the wood. She moves aside to give me a try. I pull a few times and feel the knife loosen, and I can't help but shudder at the thought of Anand's hands having been where mine are now. I give the knife a solid tug and it flies across the deck with the passports still attached, landing just short of the railing. Lena and I dash over—she gets there first and begins to pry the passports away from the knife.

"Be careful." My voice is trembling. I'm still half convinced Anand is going to jump out of the shelter of the other boats and attack us. "Hurry, though—I want to get out of here."

"I do too," Lena says. "Obviously. Do you think these will still work? Even though they're sliced? Wait." She pauses, then slides them the rest of the way off. "There's a piece of paper on here too." I peer closer at the white square she's holding. I recoil at the thought of the knife puncturing the passports and the folded square of paper.

Chills run up my spine when I consider what else the knife could have pierced while we were passed out.

"We could have been gutted like those fish," Lena whispers, echoing my thought. She unfolds the paper and I lean over her shoulder, wrinkling my brow. The sun bears down on us and I have to squint into the light to see. Lena's mouth falls open, and she lets out a little gasp. She passes the paper to me, and it takes me only a second to see why she's shocked. Anand has left us an address with a note that reads, "Quid pro quo — in exchange for settling Charlie's debt, ask Dane for the truth about his 'death,' little lamb." The address is scrawled firmly, like he pressed hard with a sure hand, though his writing is messy. I peer closely at the last line.

"Bangkok?" I breathe. But Lena doesn't answer. Her face is white.

" 'Little lamb,' " she says. "He wrote 'little lamb.' "

"It could be a coincidence," I start. "Maybe he just happened to see your tattoo." But I know it's not a coincidence. We both know it's not. I'm starting to get the terrible feeling that none of this has been coincidental.

17

Lena

"—SO FURIOUS WITH YOU, LENA. Your attitude is terrible. You're supposed to be starting school in a couple of weeks, for god's sake. Your father and I have been at our wits' end . . ." My mother's voice drones on, coming in clear despite the ancient spin-dial telephone I'm using, with the plastic phone card I purchased at the tiny Cheap Jack store in Kerala. I don't want to risk using my iPhone — they'll be able to track it and find us. Before today, I hadn't known they still make phone cards. *Cheap Jack,* meaning jack-of-all-trades, I guess. I scan the room, which is packed full of random odds and ends — glittery mirrored boxes and journals, plastic dishware, and a clown's head on a stick. Creepy. Aubrey is standing one aisle over, looking at a display of masala-flavored corn nuts. She looks as dirty and exhausted as I feel. Her tank top is torn and her white jean shorts are smudged with dirt. She shouldn't be wearing jean shorts, here in India. The locals think it's immodest, because they're stuck about six or seven decades behind the rest of the world. There's too much we both shouldn't have done.

"—just enough so you can get back to Boston. I'm assuming your friend is taken care of?" The five-second lull jolts me back to the present.

"What?"

"Lena. Really? Pay attention. This call must be costing a fortune. That's another thing. Some things are going to change when you get home. No more wanton spending. This is too much. I don't know where we went wrong—"

"Lena, goddammit, just book that flight right away, you hear?" My dad's voice breaks in, drowning out my mother's anxiety. "In fact, I'll put you on the phone with my secretary and she'll take care of it. She'll book that other girl, Aubrey, on a flight too. You said she has a credit card? I'll transfer a few hundred dollars to your bank account just in case you run into trouble. Where are Aubrey's parents in all of this? Has she called them?"

"She's fine," I tell him, avoiding the question. "Her credit card will cover the flight." I pray it's true; but if not, flights within Asia are cheap, and I know we can dip into my newly padded account if we have to.

"Well, we can help with emergencies, but that's it. We can't foot a double bill when we've never even met this girl. Her parents need to step up." My father's voice is gruff and authoritarian. He's picked up from his home office extension, which links to our family's landline. I used to think it was quaint that my parents still have a landline. Now I wish I could have dialed up and been sure of talking to only one person. Both of them at once are overwhelming.

"Dad," I interrupt, "can you just give me your credit card information and I'll take care of it?"

"Absolutely not," he replies. "If you think I'm trusting you for a second after what you've done—no way. I'm putting you through to my secretary."

"What I want to know is, where did you meet this *Aubrey*," my mom goes on. "Who the hell is she, Lena?" I roll my eyes and reach for a tube of Christmas wrapping paper that's lying in a bin near the cash register.

"You know Lena gets into trouble just fine on her own," my dad is saying to my mom as I hand the clerk one of the few remaining coins in my wallet and rip off a corner of the paper. It's helpful, this one time, that their expectations for me are so low. I hold the paper up to the receiver and crumple it a few times. Aubrey raises her eyebrows at me and I give her a thumbs-up.

"What's that, Dad?" I ask into the phone, folding and unfolding the paper next to the receiver. It makes a satisfying crackling noise. "Dad? I think I'm about to lose you. Maybe you'd better put me through to Cara?"

"Lena? Hello? Lena? Are you there?" My mom's voice becomes louder, shrill.

"Sorry, Mom," I semi-shout, knowing she'll find it more convincing. "Having trouble hearing you. Dad? Can you connect Cara?"

"Switching it over, Leelee," my dad goes. My heart clenches up at his pet name for me. I feel even worse than before.

Then there's a silence and the lines are switched, and Cara's voice breaks in loud and clear. I toss the paper ball onto the counter.

"Hi, Lena," she says. "Got yourself into a real pickle this time, huh?" I smile. Cara's always been more like a big sister to me than anything else. She used to babysit me as a kid. She's been working for my dad for ten years.

"Hey, Care Bear," I say. "A total shitshow. The Producer's not pleased." Cara and I started calling my dad "the Producer" in jest a few years back because of his secret love for Broadway (he himself lacks vocal talent). But it's all out of love. Cara swears she'd never work for anyone else, and my parents have given her a pretty cushy setup at home. "Can you book me two one-ways to Bangkok, please?" I whisper this last line, because Aubrey does not yet know we're going to Bangkok. "You can use my dad's card for both." I bite my lip. Aubrey gave me her emergency card for her ticket with strict instructions to book for Chicago. But we might need it for other things once we're in Bangkok. Since we have no money and all.

"No way, Lena," Cara says, her voice rising. "Your dad told me to get you straight back to Boston."

"Cara," I start, keeping myself calm. "Thing is, we already have return tickets booked from Bangkok." My eyes follow Aubrey's progress toward the back of the store. She's funny, like a child, eyeing all the cheap touristy stuff with huge eyes. "We were supposed to be there already," I tell her, lying. "We booked the whole thing—flights there, then flights back to the U.S. tomorrow morning from there. But we were supposed to fly in last night, and we missed our flights when a psycho Indian guy drugged us. So can you just book us new flights? My dad knows all this. Minus the psycho Indian guy." My heart's hammering but I keep my cool. I pause, waiting for Cara's response.

"You wouldn't lie to me . . . ?" There's uncertainty in her question. I squeeze my eyes shut and grind my teeth once before I answer. I've never lied to Cara. Not until now. I never thought I would, especially when it might mean her getting in trouble with my dad.

"No way!" I pipe up, feeling the receiver shift against my slick palms. "I'd never. Dad was just confused." My stomach drops. I hate what I've just done. Worse, I don't understand it. I don't know why I can't just let this mad search for Charlie go, and why I keep making ridiculous choices at the expense of everybody else.

But after Anand's note . . .

He's alive.

The voice that tells me so won't quit. There's no turning back. It's not possible.

"Okay. Eleven fifty-five p.m. into Suvarnabhumi. It's a redeye, but that way you'll still make your flights tomorrow morning. You've been there, yes? You know how it works? Or you want me to arrange for someone at the airport to escort you two?"

"Cara, please. I'm nineteen, not twelve." Cara laughs, and I feel a pang. She's always been rather protective of me.

"Got it," she says. "Give me a minute while I make the reservations." I sneak peeks at Aubrey, who's moving toward me. I can't have Aubrey catch me before the transaction goes through. She still hasn't called her parents, told them the whole story. She's trusting me to get her home. But I can't, not now, not when we're in it so far. *Surely she must know that,* a little voice in my head pipes up. Surely she can't expect anything else. A second later it's done. "You've got access to email?" Cara wants to know.

"Sure," I say distractedly. "There's loads of Internet cafés around." It's not entirely true. We're in a third-world country, after all. But I'm sure we'll figure something out. The phone beeps to let me know I have less than a minute left. "Cara? Thanks." I pause and take a breath. "I really appreciate your help."

"Anything for my girl," Cara says, her tone warm. "Bye, sweetie. Safe travel, 'kay? See you tomorrow night."

"See you," I start to say, but the phone disconnects before both words leave my mouth.

"Is it done?" Aubrey wants to know. She's wearing a stick-on bindi on her forehead and carries an open pack of sparkly faux jewels.

"We don't have money for you to buy those," I point out.

"Sure we do," she says. "I found a hundred rupees in my pants pocket. We could probably even eat something tonight if we play our cards right. I'm kidding," she says, registering my expression, which probably reads as worried. "There's gotta be enough left on my credit card for food, right? I mean, there was a thousand-dollar limit. How much was my ticket?"

"Um . . ." I start. "Only about four hundred."

"Four hundred dollars?" Aubrey exclaims. "That's so great. How'd you find tickets for that cheap?" When I don't answer, she looks hard at my face. Then she tenses and begins fiddling with her cuff. I stare back, silently entreating her not to be angry. "You didn't buy tickets back to Boston and Chicago," she says slowly. "Because tickets back to the U.S. would be much more than that." She waits for me to reply even though she knows the answer.

"Nope," I tell her. Aubrey takes a deep breath, then brings her hands to her temples and massages them, pressing in hard with her thumbs. Her short black hair looks limp, greasy. We haven't showered in days.

"Give me my credit card," she demands.

"No," I say again. "Not until you promise to go to Bangkok with me. It's kind of too late anyway. I took care of your flight. Your credit card limit is too low to book a flight home. We'll need it for Bangkok. Consider it, Aubrey. Just hear me out this time. You know I've been thinking about it a lot. Would Charlie really have planned to kill himself? Isn't that a little over the top for someone who was such a coward, who talked about running away all the time? I think Anand was trying to tell us something. I think he's alive. And I need you to consider it as a real possibility for a second."

"You do." Aubrey's voice is dull, flat.

"Yeah," I say in a rush. "And there's more. I think Charlie buried a message for me in that suicide note. I've practically memorized it by now. I read it and reread it because something kept bugging me about the language he used. Especially the eight-eighteen and death. I couldn't put my finger on it. And then I realized — some of the things he said were quotes from a crazy song we used to listen to. 'Epizootics.' By Scott Walker," I clarify, seeing her blank look. "He said things right from the song: 'all the people . . . pushing each other around'; 'Sorry, I'm so clumsy'; 'It's dense. Tense.' Suddenly it all started coming together. But I still couldn't figure out why he'd do that. Then I remembered." I pause, trying to catch my breath. "And maybe just in time. He practically spoon-fed it to me, like he knew I'd find that letter. Today is August sixteenth. In the letter, Charlie talked about death being like empty shoes at eight-eighteen. When I realized other parts of his letter were 'Epizootics' lyrics, I remembered the video. And the conversation we had about it." I shudder. I can't help it; the video was one of the most macabre I'd ever seen, full of insects crawling on skin and manic dancing and a series of bizarre images. Charlie had been fascinated by it.

"What was the conversation?" Aubrey asks, her eyes wide.

"Charlie thought the empty shoes meant someone died. Not just anyone. The woman in the video. The one dancing. I said it was ridiculous. The shoes appear a bunch of times, and the woman keeps appearing afterward. But Charlie kept saying, 'No, when you see the shoes for the last time, you know she's dead. See,' he said, and then he flipped through the video and showed me all the times the shoes appeared. The last time was toward the end of the video. 'Now it's eight-eighteen and she's gone forever,' he told me. She was only on the road to death before. I'm almost positive it was eight-eighteen he said. I remember being creeped out, but then I figured he'd just read up on the meaning of the song on one of the music blogs he was always on — that Scott Walker had really intended it to be that way, and Charlie was just recounting his intentions.

"Now I'm wondering why he referenced it in the letter. Maybe what Charlie had planned for August eighteenth had more to do with us — or me — than with him. I think it's a clue. I think he wants us to find him."

"You're crazy," Aubrey says, shaking her head at me. Her blue eyes are brighter than usual. "If he meant anything at all by it — and he probably didn't, since like you said, it seemed like he was out of his mind — I'm sure it had to do more with him than you or me."

"Yeah, maybe," I say, tightening my grip on the counter. "But I need to know for sure. And you still need your journal. Don't you want to know where that address leads?"

Aubrey lifts her head and looks me straight in the eye. She straightens her shoulders. When she speaks, her voice is clear and confident. "I'm sick of this roller-coaster ride," she starts. "I feel all over the place, totally out of whack. But I want to know what the hell is going on. So let's go to Bangkok," she says. "Plus . . ." She pauses here, and her lips curve up into a wicked smile. "If Charlie is alive, I've got some damn good ideas for making him wish he'd never messed with us."

I grin back, biting my lip. I have to stop myself from leaping across the few feet that separate us and pulling her into a hug.

18

Aubrey

It's something I can never fully explain to Lena. She won't understand, because she loved Charlie in a way I couldn't. She hurts from the loss in a way I don't. And, although I'm plagued by anger and confusion and sadness and guilt, she's plagued by heartbreak. I see it all over this crazy adventure: it's in the way she needs us to be here, searching for something as yet undefined amid the smells of saffron and turmeric in street stalls and undulating trance music in sweaty London clubs and the beautiful, polluted waters of the Arabian Sea. It's why I say yes to Bangkok, even though I'm fairly certain the answers aren't waiting for us there, even though I know it might be dangerous, even though I know my parents are probably already booking their flights out to bring me home. Lena needs something and I feel compelled to give it to her, or at least to be there while she searches. None of it is logical, all emotional. My heart hurts for Lena every time I see the loss on her face, even though technically the same exact person has disappeared from my life. I'm just not suffering in the same way.

It is no secret that I was questioning things with Charlie; but I couldn't tell anyone. None of my old friends from Liberty—the school I attended before we moved to the eastern side of the city during my junior year—kept in touch after I left. The couple of casual friends I made didn't understand why I'd date someone who didn't live right there, who couldn't make out in my parents' family room or the hub of a station wagon at the drive-in, who couldn't split a six-pack in the dark corners of someone's unfinished basement. My parents disapproved of the way I hopped on flights and trains, single-handedly (in their minds alone) sustaining the financial models of Amtrak and Southwest, industries designed (again, just in their minds) to capitalize on *Before Sunrise* moments. Industries I bought into with babysitting money alone. They called my bluff, and I couldn't bear to admit that they were right. It was all for nothing.

Adam was the last person I should have sought comfort from, but I did it anyway. Adam knew Charlie and didn't completely trust him. He never said so, but it was always there. Adam liked me, however, from the beginning. He was like a salve, a trusted friend when Charlie was impossible to trust. He was comforting, while Charlie was variable and extreme and moody.

Flash back to April: I'm sitting on the sofa waiting for Charlie to text, flipping through my parents' Netflix until I settle on a French film, the slightly steamy tale of an uptight writer whose world is blown wide open by her publisher's free-spirited daughter. It's a fairly predictable, cotton-candy plot, at least for the first half —I've seen it before—but its easy French eroticism does nothing to distract me from the dead silence of my phone. Charlie and I scheduled a FaceTime session at one p.m. my time, seven p.m. his. It's 1:10 and I'm starting to suspect it's not going to happen.

Charlie is forever promising to call, forever forgetting. Forever neglecting to respond to my text messages, the last of which read,

"Hey! Thank you so much for the book recommendation, can't wait to pick it up!" In actuality, Charlie recommended a book I had no interest in at all—a nonfiction account of the emergence of indie rock musicians in Germany. I'm not sure why he sent it in the first place. We haven't seen each other in six weeks now, the longest we've ever gone, and we're talking an average of twice per week aside from the occasional email. It's starting not to feel like a relationship at all. I used to convince myself it was better this way; it's my senior year of high school and I have to ace Honors Physics II in order to keep my scholarship to Georgetown. I don't have time for a distraction. The phone rings and my heart picks up. But one quick glance at the caller ID tells me it's not Charlie.

Still, my heart doesn't drop. It lifts at the sight of Adam's name. I pick up the phone, taking a breath first to ensure that my voice remains neutral. I swallow the guilt that's filling my chest. It's not wrong to get excited about Adam's calls, I assure myself; it's the opposite of wrong. I need a friend. Ever since switching schools, I've had pretty much no one but my dog and Charlie for company.

"Hey, you," Adam says. His voice is always upbeat and warm. The time difference between Illinois and Mumbai is more extreme than the one between Illinois and Oxford, yet Adam manages to surprise me with phone calls fairly often. "Listen, I'm just calling for a minute because I was in Jaipur during the literary festival and I picked something up that I think you'll like, but I need your mailing address."

"Have you heard of a little thing called texting?" I tease. "Or is that too Gen Y for you?" Adam and I have this joke that although we're both technically Millennials, neither of us fits the profile by a long shot. He has a fear of electronic communication—he's only occasionally on Facebook or Twitter—and both of us still like to read books printed on paper. Plus, he's living in a third-world country, on his own. That changes a person, at least in the sense that gadgetry becomes less important.

"Trust me, this surprise waits for no one. And I know how you are about responding to texts." I laugh, but I can't push away the pang I feel. Adam is basically saying the same exact thing I say to Charlie every time he sends me a two-line email and encourages me to be okay with it.

"Okay," I tell him. "You ready?"

I rattle off my mailing address and give him a quick goodbye, and then Adam is gone and I'm smiling. He's left me with a new wave of energy—kind of like after I drink peppermint tea in the winter or feel a breeze on my skin in the stifling heat of the summer. The energy of sharp contrast, I realize. Adam's voice is a momentary reprieve, every time.

A reprieve. I don't like to think about what it's a reprieve *from*.

A second later my phone pings and there's a message from Adam that reads, "Embracing the Y." Underneath it is a photo of Adam with Art Spiegelman, who created the graphic novel wonder that is *Maus*.

"OMFG," I type back, grinning like a lunatic. Then Adam responds with a big winky face because he knows I'm super excited but also half joking because I hate acronyms; we had a whole conversation less than a week ago about how dumb they are eighty percent of the time, again establishing ourselves as the same kind of freak.

I ride the glow of my talk with Adam right through dinnertime with my parents: burgers cooked on the grill medium rare with slices of dill pickles and potato chips under the bun instead of on the plate. It leaves me with a sweeping, contented form of happiness that's both tingling and peaceful, so much so that I don't notice until about seven p.m. that Charlie never called. For about two seconds, I think about breaking up with Charlie. But for what? For irrational feelings for a guy who lives on another continent and is wonderful and sweet and caring, sure, but who in all likelihood thinks of me as just a friend? Still, I think about it. And then I think about it more. And keep thinking about it.

About a week later, a battered package containing a signed copy of *Maus* arrives in the mail, with a printout of the photo Adam texted me. I put the photo in the frame of my mirror, where it lives for less than a day before I take it down out of (a) guilt and (b) worry that my mom will ask who Adam is. I return to work on my comic the same day and I don't stop after the picture comes down.

I'm working on a new comic now, at an outdoor market of sorts in Bangkok. Lena's gone in search of a bathroom and I'm eating a noodle bowl with fish balls floating around in its murky broth. Fish balls strike me as inherently weird and wrong and false—like if you tried to make goat squares or something—and yet they taste so right. They're like the chicken nugget of Bangkok, I muse as I sketch, hoping they aren't half nerve and bone the way actual chicken nuggets are. (Chicken nuggets, right up there with Cheez Whiz, are among my Worst Nightmare Foods. Lena is a foodie, and although her brand of picky barely exists in the Midwest, I've tried her kale chips on this trip, and I'm starting to think she's on to something.) I'm sketching the outdoor food stalls, the ones meant for tourists with their fried bat wings and skewered tarantulas. I realized a few months ago that making comics keeps me calm and helps me understand what I'm seeing. It's sort of like a natural filter when staring at everything directly feels overwhelming.

I feel a nudge to my chair and there's Lena, looking impatient.

"Dude," she says. "Let's get going. Sukhumvit Road is in Nana Plaza. I think we should get over there right away, before Cara blows it and lets my parents know she booked the wrong flights." I fight to suppress a wave of irritation. Lena's desire to chase Charlie is borderline obsessive, and I'm wondering if it was a mistake to agree to it. We've been traveling for almost a week, and I'm starting to wonder what's behind it besides grief and anger. Meanwhile, I'm tired and hungry and we have no place to stay. Yet a tiny part of me still wants to support Lena—a strange sentiment, given the circumstances—and another part, if I'm honest with myself, has enjoyed our adventure.

"Let's find a hostel first," I suggest, trying to remain patient. "We'll want to put our bags down, right?"

"I just wonder how long we can expect this lead to last. My parents are going to know where we are soon, and yours probably will too, since we're using your card for everything else. We're going to run out of money in, like, two seconds, and this address Anand gave us could lead nowhere or Dane could be gone by the time we get there."

"Lena," I say, speaking slowly, "I know you like to make quick decisions, but I need to finish my food, take a shower, and put down my stuff. My shoulder is killing me. I can't carry this bag forever."

"We're not on a shopping spree," Lena snaps. "We're close. *So close.* I can feel it. And tomorrow is eight-eighteen. Do you want to blow this?" Her voice rises the way I've learned it does when she's getting anxious that things won't go her way, when she thinks everything in the world hinges on this moment. And she believes that if this particular moment doesn't work out, she won't be okay.

"All right," I tell her, though part of me thinks she's this way from a lifetime of getting whatever she wants. "Let's do it. How far?" As Lena spouts off directions I can barely comprehend and I gather my bag in a half haze and I stumble after her in the direction of the busy highway, flanked on all sides by people hawking illegal DVDs and foot massages and plastic helicopters, I realize that I'm not giving her enough credit. It's *purpose* that drives Lena. We walk through the busy market and she sticks out her hand for a taxi and I see the way she squares her shoulders, where a minute ago they were slack. I see the way her eyes light up and the nod she gives the cab driver as she slips into the back seat and reaches to prop the door open for me. The thing Lena fears most is being without direction.

Now I understand why she needs to find Charlie.

I haven't allowed myself to think we might really find him here. Anand's crumb might just lead us to Charlie's estranged brother, who'll confirm what we already know by now: Charlie was one messed-up guy who in all likelihood is dead. Anand has painted Charlie as a drug addict and maybe a dealer; Adam has painted him as a misfit; Charlie has painted himself as a liar. Maybe Dane will just illuminate one more side of the turmoil that was Charlie and lend a little more credence to his suicide.

I haven't thought about what will happen if we actually *find* Charlie, because ever since Lena told me about the suicide note, it's seemed impossible. But watching Lena in action has confirmed for me what makes her tick. She only went to Bangkok once as a kid, she claims, and yet she's handling it like a pro. As I follow her around and watch her squint at the GPS device she's activated on her phone while alternately squinting at street signs—looking wholly unflappable—I wonder what Lena and the way she is means for me and the way I am, and what it says about each of us that Charlie dated us both. It's almost like together, we're a weird, symbiotic entity that hinges around the common nucleus of Charlie.

I don't want to be hinged anymore.

The recognition hits me in a rush. I've traveled to Paris, London, Mumbai, and now Bangkok only to realize that I don't want my identity to depend on someone else's idea of me, an idea that's probably pretty inaccurate. I've been half removed from Charlie for the past four months, maybe longer. Now I want to cut myself off altogether, watch myself float and see what happens and where I wind up. Lena doesn't want that, because she's been a free spirit—alone in boarding school, after boarding school, and now in college—for way too long. Thinking about it makes me furious. It makes me angrier than ever with Charlie, the way he put us each into a box. The congested streets of the city whiz past us and the traffic carries us forward in a steady stream, each vehicle part of a greater, more purposeful path, each containing within itself the option to veer off at any time. I watch Lena as she watches the cars beside us, then urges our driver forward, faster, faster, her lips pressed together in a thin, grim line—and I determine to fix this thing before we crash.

19

Charlie

You'll lead them right into it. Lambs to the slaughter; one lamb, anyway. It's a phrase you've always liked, a phrase you've used more than once. Ironically, it's a phrase you picked up from Aubrey long ago. Sometimes you don't care which one suffers, knowing one of them will. You go back and forth about which one it should be, and it gives you a thrill. Lena, the untamable one. The one who's always interfering, trying to get too close. Aubrey, the one who stabbed you in the back. It's the sweet ones who are most dangerous; you know it now.

They'll find Anand, and Dane — or is it Dana now? — because you want them to. And when they do, they'll know the truth, and they'll suffer. The truth — your plan for them — will destroy them. It's not the destruction itself that thrills you the most — though you're looking forward to it — it's the exhilaration of watching them as they learn that you're alive and in control. It's their inevitable terror. It's perfect.

You finish an email to Anand asking for twenty more ounces of hash. He'll freak out on you; he'll think you're a dealer. They'll all think, "This is why Charlie did it — he owed a guy some money and couldn't unearth the funds." Or they'll think, "This is why: Charlie was an addict. Disturbed. Went off the deep end." It doesn't matter what they think, you realize as you type. That's just the cherry. What matters is that Anand will say the right thing. You know him.

At the bottom of your email, you mention to Anand that you'll be seeing Dane in Bangkok soon. He'll tell your girlfriends where Dane is, because he'll want to destroy you. Lena will bite. Dane will play his role flawlessly, because he thinks you have the power to blackmail him. But the pictures you threatened him with? They were fakes.

He thinks you can ruin his life, but you can't.

It's all a lie.

But it doesn't matter what's true. It only matters what Dane believes to be true.

It hinges in part on Dane, on his ability to deceive.

And it hinges on Anand's inability to keep his mouth shut, without even realizing it.

How much does it take to derail someone who trusts you?

It takes twenty extra ounces of hash. That's the beauty of it. That's all it takes.

20

Lena

THIS WHOLE TIME, AUBREY HAS BEEN morose and silent. The enthusiasm—or acceptance—that she had yesterday when I told her I'd yet again pulled the rug out from under her has failed to emerge today. She's all scowly. We haven't talked about what will happen if we find Charlie. A big "if." I haven't told her about where we're going. A big shitty mistake.

Where we're going is part of the reason I wanted to go now, like *right now*, during-the-daylight hours "now." Aubrey thinks I'm just eager—I can tell by her patronizing looks and the way she rolls her eyes—but there's more to it than that. Much as I would like to find a place to stay and shower and all that, I do not want to get to Nana Plaza too late. Partly because I'm afraid of what Aubrey will think. She's so nice, so sheltered. It pains me to be the one to introduce her to the harsh realities of the world. Nana Plaza at night is a shitshow.

Unassuming in the daylight, it looms ahead of us now as the meter clicks its way up to 310 Thai bahts. Right now, you'd never guess Nana Plaza is a Bangkok nightlife gold mine. Club after club after club line streets that were developed in service of the sex trade industry. I know this because my mom is passionate about the human rights movement and donates major green to campaigns that fight violence against women, so guess what? Maybe it's rubbed off a little. Music isn't the only thing I care about.

We've arrived at one of the main streets where ladyboys work. I'm not sure what we're going to find when we meet Dane, but I have my suspicions. It's strange that Charlie never mentioned Dane, stranger still that he's hanging out in a Thai nightlife strip known for being "fun" in a sketchy way. When the car lets us out in front of one of the prominent buildings on the street—a four-story concrete structure that's open air and lined on each level with bars—I suppress a shudder for Aubrey's sake. I've got to look in control; that's what I do. Everywhere we go, it's so obvious she's never *really* traveled, and it brings out the protector in me. I mean, I guess this is scary if you've never done it before? I wouldn't know, since I pretty much came out of the womb holding a passport.

It's early—not yet eleven—and Western tourists are already hanging out at the bars. At other bars in other places, tourists sit in clumps, but here they're mostly solitary. It's the creepiest side of sexual tourism: men in their sixties with wedding bands on the same hands they use to clutch underage Thai girls' waists. My gut clenches at the thought of Charlie in a place like this.

We approach the front of Darkside Bar on foot a couple of minutes later, me picking my way confidently down the cobblestone road and Aubrey trailing behind, barely concealing her growing irritation as she drags her bag behind her. I'm half expecting the bar's exterior to be dark and shuttered, but its windows are flung wide open and people are already trickling from its entrance to neighboring venues. The crowd is varied: college kids around our age, older Western tourists, a few locals. I motion for Aubrey to follow me, and just as we near the entrance, a man stops us. He's a local, short and wiry, and his eyes flash as he grins and extends a laminated menu our way. Aubrey leans over to see what's on it but I slap the menu away, shaking my head sharply. I know what the list is. I've seen the same list in other countries, seen groups of drunk men laugh at its offerings and hand over money to be escorted into dingy, curtained rooms.

It's not prostitution, this particular list. If it were, the man wouldn't have offered it to us at all. In some ways it's almost worse — "novelties" you can watch for an extra fee, if the dancers on the bar aren't enough. I don't want Aubrey to see it. I grab her hand and pull her inside the large complex, which isn't just one bar but a long hall, as it turns out, with maybe a half dozen separate bars within. Some are decorated garishly with Scooby Doo figurines and papier-mâché Hello Kittys. Some have racecars suspended overhead. All have dancing women atop surfaces usually meant for beers and shot glasses, their Lucite, platform shoe–clad feet twisting and turning at eye level, where if you look up . . .

I don't look up. Obviously.

"Classy establishment," mutters Aubrey, and I smile a little. She's learned something this past week, and I like to think it's from traveling with me. The simple act of dragging your jaw up off the floor can get you far in this world. "Fake it till you make it" was always my dad's favorite expression, and Aubrey's show of bravado is almost convincing. *Almost.*

"They're not women," I casually let her know, pulling out a bar stool. Aubrey leans against the bar next to me.

"Excuse me?" She looks at me like I'm crazy and I signal over the waiter. While I didn't want Aubrey to see the menu—like I said, I've been feeling protective—ladyboys are something different.

"We'll have two Amstel Lights, please," I tell the waiter, and Aubrey doesn't even balk at my consistent compulsion to order on her behalf. Either she's used to being bossed around or she's still processing what I've told her. "They're ladyboys," I say. "Boys who look like girls." I watch Aubrey's eyes move from where we're sitting up the long-legged figures of the three sultry dancers in front of us. She mentally traces the curves of their hips; the roundness of their chests, made rounder still by boob jobs and pushup bras, undoubtedly; their delicate facial features; and their long, wavy hair. Aubrey lets out a short laugh.

"Shut up," she says, a note of doubt creeping into her voice.

"I'm serious," I tell her. "Some of them really are girls now, I guess. The ones who have already had sex change operations. The rest are transgendered. Hence 'ladyboys.' They're actually kind of considered a third gender around here."

"But . . . some of them are *gorgeous*," Aubrey whispers. "I would literally never be able to tell."

"Totally," I agree. "They're hot. That's part of the allure. There's a huge ladyboy component to tourism over here." It's a topic that's fascinated me ever since I came here as a kid. Which maybe would be weird for most kids, but no topic was taboo in our house. It's not exactly why we're here, but I suddenly feel compelled to tell her all about it. "My mom does a lot of campaigning against sexual tourism," I go on, "so I've grown up hearing all about this stuff. She donates but also travels internationally and speaks out against exploitation and such. She's also really into sexual identity in general, LGBT rights, gender rights . . . it extends in all these other directions. She's not a career woman exactly, but she's also not a trophy wife taking it on as a trophy cause. She cares a lot about it, and I guess I kind of do too." I blush a little, only because I don't usually admit that to anyone. Not that I'm ashamed; it's just that it's never come up, not really, not outside the sphere of my parents' dinner table. The couple of times I mentioned it to Charlie, he laughed like he thought I was being cute and said something like "Stick to music, babe." Like this is an interest on a par with records or concerts. I search Aubrey's eyes for similar derision but she looks interested. Even transfixed.

"You never mentioned it," she says.

"Why would I?" I shift awkwardly on my stool, sipping the beer the bartender has placed in front of me. I get emotional talking about it. I don't know why.

"It sounds pretty fascinating." Aubrey looks thoughtful. She grips the side of her own glass, and condensation decorates her fingers and drips down the side of the glass onto the countertop. "It's funny —I feel like none of that stuff ever comes up, where I'm from. I'm picturing you and your family around the dinner table and it sounds a lot more interesting than our tuna-noodle-casserole convos."

I laugh. "What does the food have to do with it?"

"Not the food . . . I mean, yeah, the food. But, like, tuna noodle casserole is the metaphor. Our dinners are pretty much, 'How was school, how's your essay, what's the latest blockbuster at the local theater, how did cheer tryouts go, what's the football team ranked?' There's none of this . . . exoticism." Aubrey gestures at the room we're in. "I kind of wish there were. I wish I hadn't had to be eighteen, here with you on this random trip I never would have taken *without* you, to hear about it."

"You should watch the movie *Beautiful Boxer*," I say, getting braver in response to her enthusiasm. "It's about this famous lady-boy, Nong Toom. She's, like, gorgeous. She's a model and an actress and she was a boxer. And a monk."

"A monk?" Aubrey nearly chokes on her beer, giggling a little.

"Yeah. Probably, you know, to suppress her nature or whatever. Religion. It sucks for that. Everyone's always turning to religion when there's something to squash down that they're ashamed of." Aubrey's quiet. *Shit.* For a second I'm worried I've offended her. I don't even know if Aubrey's religious. Sometimes I just assume everyone's atheist, like my family.

"Sorry," I say. "A lot of people are into religion. That's cool too." My words sound ridiculous, and I can't help laughing. "I mean," I say, "shit. I'm sorry. Are you religious?"

"Not particularly," Aubrey says. "I'm Presbyterian, and we go to church and stuff. I can see what you're saying, for sure. But the way I was brought up, it was about tolerance and respect and being nice. Good Midwestern values and all that," she jokes, mocking the phrase with air quotes.

"Don't make fun of it," I tell her. "If that's what you believe, it's cool. I mean, I don't believe in God. At least, I don't think so. But sometimes when stuff happens — stuff that feels bigger . . ." I pause, wondering if I should continue. Then I think, *Fuck it,* and go on: "Like being here with you on this strange mission to find Charlie. Getting robbed. Living life. Opening up to experiences. Saying yes wherever possible because it feels like if you ride the ride, it'll pay off. This kind of thing, and the fact that it wasn't even in our heads two months ago, makes me feel small. But in a good way — like there's something more out there. That's religion to me. That's why I get why people want to buy into spirituality."

Aubrey laughs. "It's a little more than that . . . at least for my parents," she says. "But I get what you're saying. Maybe you're spiritual, just not religious."

"I'm into people believing and doing whatever the hell they want," I say, my words building momentum, "as long as it doesn't hurt other people. It's the same principle as ladyboys. Live and let live. Do what makes you happy. Don't tamp it down, don't be embarrassed. Just don't be an asshole." Even as I say it, I realize how long I've been suppressing these words, these thoughts. *Oh, the irony.*

"Hear, hear," says the bartender, winking at me. She puts two fresh beers in front of us, and I feel myself blushing again. I didn't realize how loud I was being. "On the house," she says, wiping her eyes on the bar rag and sauntering off.

"Holy shit, I'm tipsy," Aubrey says. I laugh because she only really swears when we're drinking . . . another fun fact I've discovered about her lately.

"Oh my god," I tell her. "It's been a half hour. We so didn't come here for this." I start to stand, craning my neck. I'm wondering who we should ask first. Does Dane use the same last name as Charlie? Will he look like Charlie?

"Lena." Aubrey's hand is on my arm, even as I begin to stand. "Hold on a sec."

"What?" I ask. "Don't you want to get this over with?"

"I do," Aubrey says slowly, nodding. "In a second." She stops, like she's thinking, and I drum my fingers against the bar impatiently. Aubrey only speaks when she's ready, though. So I wait.

"I'm into comic books," she says finally. "Graphic novels, if you will."

"Uh-huh," I say, wondering where this is going.

"Maybe you didn't even know that, because I've never mentioned it."

"I've seen you doodling in that little tablet of yours," I say. "Not doodling," I amend as Aubrey winces. "Just. Whatever. You know."

"It's okay," she continues. "That's not my point. My point is that there's this one artist I love. Like, really love. She's smart and profound and emotional but unsentimental, and everything she does makes me cry. And she has this theory, this test. The test is this: In a book or a film, when there are two girls talking . . . do they ever have a conversation that isn't about a guy?"

"Uh-huh," I say distractedly, still not sure where this is headed.

"Lena." Aubrey's voice is serious, and it causes me to look up. "I'm like ninety-nine percent sure this is the first conversation we've had since we met that didn't revolve around Charlie." She stops, letting this sink in, and finally I understand.

"We failed the test until now."

Aubrey nods. "I liked it," she says quietly. "Not talking about him, I mean. I kind of wish . . ."

"We'd do it more often?" I finish for her.

"Exactly."

"Done," I say, and she grins. She's totally right. I feel like I've been more *me* in the last forty-five minutes than I've been on this whole trip, or since Charlie died, for that matter. And sometimes I feel close to Aubrey. Almost as if I'm starting to trust her. It's enough to make me hopeful.

"And, um," she says, "let's go ahead and finish this thing. But if we find out that Charlie's alive, *fuck him,* Lena. Charlie is a fucking asshole. And it's time we owned the truth that he treated us like garbage. So let's be angry. Promise me you'll stay angry."

My mouth drops open, not just because she's swearing up a storm, but because I've literally never witnessed her this fiery. Aubrey's stronger than I thought, and she's right. We've been consumed by Charlie for too long. Especially me. My heart aches at the admission. But she's right.

"Let's finish this," I say, in agreement.

21

Aubrey

I THINK AT FIRST IT'S GOING TO BE TRICKY to find Dane. The bar is big and sprawling—really a collection of bars, almost like a marketplace—and I'm tipsy from the one and a half beers I downed as Lena and I talked. But it turns out to be easy—almost too easy. The first person we approach knows him.

"Dana?" the man asks. "Dana Price." I assume at first it's his accent that twists the name into its feminine version, or that we got the name wrong—"Dana" is a guy's name too, in some circles. But Lena's eyes darken and narrow, and I can tell she thinks different. She nods carefully, her posture tense and poised, like she doesn't know what to expect. It hits me that if Dane is bad news, we could be in more serious trouble than we already are. "Yes, Dana," the barback tells us, his manner relaxed. "Everybody know. Dana go onstage tonight. She . . ." He trails off, seeming to search for words. "She in house, wear lipstick." I feel my eyebrows shoot up. Lena looks unfazed.

"She onstage, wear lipstick," the man clarifies. I'm still baffled, but Lena nods.

"She's getting ready," she says to him. "For tonight?" The man nods. "Can you tell us where?" she asks, smiling and leaning toward the man in a friendly, ingratiating manner. Like they've known each other for years. The old paranoia hits me, the kind I've fought to move past in recent days. *How well do I know Lena? What does she know that I don't?* But I push it aside. I'd rather have no room between us not to trust.

"Yes," he agrees, smiling back. His smile is less toothy than Lena's. There are gaps where teeth have rotted out. But he's affable and seems totally unconcerned about why we're asking. "Go down road, take left. Then after four buildings you turn down alley. That house of Dana."

"Are there any details that might help us recognize it?" Lena asks. "Paint color, or . . . ?" The man squishes up his eyebrows like he doesn't understand. "Color," Lena clarifies. "Red house, green house?" She points at a grease-streaked placemat sitting on the bar. "Red," she repeats, as she might for a toddler. "Brown?" She points to the bar. The man's face clears and he nods again.

"Yellow house," he says, pointing to a container of mustard.

A minute later we're off, after Lena asks a few of the performers, already warming up onstage, to confirm the location of Dana's home. One of them speaks proficient English, and we have no problem following her directions to the opposite end of Nana Plaza and over to a side street, where the yellow house turns out to be a crumbling, faded high-rise the color of dirty buttermilk. It's covered in graffiti, and although I can't read the wording, the house still looks charming in a gritty way. We walk through the throngs of peddlers at the building's exterior, enter a dingy corridor, and push our way back to the elevator shaft.

"Are we sure we want to do this?" I ask Lena as she pulls open the creaky metal accordion grate that separates the elevator from the hallway. The tiles that decorate the floors of each, once probably cheerful, are covered with years of accumulated filth.

"Are you kidding? We've come so far." She steps into the elevator and presses the button marked 6.

"I just mean the elevator." I take a cautious step into the creaking beast after her, trying not to dwell on how frayed the suspension cable must be.

"Oh." Lena laughs. "Right. Too late now." The platform starts moving upward almost before she can close the door behind us, and I watch the floors pass by one by one, the elevator grating against its gears all the while. The stairs and ceiling bear thick cracks, insinuating that the building might collapse at any minute. I recall an article in the in-flight magazine that cited building regulations for cities like this one, regulations put in place to prevent buildings in certain areas from being built over four stories high. I wonder nervously if this building is illegal. Buildings collapse all over Asia all the time. I try not to think about it. It's Bangkok. Bangkok is more developed than, say, Bangalore. *Isn't it?* I wonder if I'm getting my cities straight. My thoughts converge in a haze, and my palms turn sweaty as the elevator screeches to a halt.

Lena pushes open the door, and more black sediment attaches itself to her palms. She brushes them casually on her jeans, and I feel another flush of admiration. Lena is remarkable in so many ways: she's bold, fearless, and street-smart; I'm sure she doesn't even recognize all her strengths. I follow her down the sixth-floor hallway, even dimmer than the hallway on the first floor owing to a burned-out bulb—its cord dangles frayed and helpless from a patch of crumbling concrete in the ceiling. Footsteps echo upstairs and dust peppers our heads as we walk. When it touches Lena's hair, it disappears into her white halo. I'm sure on me it looks more akin to dandruff.

"I think this is it," Lena says, glancing at her palm. Sing Lee, a dancer at the bar, drew a map of the building's interior, holding her pen in a firm hand while her red-lacquered nails dug lightly into Lena's forearm to keep it steady as she wrote. There's a small, narrow corridor off the main hallway on this floor. It leads to a plain brown door with a brightly colored sign on red paper tacked to its surface, with a word scrawled across its front in Thai. I imagine it means something like "Welcome," and I say as much to Lena.

"Fingers crossed it doesn't say 'Keep out,'" she shoots back. I suspect she's only half joking. I reach out to press the black doorbell just within the metal grate that stretches across the shabby door, and Lena gives me a reassuring smile. "I'm sure Dana's great," she tells me.

"How are you so sure?" I ask.

"Charlie's parents are awful," she replies. "Well, his dad, anyway —his mom's just sort of a mess. Any enemy of theirs is a friend of ours." I make a mental note to ask her more about that later—I never met Charlie's parents, and it was more difficult than anything to get Charlie to open up about them. All I ever knew was that he and his dad didn't get along; but when I saw his dad from afar at the memorial, he seemed engaged and charming. Odd, actually, how he was smiling and greeting people like it was a receiving line at a wedding and not a funeral. I'm thinking this as the door swings open and a young girl, or ladyboy—I'm not sure which term is correct —smiles up at us. She's wearing a tight black pleather skirt and glittery stilettos that must be at least six inches high.

"Dana?" Lena asks, sounding shy for the first time since I've known her. The girl shakes her head and leans back into the room behind her, yelling out a few words in Thai. A few seconds later, another girl approaches, also Thai.

"I'm Dana," she says in perfect English, twirling a long strand of hair in one finger. It's so reddish purple it's almost magenta; but it looks pretty, contrasted against the smooth brown of her skin.

"Dana Price," Lena repeats, disbelieving.

"The one and only," Dana replies.

Lena looks confused, and for the first time I wonder what the trajectory is with this black sheep half brother-sister. I can tell Lena was expecting a Westerner, someone white like Charlie. I hadn't thought that far ahead, but now I'm wondering about this supposed brother of Charlie's who's clearly half Thai and wound up back in Thailand after years in elite boarding schools, presumably, like Charlie. Many questions are whirling through my mind.

"We're friends of Charlie's," Lena tells her, raising her chin just slightly. Dana counters with a level gaze. "We have a couple of questions, if you're free."

"You're the girlfriends." Dana's voice is flat, unfriendly.

"Yes."

Dana's eyebrows furrow, and then her face hardens. She purses her lips, takes a step back, and starts to swing the door shut. I manage to wedge my wrist through the partitions in the cold grate, catching the door before it latches. I hope fervently that the grate hasn't cut my skin; I can't tell just yet, but blood poisoning is something I'd like to leave Asia without experiencing.

"Please talk to us," I plead, raising my voice so Dana can hear it.

"I'm busy," she says, the pitch of her own voice sinking low in its aggression, the only betrayal of her origins as a boy. "I'm getting ready. And I hardly talk to Charlie anymore."

"Did you know he died?" I burst out. I can't help myself. Lena looks at me and glares. There's a long silence. Then Dana eases the door open just a crack.

"Oh, honey, Charlie's not dead," she tells us. "He's just being a grade-A asshole. If I didn't hate our parents so much I'd probably have it in my heart to tell them. I just saw Charlie last week." Though she's friendlier, she is still guarded.

"He's not dead." Lena's voice is flat but registers no surprise. I'm so shocked that I can't say anything at all.

"No," Dana replies, and then she sighs through the slight opening of the door.

"We've traveled halfway around the world," I hear myself say through the buzzing in my brain. "Please." The noise grows louder and I feel like I might pass out. Dana's face looks like a cauldron of warring emotions. She hesitates for a second longer, then removes a key from her pocket and unfastens the padlock that secures the grate. "Come in," she says, foisting the grate open. "I don't know if I have a lot of answers for you—Charlie and I were never exactly BFFs." She waves us in impatiently; and, as I cross the threshold into her chaotic, filthy home, my nerves shoot adrenaline through my whole body—so much that it's nearly impossible to keep my balance. It feels like Lena and I are crossing a bigger line than the threshold of Dana's home, and that this time, we may not be able to turn back.

22

Lena

CHARLIE'S NOT DEAD. DANA'S WORDS RING in my ears, confirming everything I've suspected all along—and known without a doubt since our encounter with Anand. I don't know whether to jump for joy or cram my head into a vise and squeeze. I've been right this whole time, but I'm not prepared to be.

After I found the suicide note, I sat in his parents' living room and held his mother's hand while she chain-smoked, her hair wild and untamed, a badge of the girl she probably once was. I didn't think Charlie's mother could fall apart any more than she already had, and then she did. But even in her disintegrated state, she told me: "Lena, honey, we have to let him go. We'll lose ourselves too, otherwise." I think she was saying it for my benefit, because the way she was clutching a photo of him as a toddler, cradled in her arms and smiling shyly into the camera—it seemed to me that she wasn't letting him go.

No parents should lose their child.

Nobody—my age, anyway—should lose her boyfriend.

Nobody should lose her brother, nobody should lose herself. When I found the letter I thought, *Charlie lost himself.* But I still didn't believe he was dead. And I didn't think, *I lost myself when I met him. I lost myself a long time ago, long before losing Charlie, maybe the second he walked into my life.* I feel selfish, thinking it now. But it's there and it's true.

When he disappeared, I felt like my grief was bottomless—because even if he was still alive, he'd chosen to leave me behind. And my own mother said, "Someday, you'll fall in love again." I didn't want to. I only wanted Charlie. I felt like someone had ripped my heart out, ended things before I'd given it the okay or even had a chance to adjust to the idea. Then I did adjust, somehow. After the grief there was the numbness, which stretched all the way up to the memorial service. During that phase, I realized I didn't have anyone except Charlie. Charlie swooped into my life at the expense of all my other friends, who slowly faded into the background, where they remained, semi-forgotten, just people to say hi to at parties and follow on Instagram. After Charlie came into my life, everything was always all about Charlie. When he disappeared, as easily as the retreating of the tide, my old friends didn't rush in to replace him. There was just barren, empty numbness. Then, after meeting Aubrey, there was the fresh pain of what he did. And the anger that's consumed me ever since. And the relief.

No one wants to talk about the relief.

I don't like to think about the pale, soothing calm that has swept over me in the more recent days following his "death." I don't want to know what it makes me. But I can tell Aubrey feels it too. Charlie may have been a liar and a cheat, but he didn't deserve to die. And yet . . . I've been feeling relieved. There's no other word for it. I've felt lighter. Charlie is missing from my life, but so are the worries, the letdowns, the disappointments.

And now I don't know what to feel. Or what I'm supposed to

feel, now that I know I was right and he's really out there. There's no instruction manual for this: *What to Do When Your Boyfriend Supposedly Commits Suicide and You Know Your Boyfriend Cheated and You Find Out Your Boyfriend Is Alive After All and for Fuck's Sake, You Wasted Three Very Important Years on Him.*

These thoughts are running through my head as Aubrey and I follow Dana through what can only be described as a foyer — though not a very nice one — into a large common area where dancers in various stages of undress are applying makeup. Aubrey reaches out and squeezes my hand unexpectedly, then drops it again without looking at me. I glance at her, surprised by the random burst of affection. She's not exactly the touchy-feely type.

"Meet the ladies," Dana says wryly. "We all live here. Sleep here. Do pretty much everything here. The younger ones go to school here."

"In this room?" Aubrey whispers, incredulous. Her expression is a mixture of guarded and shocked, like she's doing her best not to offend Dana.

"Yeah. It's a pigsty, but it's free, okay? I'll get my own place someday soon. This is just . . . my starter pad." She cracks a grin and glides gracefully toward one of the mirrored tables. I notice that the room is lined with small vanities, almost as if it's a makeshift dressing room for a bizarre, low-budget stage act. Then I get it: that's exactly what it is.

"Who pays the rent?" I want to know. Dana grins again.

"Ignorance is bliss," she says, rolling her eyes. I raise my eyebrows. "Just kidding," she adds. "It's the guys at the bar. They let us crash here in exchange for a certain number of hours. Anything after that is take-home pay. But," she sighs, plopping herself down on a rickety folding chair and reaching for an eyeliner, "you're not here to hear about that. You want to know about Charlie." At this, one of the other dancers nearby glances up at us suddenly, knocking a tube of mascara from the vanity as she does. She has long dark hair and wears a sequined red bra with a black pleather skirt. Dana frowns in her direction, then turns her attention back to us.

"You say Charlie came through here." Aubrey's voice is tense. We're standing next to the mirror, huddled in a clump like agitated birds. Dana pulls two pillows out from under her chair and tosses them in our direction, motioning for us to take a seat. I sit cross-legged and Aubrey tucks her legs up under her modestly, and now it's like we're two children at story hour.

"Charlie and I didn't grow up together," Dana starts, lowering her voice by a few pitches. "At least not consistently." She lines the slope of her mouth in between words. I watch her fill in her lips with a dark wine red color. I try to picture her as she must have been before she became a kathoey. Thin and angular, with the cheekbones of a model—all of that would have remained the same. What might have changed is the curve of her hips, the fullness of her chest, the lack of facial hair. Maybe she changed her gender before she ever grew facial hair; maybe she never really felt what it was like to be a man, only a young boy. "I actually never liked Charlie when I did see him," she continues. "He used to make fun of me, I guess because he sensed I was different. I tried to hide it for a long time." Dana pauses again to apply another coat of lipstick. I feel restless and eager to get to the point, and I can tell Aubrey feels the same way; she's picking at her sleeve the way I've seen her do so many times.

"He's no good," Dana says unceremoniously. "He only came here last week because he was desperate. He was in a bad place. Needed some cash. Needed to disappear."

"Why did he need cash?" I ask. "Charlie had tons of money."

"And why did he need to disappear?" asks Aubrey, who is practically jumping out of her skin. "Do you know where he went?"

"I wouldn't try to find him if I were you," Dana says. "Look at what he did to you. And you should have heard the stuff he said. But you won't. I wouldn't tell you if you were my worst enemy. Just trust me, you're better off."

"Can you just start at the beginning?" I elbow Aubrey and give her a hard look, hoping she'll take the hint and hold back instead of pelting Dana with questions.

"Look," says Dana. "I have to be onstage in two hours. I have this whole routine I do before going on—get my som tam, chill backstage with the girls, play a hand of solitaire. It's kind of my thing."

"That's fine," I tell her. "Just the basics."

Dana sighs. "I don't know how to tell the basics without getting into the backstory," she says. "I'm Charlie's half brother. Obviously. Both Price parents are white as snow. I never knew my mom—she was probably some sex worker my dad knocked up while he was out here on business. I never really found out. Charlie's parents—our dad and his mom—they're a train wreck. I'm sure you know that if you've spent any time with them." She looks to us for confirmation, and I nod. I actually have a soft spot for Charlie's mom, who despite being super screwed up and depressed and boozy is a good person deep down.

Charlie's dad, on the other hand, is a jerk, down to the core. Never there—and when he was, nothing was good enough. To me he was always engaging and friendly, but in a sort of fake way. Like you couldn't tell what he was really thinking. Charlie's mom had the shakes every time he was around. It was sad to see. It was something that always made me feel compassion for Charlie . . . until I realized belatedly that it probably also messed him up in ways that would affect me.

"So, all along I know I'm different, right?" Dana continues. "I know it, they know it, everyone knows it. I mean, I regularly raid my aunt's closet, I clearly like boys, I feel uncomfortable in my own skin. It's hard to explain to people who don't get it. I referred to myself as Charlie's sister. People were confused. Their friends thought it was weird. Charlie's dad — our dad. Sorry. It's been a while since I've thought of him as my dad too." It's odd the way she stumbles over calling him *her* dad . . . but it occurs to me that when you've been ostracized, you have to cut yourself off emotionally.

"Anyway, our dad was gone all the time, totally uninvested in the whole family thing. They're still married, but I guess it's for appearance's sake or some bullshit. His mom actually tried, when I came along — at least at first. Like really tried, took me in. Treated me like her own kid — this was back when she still had her shit semi-together. And then everything worsened between his mom and our dad, and I guess I reminded her of the things she was trying to forget — his string of affairs, the reason I was there in the first place. Her anxiety got worse, and she kind of cracked. She raised a huge fuss and said she couldn't deal with me anymore, she had enough to handle, and my dad needed to be more present in my life. So I started to travel all over the world with him. I went to schools in the cities where he was stationed. He tried to instill some 'real discipline,' tell me how to walk, talk, dress." Dana's face darkens at the memory. "But at least he didn't discipline me the way he did Charlie."

"How did he discipline Charlie?" Aubrey asks.

"Charlie was tougher than me," Dana says. "More rebellious, and he used to piss our dad off royally. I remember this one time when we were very little, Dad held Charlie's head underwater in the bathtub for a really long time after Charlie misbehaved. Like, long enough that I was freaked out. I tried pulling my dad's hands off him, but I was only, like, seven or something. I think I knew I couldn't do anything. I remember feeling like Charlie was going to die and there was nothing I could do. Finally my dad let up, but he was laughing, like it was a big joke. He said he was teaching Charlie a lesson. It was fucking scary."

"My god," I whisper. I had no idea it was like that. Charlie never said. "Where was your mom?"

Dana wrinkled her forehead, thinking. "She was out with friends or something. I don't really remember. I was going to tell her, but Charlie yelled at me. He swore he'd kill me if I told. Said I was being a pussy. He actually said that, at, like, age five. Stuff like that happened a lot back then. Our dad really beat up on him, and Charlie would never tell. Like he was defending our dad, even though our dad almost killed him. He was so calm about it. I was the one freaking out. I would feel bad for Charlie if he hadn't gotten so mean as we got older. I was scared of them both as far back as I can remember.

"We'd all get together on the holidays and stuff back then, up until we both finished middle school. I wanted to be close to Charlie. He was nice sometimes, when we were hanging out alone. But sometimes he'd change . . . just be a totally different guy. I think maybe he was afraid of what our dad would do if he thought he was spending too much time with me. He started beating up on me a lot when we were in elementary school even though he was two years younger. I think he thought if he showed our dad he was tough — that stuff like that didn't bother him — he'd be proud. He was still living in Paris back then."

"You were just young kids," I say. Charlie was fourteen when he moved from Paris to Bangkok.

"Yeah," says Dana. "I split when I was fifteen. The bath thing happened when we were really little. I think I was maybe seven. But that was just one example. God," she says, shaking her head. "I'm almost twenty-two now. It feels so long ago. Anyway." She shakes her head again quickly, as if ridding herself of the memories. "You don't care about these sob stories. I only saw Charlie twice after I left. Coming here was the obvious choice for me. We'd traveled here when I was young. I knew my way around. Like I said, I saw Charlie twice after that. Ran into him once when he was a freshman at the American School here, just after I had split. It was a shock." Dana shakes her head yet again, laughing a little. "He shows up at the bar where I'm at and I'm like, 'That's Charlie. That's my little brother.' But he doesn't recognize me at all. I go up to him and I pretend to be a random girl just to mess with him, but he freaks. He thinks I look familiar and he can't figure out why. Then it dawns on him and he's totally spooked." Dana laughs and runs a brush through her long hair, then twirls it into a haphazard bun at the nape of her neck.

"Back then I didn't look like I do now, but I looked different enough. We talked for a while. He seemed okay. He apologized for what he'd done to me, how mean he'd been. Playing me against our parents and all that crap. He apologized but he still didn't seem trustworthy. I asked how his best friend was, this guy named Phil.

And he was all, 'Who?'" Dana raises her eyebrows like a clown, in a mock expression of confusion, and laughs. "And I was like, 'Dude, you've known that guy forever,' and he claimed he'd never been friends with him at all or some shit. Same thing with family stuff. I was laughing about the time we rocked out to the Dr. Dre our mom wouldn't let us listen to—we had to sneak that kind of thing around her—and smoked a joint and accidentally spilled cranberry juice on our parents' white sofa—and then our parents thought the cat knocked over the glass, even though it was all Charlie. I was cracking up over it, and I remember he gave me this blank look. And he swore up and down it never happened. Like *I* care. Like I'm going to rat him out or something after all these years. It was the most pathetic thing." Dana shakes her head, frowning at the memory.

"It was like he needed me to believe he wasn't there. Or like he needed to believe it. He got all upset, said I was thinking of somebody else, because he doesn't smoke, he's straight edge, and furthermore he doesn't even listen to rap, never has, couldn't name a Dre song if you held a gun to his head. But like, we had had good times that night. We bonded over the whole sofa thing." Dana looks disturbed. "I thought he was fucking with me. Then I realized. He didn't remember it. It was like he blacked it out." Dana trails off, seemingly forgetting about the makeup in front of her, the show she needs to dance, her preshow routine that should have started five minutes ago.

"And what about the second time?" Aubrey asks it so softly I can barely hear, but Dana seems to snap out of her reverie.

"That was two weeks ago," she says. "Or maybe not quite. Maybe ten days. And seeing him . . ." She trails off, her eyes widening. She has caught sight of the tattoo on my wrist, exposed when my sleeve drooped back as I was tucking my long blond waves behind my ears. She pales.

"What?" I ask, confused. The tattoo is crude, even ugly; but her reaction seems extreme.

She appears to recover easily. "Nothing," she says. "I'm just afraid of needles. Your tattoo looks . . . painful."

"I wouldn't know," I tell her. "I have no memory of it."

"Really." The word is loaded. "How did you pick a lamb? That's what it is, right?"

"Again, I don't remember," I say, my tone sharper. "What were you saying about Charlie?" She takes a breath, dragging her eyes from my wrist back to my face.

"I was saying that seeing him scared the shit out of me. He's seriously fucked up, that one," she says. "If I were you, I'd get the hell away from him as fast as you can." Then she frowns, looking worried. "Do you have flights back? Because I can book you. I have a guy. He can hook it up for cheap. Like less than two hundred. He's got an in at United. You should go, really," she says. "I don't know where Charlie is now, but I'm pretty sure he's still in Bangkok. You should go before he finds you." The last line sounds like a warning, and I tense. I'm quite sure there's something Dana isn't telling us.

"What do you know?" I ask. "What aren't you saying?"

Dana brushes on a quick coat of mascara but doesn't answer me. "I've gotta go," she says, then stands up quickly. "That's all I've got for you. Sorry." Aubrey and I pull ourselves to our feet. My heart is beating fast, and I feel the back of my neck dampen.

"No," I say. "There's something else. I'm right, aren't I?" Aubrey looks uncertainly from me to Dana. I'm blocking Dana's path to the door, and a few of her friends are giving us wary looks. I'm not sure how long my confidence will hold.

"Look," Dana says quietly. "There might be more. But you don't want to know it. Take my advice and get on a plane soon. Tomorrow. You can stay here tonight. Just stay here while I'm gone. You're safe here for now. I'll hook you up with tickets, but you'll have to give me a little incentive."

"My ring," I blurt, pulling my sapphire band off my right hand. It doesn't matter now that I'm losing an heirloom; all that matters is getting home. Dana examines it closely while Aubrey watches my face. Finally, Dana nods. I breathe a sigh of relief but place my palm over her hand, the one that cups the ring.

"I'll give it to you when you hand over the tickets," I tell her.

Dana releases the ring from her grasp without hesitation. "You seem like nice girls," she says. *"So get the hell out of here as soon as you can."*

23

Charlie

You know it'll take something else, something more than just an explosion and *poof*, vanished. There's your mom, for one. She's not dumb, and she cares. She cares more about you than you've ever cared about anyone. You know she won't settle for a downed plane and a missing body—she'd have the cops plus a dozen private investigators all over that one until the money ran out, and the money isn't ever going to run out.

And there's Aubrey. She has so much hope underneath her fragile shell. She acts like she's made of something hard, but glass shatters if you want it to. She *wants* you to care, she *wants* you to show her, she *wants* you to visit her, she *wants* you to be this thing she can parade in front of her parents, but she *needs* you to keep up the act even though you know she knows there's something going on with you that she can't explain. She *needs* you to stay alive for the sake of her guilty conscience. Because if you were dead, it would destroy her. She'd feel responsible because of what she did with Adam. You've known about her and Adam for a long time, even before she finally confessed. You know all about her guilt. She needs to feel like a good person, even if she's a cold, heartless bitch.

You used to be a good person. You don't know what happened.

You don't know why you couldn't manage it all, the way your father manages things. His lives, his homes, his mistresses.

For all this to work, you need your mom to let go of you and you need Aubrey to hang on.

Lena's a smart girl. She comes off wild and impulsive and flaky, but she's got a crazy sixth sense. She'll know exactly what happened . . . eventually. She'll find the note you're about to leave in the top drawer of your bedside table at your parents' house, the drawer she likes to snoop through when she thinks you're not looking because she thinks by doing so she finds out more about you. Lena's always one step behind you, but she'll catch up. She's no fool. That's partly why she's become so much trouble. She sees the Bazooka Joe wrappers you put there and the set of pogs and the note to the Easter Bunny from when you were (supposedly) five. She assumes you're hoarding remnants from your past. These things make her feel safe, make her feel like she knows you. But why does she need them? Why did you need to plant them there for her to find in the first place? Because she *didn't* feel safe. That's why. Because she sensed something about you that was off. Something she'd rather ignore.

You need your mom to let go and Aubrey to hang on and Lena to know the truth . . . at some point. You need Lena to be the leader of this charade. And besides, you've always loved her. She deserves to know the truth. (*Aubrey you could have loved, but she ruined it. She went and cheated with that douchebag from the American School in Bombay. Is there a way to get rid of him too?*) So you plant a note, may as well be a note to the Easter Bunny because it's just as fake as that one was — and you phrase it like maybe you want to kill yourself. It's almost too easy. Then you put it right on top of that drawer for

Lena to find, and you address it to "Mom." (*Your mom knows better than to dig through your drawers.*)

Suicide is not what you want. You don't want to die. Why should you suffer more than you've already suffered?

You want someone else to suffer for a change.

Once the note is in place, you drive a knife into your thigh and stanch the wound with your Oxford blazer. You twist the knife deeper, biting down on a rag to quiet your urge to scream. There needs to be plenty of blood.

It's perfect. Aubrey will think, *He's dead, I'm safe.* Your mom will think, *I don't want to accept it but I have to now.* Lena will think, *Trust Charlie to fake a big, brilliant suicide this way.* You don't use the boning knife from your mother's kitchen. You buy another one especially for the project, with cash. You blow a fortune on one with a mother-of-pearl handle. It feels better that way, ceremonial. You hate yourself for having to inject Lidocaine first; but then you do and it's over much more quickly and easily than you expected. You sterilize with peroxide, add three thick layers of gauze, and top it off with bandages. Still, your thigh throbs when you're finished.

Now you disappear, high in the sky, jumping out of a plane no one knows you knew how to fly, using a parachute no one knows you knew how to use. You have so many secrets. It wouldn't have worked otherwise.

You watch the plane explode just as it should, right on time. The bomb was the easy part; any fool could have made it. You're no fool.

Later, you plant the blazer you've bloodied and charred.

The note is just in case the bloody jacket isn't enough. Everyone needs to give up on you. Everyone but Lena. Aubrey will come for what's hers whether she thinks you're dead or alive.

24

Aubrey

WE DON'T STAY.

We've been through too much to sit around, docile as sheep. This time I'm the one who speaks up. Because Lena, she's immobilized. Something peculiar passed over her face when Dana was talking, and she's been silent ever since. Dana's just left us with strict instructions not to move, not to go anywhere. Her words were chilling. So Charlie is alive, after all. He's alive and wanted to disappear—and it means *he crashed a plane and spilled his own blood* in order to do so.

I'm afraid of what this means for me.

In the last weeks, when we talked, Charlie seemed scattered. He got dates and other factual things wrong. But it was all trivial. He thought I liked brussels sprouts, he remembered a pink dress I never owned. After I met Lena, I assumed he was just getting the two of us confused. But if he faked his death, he's not just a liar, he's unhinged. With a bunch of evidence that could ruin me. Just like that, all the old fear I felt when he was blackmailing me before his disappearance is back. I almost sob from the weight of it.

"What are you thinking?" I ask Lena. She's biting on her thumbnail, a habit that seems to have developed in full force just after

Kerala, which is about when she started becoming visibly anxious. She shakes her head and remains silent. It's unlike her to say nothing. Something's seriously off. All around us, the ladyboys in the room are pulling on slinky dresses, spritzing on perfume, decorating their faces, bedazzling their long nails. Generally, they are paying no attention to us at all as they ready themselves for work. Dana's pretty much the only one who's already left, our passports in hand.

"We shouldn't have given them to her," I tell Lena, pulling myself to my feet. Suddenly I'm terrified and starving, and I nearly pass out from nerves and low blood sugar.

"What?" Lena asks distractedly, her brow furrowed.

"The passports. That was stupid. After what happened in Kerala . . ."

"She's not Anand," Lena points out, getting to her feet. "And she needs them for our flights."

"Flights she's getting a 'special deal' on," I say. "We need to get them back, Lena. We barely know her."

"She's Charlie's brother," Lena says, then snorts when she catches herself. "Sister. *Was* Charlie's brother? God, that sounded weird." I'm barely listening to her. I'm already moving toward the door, every nerve end in my body firing away. "Aubrey, we're probably better off here," Lena insists. "What if we can't get back in, or miss her somehow?"

"That's why we're going back to the bar," I explain. She's being oddly dense for someone who's usually so streetwise. "We're going to sit there and watch her and make sure she doesn't leave our sight until we get those passports back, along with our plane tickets."

"What about finding a hostel?" Lena asks. I'm halfway out the door but for some reason the question sends a searing pain through my temples and into my skull. I whirl around.

"Why are you being weird?" I demand. "Dana was being weird. You're being weird. Who cares about a hostel? I'm pretty sure we're both past placing that high on our list of concerns for the evening. What's your deal?" Lena avoids my eyes. Tugging at her black T-shirt, she follows me.

"I'm probably just being insane," she starts, skipping a little to match my stride. I'm the taller of the two of us, and although I usually match her pace, I'm tired of being courteous all the time. I just want to find Dana again, see our passports in her hand, figure out what it is she wasn't telling us, because all of a sudden it's feeling pretty important. We're missing a crucial piece of the puzzle, and Charlie's nearby. That's part of it: I half wonder if Charlie will get back in touch with Dana.

"There is no part of this that isn't insane," I inform her. "But I think we need to be open with each other." I hesitate before deciding whether to finish my thought. Then I go for it; Lena and I have only each other in this whole crazy mess. "Just tell me what's on your mind. We need to have each other's backs. There's a chance I'll even have something useful to add," I say wryly. I quicken my pace and Lena hurries to catch up, and for a few seconds it feels like role reversal. It's the first time on this trip that I've felt in charge. I'm filled with an unfamiliar surge of confidence as I retrace our path to the bar. I'm not expecting what Lena says next. When she speaks up, it nearly knocks the wind from my lungs.

"I have the letter with me here," she tells me. "I keep reading it and rereading it." I stop, disbelieving.

"The letter," I repeat. "The suicide letter?"

"Yeah," Lena says. She looks at the fruit stall beside me, the beer vendor to our left, the smog-sodden sky. Anything but my eyes.

"Why didn't you show me?" I ask. Still, I resume my pace. I won't show her how this latest betrayal hurts me, but it does. It sends a pain through my heart so sharp that I wonder how, in such a short time, I could have come to rely on someone so much.

"Mostly, I didn't want you to have to see it," Lena says. "But I don't know. I guess part of me wanted to keep it private. I know it's just as much yours, though. You can see it now if you want."

"It belongs to his mother," I point out. "And I don't want to see it. I don't need to anymore." Lena is quiet. "Look, there's no room in this for us not to be on the same side," I say. "It's okay. I get it. I understand why you think Charlie was more yours than mine. I just wish you would have trusted me with it. And I wish you weren't still wanting to keep any part of him close. Mostly because I can't understand why you'd still want to."

"I don't want to," Lena says quickly. "I don't think I do. I did. It's different now, though. I just . . . I don't know. But there's something in the letter that he says. He says 'When I'm gone' and 'death takes a long time to orchestrate.' But he never actually says he's going to kill himself. Not verbatim."

"Right," I tell her. "It was a setup. He disappeared."

"But why did he disappear?" Lena presses on. "Why was it important to vanish?" The bar is twenty or thirty yards away now. It's late Saturday afternoon, and because it's open air I can see the crowd that's begun to form within. It looks like a healthy mix of tourists and locals. My heart is in my throat; part of me wonders if Dana will be there at all. Part of me wonders if all this is a trap. Charlie feels so close; Dana's story was so bizarre.

"You're still thinking this was a setup?" I ask abruptly.

"I think maybe he never meant to disappear for long," Lena responds. "I think he meant for us to find him."

"How is that possible?" I mutter. I push through the entrance to the bar and shoulder through the crowd of people. It's early but the ladyboys are already moving sensually to the rhythms of Lady Gaga and Rihanna. "We tracked down all these people ourselves." Lena's jaw clenches, but she doesn't say anything. We're both beginning to realize that anything is possible. But the thought that this is all some sort of master plan to . . . what? Confront us both? Make us fight over him to feed his already overstuffed ego? Seems nuts.

"I don't know," Lena says quietly. "But remember the music lyrics in the suicide note? What if it's some sort of message to us? I can't figure it out. The eight-eighteen has to mean something. Maybe you should take a look too."

"I don't want to see the letter," I repeat. "Keep it. I can't analyze or wonder anymore. I just want to get our passports back and go home." It occurs to me that "home" means returning to a life without surprises, save whether I'll get along with my new college roommate and whether I'll like my courses. Suddenly I feel very old and as if a chasm has opened up between me and the people who will soon be a part of my life but who haven't shared this experience with me. It's as though, in this one week, my identity has shifted, toppled, and rebuilt itself into something that makes me different from everyone I know—everyone who's not Lena, anyway. I wonder if I can ever go back and be happy the same way I was. The thought of the preprofessional studies program I'm enrolled in — with its safe career trajectory and solid job prospects and predictable curriculum — makes me feel like I'm looking backwards and forward on someone else's life. Not mine. The life I had, it seems, no longer belongs to me at all.

We have to go back. But I'll never go back to the way things were.

"But eight-eighteen — August eighteenth — is tomorrow, Aubrey," Lena reminds me. "What if that moment he referenced — the shoes at eight-eighteen — means something? In that conversation, he kept saying, 'The woman dies.' Why would he have referenced that particular moment if he was talking about his own death?"

What if it means something?

Her words echo in my ears a million times over, but I don't bother to respond. Part of me wants to chalk this all up to the delusions of a heartbroken girl, but I know by now it's more than that. If it means something, we'll know soon enough. Tomorrow is coming for us; and for once, I feel brave enough to meet it head-on.

We return to the dark wooden bar where we spoke to the barback this morning. Now, at nearly four p.m., it's lined with patrons. It's hard for us to push close enough to get anyone's attention. An unmistakable wave of relief overcomes me as I spot Dana's lithe form in the far recesses of the bar, talking to a pretty Thai girl with long dark hair, high cheekbones, and dramatic eyes. They're near a door that seems to lead into a kitchen or washroom. Dana glances over, sees us, and moves toward us. The other girl disappears hurriedly through the door to the other room.

"I told you to stay put," she says, her brow creased. She looks over her shoulder, grabs me by the wrist, and yanks me toward a small table that's set off from the adjoining bar. Lena trails behind us.

"We came for our passports," I say. "We'll handle everything ourselves."

"I'm getting you on a flight tomorrow," Dana says. "It's the earliest I could get — tonight's booked full. I can't talk long or I'll get in trouble." She turns, craning her neck to look at the bar behind us. "It's routing through Boston, then on to Chicago. I know a guy who works for the airlines. He's going to pull his discount."

"We'll take care of it," I repeat while Lena watches us.

"I already handed off your information," Dana says. "I have your passports here — I just made copies — but I guess I can call to see whether he's already made the booking."

"Why are you being so nice to us?" I ask.

"I told you, you seem nice. I'm trying to help. I'd rather not see you get screwed over again by my brother. Besides, you're giving me that ring. It's not like I'm giving you a freebie. My act's about to start. So if you'd like to talk more, we can do it tonight. Here are your passports." She fishes around in the small sequined clutch she's carrying and produces them. I grab them and she stands up to go. Lena glances down at the sapphire band she's promised Dana in exchange for the tickets. She twirls it once, twice around her middle finger, her mouth turned down.

"Cancel the flight," Lena says suddenly. "I think I'd like to stick around Bangkok for a while." I stare at her, astonished.

"What are you talking about?"

"I'd like to hang out around here," she repeats, meeting Dana's eyes. "There's no reason to run off just because Charlie's nearby. Why let him dictate what we're going to do?" I start to protest but she jabs me hard with her heel under the table.

"No." Dana shakes her head and sits back down. "No. You have to get on that plane tomorrow."

"Why?" Lena asks, and now I know what she's doing: she's provoking Dana in order to get more information.

"You just do. It's safer that way."

"I feel perfectly safe right here," Lena says breezily. "I'm not afraid of Charlie."

"You should be." Dana's voice is pointed.

"I don't think so," Lena remarks. "I'll just find a hostel—"

"He's planning to kill you." The revelation comes with a force too overwhelming to absorb. Even Lena looks shocked. "There. You wanted to know? Charlie was going to murder you. All along, he was planning it. As of ten days ago, he still is."

"What are you talking about?" Lena's voice sounds muddy, and there's a rushing noise in my ears.

"I thought he was crazy. I thought he was just talking up a fantasy, you know, the way he always did—saying stuff he didn't believe in. He kept saying he was going to lead you two here, 'like lambs to the slaughter.' And that he was going to kill one and make the other suffer. He said one of you is branded. He didn't want to pull the trigger himself. He was planning to hire someone. So you needed to be branded. Like I said, I didn't believe him, thought it was all some elaborate game. Then you two show up, lured here by Charlie like he said you'd be. And then this." She grabs Lena's wrist, turning it over so we can all see the crudely etched lamb tattoo. "You're branded. 'Like lambs to the slaughter.' He wasn't making any of it up. If you stay here, you'll die." Lena's face is bright red, as if she's angry; but I can see that she's trembling from fear. "Charlie said," Dana continues, standing up and poised to leave, "that he had too many selves. That he had to kill one off, to simplify things. And that killing one off meant killing it entirely. Don't you get it?" Her voice is animated, tense. "He couldn't handle it anymore. In order to simplify his life, he has to kill one of you. Maybe then he'll reappear. He kept quoting something to me, something from a book he read. *The Lazarus Project.* And showing me this crazy music video." Lena pales at this. "You know what I think?" Dana asks. "I think he plans to rise again like Lazarus. With a clean new life. Once you're dead." She stares at Lena as she says it, and Lena blinks.

"The music video," Lena says. "Can I see it?"

Dana shrugs, then pulls out her phone and accesses a video on YouTube. Lena stares at the screen, transfixed.

"Here's the part he kept showing me," Dana says, scrolling through the video. "Around eight-eighteen. Here." I look over Lena's shoulder now. An image of shoes—empty but for rose petals fluttering from above—fills the screen. "He said for him, it's about death. The death of a woman who's been walking straight into it all along." Then Dana pockets her phone and delivers the final punch. "I'm only trying to help you. I have no idea where Charlie is right now. He could be in this bar, he could be down the street. But one thing I do know: If you don't leave Bangkok as soon as possible, Lena is going to die."

25

Charlie

You need to take extra measures to ensure the plan goes smoothly. You need to dot every *i*, cover every base. For a while, you aren't sure it will work. You hold your breath, watching them from afar. That part's easy; you have access to their email accounts, their smart phones. What's hard is that you're losing patience. And you're running out of money. There's the money you owe Anand, and there's money you owe Dana. You owe so much money. The thought of it makes your palms sweat. It makes your heart pound, because there's no way out. Or maybe there is, but it's narrow and risky.

You've got to pay Lena's killer, too. You put a deposit upfront and the rest is due on execution. *On execution,* ha ha. It's a private joke between you and Dana's guy. Dana's role, it's just to get them where they belong. Dana will do it; she thinks you've got dirt on her. As long as she keeps thinking that, she'll follow through. Dana will get them to the final destination on the transatlantic adventure you created for them. Everything they've done they think was their idea. But it was all you, lining up the dominoes. Sure, there were wildcards. You weren't sure Anand could be trusted. There was the chance Lena wouldn't find the letter. But that's been part of the fun.

Part of the game. Dana was the most reliable player. She's good. The best con artist you ever met. She told you she could act, and she can. She's the one who spun the story about your parents, to get Lena's and Aubrey's sympathy. It's been fun watching it work. It was a brilliant touch, how Dana turned them away at first. It was her idea, telling them outright that you plan to kill one of them. And it's worked. Every step of the way. The way Dana laughed when she told you about all of it from a noisy pay phone at her bar in Nana Plaza . . . it was like the best cacophony. *Cacophony.* Phony. Like Dana. A lipstick-slathered phony, everything about her.

Now they're at the final stage, and you get to watch it unfold. The money you'll deal with later. Sure you're feeling heat, but they all know you're good for it. They know you were stocking up to disappear, but they don't think you'll run with it. You've always paid your debts. You just need a little more time. You need to send out the ransom note to your parents: from Charlie—though they won't know it—about Charlie. They'll fork it over, a huge sum, anything to get you back. You'll take the money and pay off your debts and kill your girlfriend, not necessarily in that order.

And oh, the relief. To be rid of one of them. To be rid of the thing that you are as long as she's alive. *You're still that thing; she's not gone yet.* You're impatient for it to happen. Fidgety. Restless. But you know you have to be strong. It's an exercise in willpower, this waiting for Lena's death.

Once, you thought you could break up with her. You thought that would be enough. And you tried. But Lena is headstrong. She doesn't just disappear. She hangs on, asks questions, demands answers and what she calls "respect." What about you? Why does she always think about herself and her feelings? What about what you're feeling? She wants you to be reliable, but you want her to disappear from your life. You want that entire life, the one you had with her, to disappear along with her. Finally you realized: you can't do that unless she's dead.

But why Lena? Why not Aubrey, the one who cheated?

It's simple: because for Aubrey, you have something better planned. Aubrey will disappear on her own. She *wants* to disappear. She's been waiting for a way out since the beginning. Lena's like a tumor that grows bigger and more poisonous, threatening to take you over. Lena is the one who can't be dismissed. She needs to be destroyed. Or she'll destroy you. Like she was starting to do. And you can't have that, can you? No. Everything is in place. Everything is set to happen the way it should. The day you've chosen—August 18—is tomorrow.

26

Lena

WHEN SOMEONE TELLS YOU YOU'RE GOING to die and you don't know how it's going to happen, or when—just that it's going to happen within a day, unless you can somehow dodge the bullet and hop a plane home—everything slows down. It feels like time's on hold, maybe because everything revolves around the moment when I step on that plane tomorrow and know I'm going to be okay.

If I could call the cops, I would. But I can't. What would I say? *I think my dead boyfriend is alive and is trying to murder me. No, officer, he hasn't contacted me. No, nothing in particular has happened other than a mugging in Kerala that can't be traced back to him, exactly, and a tattoo of a lamb that I got while blackout drunk, and a suicide note with tomorrow's date on it.* None of it is substantial; and yet, I'm more and more certain that Dana isn't making anything up.

The wildcard is Adam. If Charlie led us here, to Bangkok, there was a reason, and Adam was instrumental. But Aubrey swears up and down that Adam couldn't have been involved. And yet—she hasn't reached out to him since we left Bombay. Neither of us has been on a computer. We don't have local cell phones. Adam, to me, seems too good to be real—how else could we have found Anand and Kerala and Dana? How did Charlie manage to orchestrate that? And why Bangkok, why like this? For his plan to move along without a hitch, everyone we've spoken to would have had to have been in on it. All the whys no longer matter. All that counts is getting through this day and making our way back home. In the end, we decide to let Dana book us the earliest flight. It takes off at 5:15 a.m. tomorrow and lands in Boston at 8:40 p.m.

We wait until Dana hands us the printed confirmations. Then we split. We're sitting curbside a few streets away from the bar, our tickets in our bags. I had to give Dana my gold and sapphire ring. It's the only piece of jewelry Anand left behind—and probably because it fits so tight in this heat that it's difficult to remove it without a good dollop of soap. Neither of us feels safe staying at Dana's overnight.

"We should go straight to the airport," Aubrey says. "Right?"

"If Charlie has big plans for me, he'll find me there, too," I tell her.

"They have security. It's safe. Unless . . ." She hesitates.

"What?" I'm antsy, fidgety. My heart's been beating fast ever since Dana told us about Charlie's plan and I feel consistently light-headed, as though I'm experiencing some low-level, steady state of shock.

"Lena," Aubrey says, "we can beat this thing. We can outsmart Charlie. We're better than he is. More stable. Crazy people always get impatient, make mistakes. We've got sanity on our side. Charlie thinks he knows us better than anyone . . . and that's why we're here. But we know him better than anyone—all sides of him. And we've changed. He doesn't know us like he did. He brought us together, but maybe that's what's going to save us."

I hope that what I'm about to say isn't the byproduct of my panic. "You mean, we beat him at his own game?"

Aubrey nods. "You know he was able to hack. He might be able to check our email, wherever he is. So let's lead him to us the way he led us to him. Except we'll lead him in the wrong direction—and then we'll spend the rest of the night doing all the things Lena and Aubrey, as Charlie knew us, would never do." I draw my knees to my chest and think. Aubrey taps her foot while I consider the implications of what she's saying.

"Okay," I begin. "Let's try to get into his head. And out of ours. We can't go to the hostel or the airport. That's where he'd expect us to go if we were running."

Aubrey looks at me hard, her eyebrows furrowed.

"You're really okay with this, though? Are you sure you're not just . . . reacting?" she asks.

"Of course I am. I'm reacting to everything. That's all we do, react and react and react. How do you think we got here in the first place?"

Aubrey's voice is quiet. "I just want to make sure you're okay. I'm not okay."

"You're not the one who might only have one night left to live."

"We're leaving first thing tomorrow, Lena. You'll be fine. We were never supposed to know about this—we were supposed to stay in Bangkok and walk right into whatever spidery mess he laid out for us. We have choices now. Just don't fall apart."

I flash her my widest grin, though inside, my heart is hammering and tears are welling up at the back of my throat and behind my eyes. If Aubrey weren't here—if there were no one to put on a show for—I don't know what I'd do. Aubrey's asking me not to fall apart, and I won't.

"I think it's time to call home," I say. "Shake them up a bit." I give her a wink to show that *I'm okay, I'm fine, totally! See?* But she gnaws on her lower lip and shoots me a sad smile. It's all I can do not to burst into tears. I can't look at her anymore. I can't stop myself from feeling like I've gotten the raw end of this deal. I spent three years with him, she only spent one; I fell in love, she kept her heart under wraps; I'm the one he wants to kill. She plays it safe and she stays safe. I'm the wild one, the one always getting into trouble for leaping before I look. And now it's caught up with me. My throat tightens. I'm afraid of what I'll sound like when I call home. I'm afraid I won't be able to pull it off. I turn on my phone. This is the last time I'll use it; I'm too frightened now that he's tracking it somehow.

It rings four times. No one picks up. Then I remember: 7:30 p.m. here is 6:30 a.m. there. They're still asleep, and their phones are on silent.

"Hi, Mom; hi, Dad," I say into voice mail. "Hi, Cara. Hi, Chester; hi, Freud!" This last group shout-out is to Cara's canaries. "Hope you guys are doing okay. Just wanted to let you know that, um, I'm going to be home in a few days. Don't blame Cara, Dad. It's my fault the flights were wrong . . . as I'm sure you've guessed." I laugh at this, my eyes welling. "I can't wait to see you guys in a few days. We have midnight flights on Thursday," I say, hoping there's a flight that really exists around that time. "I've missed you a lot. Please trust me—there are just a few things out here I need to take care of. I met Charlie's brother, and he's great. We're safe with him. Later today Aubrey and I are going to Chatuchak. And we're going on a riverfront cruise," I say, improvising. "Remember how you told me you guys loved that on your anniversary? We might even get foot massages." I pause, trying to breathe. I'm rambling, and it's got to be sounding weird to both my family and Charlie, if he's listening. I want to say a proper goodbye, something profound, but when I open my mouth I find that I can't. I need to stay breezy and casual as always, or Charlie will be suspicious.

"Anyway, I'll see you at Logan on Thursday," I say keeping it up-beat. "Can't wait! I'm—I'm sorry . . . to—" There's a long beep and the message cuts off. I was going to say, *I'm sorry to put you through all this.* I just hope I have the chance to say it in person. I hand the phone, with clammy palms, to Aubrey. "You should call yours too," I tell her.

"I can't," she says. "I'll send them an email. I can't get them on the phone. I won't be able to go through with it."

"Say the same things I said," I tell her. "I want him thinking we're here, not there. I want him thinking we're doing all the things we'd normally do. I figured a riverboat cruise was something you'd like. The massage is my usual deal. We're not doing any of that. When we do get home, we'll go to the cops. Tell them everything—tell them someone out here saw Charlie." Aubrey nods, typing quickly on my iPhone. She flashes the screen at me when she's done.

I'm safe, it says, after the other stuff I told her to write. *I'm flying home Thursday. There's so much to talk about when I get home. I love you both.*

It's just a few lines, but when I'm done reading, I nod in approval.

"I had a million emails from them," she says. "They're so worried."

"They must be good parents."

"They are," she says. "When I called them the one time from

London, I told them I'd be gone for a while and asked them to trust me. I don't really deserve it, but I think that's what they're trying to do."

I nod. My parents have always given me a lot of freedom; but by now I know that Aubrey's are more helicopter style.

"So we'll just lie low?" she asks. "In, like, random places?"

"Fuck, no," I tell her. "We've got to go to places he'd never expect us to go. Charlie expects us to be scared and to hide right now. But I'm not going to let him do that to me. We're going to see this city and do all the things I'd want to do if this were actually the last night of my life. Because it's not," I clarify. "But if it were . . ."

"It's not," Aubrey says firmly, handing my phone back to me. "I like this plan." My bravado is mostly show, and I know she can tell I'm scared. But I'm determined not to give in to it. I do a quick scan of my own emails and notice a hello from Carey in Paris. I open it and read quickly—he's dating a new guy, wants to tell me about it. My heart sinks; it's been so long since I've messaged him. Carey's always been the better friend. But messaging him now would be too risky—too traceable. I pocket my phone, vowing to focus more on him when this whole mess is over.

"Still, nothing like the threat of death to push a girl outside her comfort zone." I stand up and brush my palms on my jeans. They're dotted with little indentations from the gravel on the sidewalk. There's this nagging voice inside me that says, *This might be it.* I can't explain what it's doing to me. I can't explain how it makes me feel, other than reckless. I just know that I'm infused with adrenaline, and I'm going to live this night like it's my last. Because maybe it is.

"I can think of a couple things he'd never expect," Aubrey says, taking a big breath. I look at her, and I feel myself breaking out into a grin. She meets my eyes and grins back, and my heart expands.

"How much money's left on that credit card?" I wonder aloud.

"Enough to make this the best night we've ever had," Aubrey says.

"That's what we're going to do. For tonight, let's let it be just about us. About living and doing all the things two girls our age are supposed to do when they find themselves semi-stranded in Bangkok." Aubrey giggles at this.

"I don't know what life I've entered," she tells me, "but it doesn't feel like mine anymore."

"It's your new life," I say. "Our new lives. So here's the plan," I continue, before I get too sentimental. "You're going to walk up to that guy over there," I tell her, pointing at a random scruffy back-packer in board shorts and flip-flops who's standing at the opposite side of the road. "Ask him what his favorite thing to do here has been in the past twenty-four hours. Then we're going to do that thing."

"I like the way you think," Aubrey says, her blue eyes lighting up. "I'm going for it." I watch as she picks her way across the street, her shoulders squarer and her posture straighter than I remember it being. It's like I'm watching a different version of Aubrey, one this trip has born, and I feel a swell of pride, because maybe in some small way, I've rubbed off on her. I like thinking of a more fearless Aubrey returning to sleepy Illinois, then blowing it apart. Aubrey nods, and the man scribbles something on a piece of paper, handing it to her with a friendly expression.

Aubrey skips back over, her face dimpling in a mischievous smile.

I grin in return; it's like we have a tacit agreement not to talk about what might happen. For today, it's like we're just girls on a backpacking trip. Still, the urge to run anywhere, everywhere, is almost overpowering. I discipline myself. I force myself to wait.

"He told me to go to the floating market. In . . ." she trails off, squinting at the receipt the man handed her. "It's called Khlong Lat Mayom," she finishes, hardly stumbling over the words. "He said it's a little outside the city, on Bang Lamad Road."

"Can we get there by tuk-tuk?" I want to know.

"He says taxi's best and super cheap."

"Taxi it is," I say.

We flag a taxi and slide in the back. Aubrey directs our driver toward the market. He nods and she relaxes in her seat, glancing over at me. A look of understanding passes between us; for a second, it's like she can see into my soul.

"When this is over for us, and we're safe and free of this nightmare, I'm going to art school."

"What?" I laugh. As far as I knew, Aubrey was going to enter some kind of preprofessional program in the Honors College at Georgetown.

"I can't do it right away," Aubrey continues. "But I think I'm going to switch my major to art, then maybe transfer to SVA next year if I can."

"That's amazing," I tell her, and I mean it. "That's what you really wanna do, yeah?"

"Yeah," she says. "And I guess I just realized while I was here, I'm sick to death of doing what other people want me to do. And of having this predetermined plan all the time. That's how I wound up with Charlie in the first place. I figured my parents would like him.

I'm not always right, I guess. Since then I've figured out that I need to do the stuff that makes me happy. I need to let things unfold on their own. Charlie didn't get that, and neither did my parents."

"What makes you happy?" I want to know. "Besides graphic novels, I mean."

"I'm still figuring it out," she says. "I'm not totally sure. But I won't ever know unless I try some things."

"What about Adam?" I've been wondering about this for a few days, but haven't wanted to ask. Part of me still wants to know what Adam's larger role in all of this was, if he had one.

"I'm not sure," she says carefully. "But if I had to guess, I think I'm going to let that go."

"After all that," I say. My voice is flat.

"I think Adam isn't right for me either," Aubrey says. "I thought it could work because he made me happy in ways I didn't expect. He made me feel cared about in a way that Charlie didn't."

I nod. It sounds reasonable. As usual, Aubrey is way ahead of me in terms of seeing inside herself.

"What about you?" she asks, as the cab pulls up at the marketplace. "What's waiting for you back in Boston? You're off to Rhode Island in a couple weeks, right?"

"Yeah," I say. "I don't know. I haven't thought about it that much. I'm excited to go back to school. I'm excited to meet people. I wasn't doing that as much before, because I was so focused on Charlie." I pause, thinking hard, wondering how exactly to articulate what I'm feeling. "I don't have anything I'm passionate about like you do with your graphic novel thing," I tell her. "I like music, but I have no musical talent. It's not like I can pursue that as a career." Aubrey nods like she gets it, so I take a breath and continue. "I think for

whatever reason, it's enough for now that I just feel okay about being back and being on my own."

"Without Charlie, you mean," Aubrey finishes for me.

"Yeah. I guess I haven't experienced me without Charlie for a
long time. And it's enough to get to do that. I feel okay about it."

"That's great," Aubrey says. I can tell she means it. It's not, like, a
major step for other people, maybe . . . being without a boyfriend.
But right now, for me, it means something that I'm not scared. I
want to figure out what I'm like without him, put more time into
the friendships I have managed to hold on to. I think about how,
when I get back, I'll give Carey a call. Maybe go out to Paris to visit
him over fall break. Aubrey reaches over, takes my hand in her own,
and gives it a squeeze. "We're going to get out of this," she assures
me. "Tomorrow at this time, we'll both be safe at home."

I blink back tears. All this time she's been trying to point me
toward the future so I won't focus on the danger that we're in right
now. "Aubrey," I say, forcing myself to give voice to what I'm feeling,
even though it makes me nervous in a way I'm not used to. "Thank
you." The words sound stiff, like cardboard—a pale imitation of
what I'm feeling inside, which is intense and powerful. Still, she
seems to understand. She doesn't say anything, but she doesn't have
to. At moments like this one, I'm beginning to see, words aren't
important.

27

Aubrey

CARING — REALLY CARING DEEP INSIDE, where it wells up and threatens to topple you — takes a certain amount of letting go. Staying intact — not letting yourself be toppled — means guarding your heart at least a little. So where's the balance? How do you find the precious middle ground? I think maybe you find it in the knowledge that even if you are in a safe space, there are certain things you can't control. I think you find it by taking risks, but the kind that are calculated — designed not to throw you headlong into danger but embraced with the knowledge that you can't live, not really live, if you're locked inside a crystal ball. Crystal balls break.

I watch Lena carefully as we pick our way across the market. What I didn't tell her when we talked about going home is that I've made a decision. When I return to Chicago, I'm going to tell my parents what happened the night of the hit-and-run. I'm going to accept the consequences. I'm still filled with a cold fear every time I think about what I'll have to say — and how it will hurt them — but whatever happens, it's got to be better than continuing to run from it. Living this lie has made me hate myself; and I don't want that, no matter what it means I have to face.

As for Adam, I'm going to have to let him go. Who would want to be with me after what I've done comes to light? Yet for the first time, the sadness and fear I feel don't outweigh the relief of not having to carry my lies any longer.

The market is lovely, just a series of little boats bobbing along a narrow canal. Each vessel bursts with brightly colored fruits, spices, and flowers. Lena looks at everything with the eagerness of a kid. Her eyes glow in the same way they always have. Her enthusiasm hasn't been dampened by the day's events. If anything, it's grown stronger. She is the first person I've ever known with such an insatiable curiosity for the world and its beautiful minutiae. Half of me expected her to self-destruct when Dana told us what Charlie had said. This whole time, Lena's been impulsive, borderline reckless. But now in addition to the way she embraces everything, she's looking measured. Even the way she picks up the fruits and vegetables, turns over a starfruit in her palm to examine it for imperfections, demonstrates a difference in her demeanor.

We're all mirrors to some extent, I remind myself. It's something I read somewhere and forgot until now, mostly because until now, I've surrounded myself with people like me. Even Charlie was like me for a while, the me I thought I should strive to be, anyway: smart and stable and presentable. A walking résumé. Now I'm not so sure. Everything has been called into question. If we're mirrors, I'm seeing reflections of myself in Lena and of her in me, and I'm liking what I see and how it makes me feel.

It's the first time in my life I've felt an unaccustomed sort of passion bubbling beneath the surface. It's the first time in my life I've felt fearless, especially in the face of so much to fear. The new intensity overwhelms me. I have to bite back all the emotions that work their way to the surface. They lie just beneath my rib cage, threatening to spill out. Every second is charged. I can sense it, feel it. The air is thick with it. A man floats by in a boat laden with bunches of yellow flowers that look almost as delicate as lace.

"Ratchaphruek," Lena tells me. "It's the national flower of Thailand."

"How do you know that?" I ask her. She just shrugs.

"I like beautiful things."

Among the ratchaphruek, I recognize orchids in all their firm, solid extravagance. It's growing dark quickly, and some of the boats are alight with candles, though others pull aside and shut down for the day. Lena waves to one woman whose signage trumpets coconut pancakes, and I realize it's been hours since we've eaten. Lena uses what little cash we have left to buy two pancakes and a small paper basket of grilled shrimp. We sit in silence along the edge of the canal, eating our modest dinner as the market vendors close up shop. I glance at my watch.

"How long?" Lena asks softly.

"It's just after nine," I tell her. "I'd say we have until about two, two thirty, to amuse ourselves before we leave for the airport. What's up next?" I want the night to be everything she wants it to be. I'm surprised to find that I don't want it to end. The dreaded eight-eighteen—the date Charlie hinted at on his fake suicide note—lies unspoken between us, its import too dreadful to discuss.

"I'm up," she says. "My turn to ask." She polishes off her pancake, wrapping the last bit of shrimp inside it like a taco. "I'm waiting."

"For . . . ?"

"You pick." Right. I'd forgotten the rules of our little game.

"Okay." I scan the crowd. There are hundreds of tourists around us, but what are they going to say? This market was a good recommendation, but I think I lucked out—most visitors, like us, don't know what they're doing here. They've read some article in the *New York Times* or looked up a list of must-dos on TripAdvisor, and they feel equipped to explore and come back with a grownup scout badge on their metaphorical vest of achievements. Nope, for our next experience, we need a local. Once I've decided what I'm looking for, I spot my girl right away. She's standing nearby and seems curious about us too; she keeps glancing in our direction and smiling.

"That one," I say. She's perfect, about our age and stylish, leaning against a stall of decorative lights, their bulbs twinkling brightly against the night sky. She's making eye contact. She looks approachable but also like she belongs there, maybe like she's the owner or the owner's daughter.

"Nice choice," Lena says. "And if she doesn't speak English?"

"She will," I say. I'm not sure why I say this. I realize I'm making all kinds of assumptions based on appearance, but the girl has the same adventuresome glint in her eyes that initially drew me to Lena. Lena may not know Thai, but she knows basically all of the Romance languages . . . at least according to her. I think it's a safe bet that this girl knows what she's doing, has been around and seen some things and knows some stuff. Seeing us staring, she smiles again and motions me over. I roll my eyes in Lena's direction; I'm sure she's going to try to sell us something, but at least she's friendly.

Lena stands up and brushes off her pants. I watch as she approaches the girl. Unlike Lena, our new friend has a long mane of thick dark hair. She's slim with high cheekbones, and black eyeliner makes her eyes look wide. Lena's back is to me, but I can read the other girl's expression. At first her brows furrow, and then she breaks

out in a wide grin and nods with enthusiasm. The two talk animat-
edly for a couple of minutes longer, the Thai girl gesturing with her
hands. I'm growing curious, so I join them. Lena is nodding in response to something the girl is saying as I approach. The two almost
look like twins from the way Lena is standing, slight and lanky in
her jeans.

"Aubrey!" Lena exclaims. "Charanya here is going to take us to a
karaoke bar!"

"Okay," I say slowly. I'm not sure how I feel about this random
girl tagging along, but maybe it's not that big a deal. Maybe it'll be
fun. Great, even. So why is a prominent part of me bristling at the
idea of someone joining us on what I've come to consider an important night for the two of us?

"Charanya's from here," Lena says. "But she studied at NYU. She
just graduated."

"Hi," says the languid Charanya, extending one hand in my direction while the other busies itself with a cigarette. Almost as soon
as I take it she snatches it away, as if it's something breakable that I
can't be trusted with. She looks me up and down slowly, then turns
and saunters away, beckoning to us over her shoulder as she calls
out something in Thai to the man behind the booth. In contrast
to our worn and dirty clothes, Charanya is wearing a simple white
T-shirt, distressed pegged jeans, and low black heels that fasten with
an ankle strap.

"I go by Cha-cha," she tells us, as we hurry along after her in the
busy, thronged streets. It's hard to keep sight of her in the night, and
I find myself exchanging a look with Lena as if to say, "What the
hell have you done this time?" At least I hope that's what it conveys.
But Lena's pepped up, high on something like fear, if I had to guess.

We have four hours. Four hours to kill until she is — we are — presumably safe on a plane. But what if our efforts to evade Charlie before that are in vain? There have been so many surprises thus far that I can't discount the possibility that both of us are in danger, not just Lena, and that our plan isn't foolproof.

"What?" Lena shoots me an irritated look. "She's a local. This is fun. This is what we're supposed to be doing." I look closer and her smile, while wide, seems off. Something's not right. I'm losing her. Instead of arguing I hurry after her, anxiety building in my stomach. I think back to what she told me when we first met. *I say yes a lot. Sometimes to my detriment.* I think about what this means. How often it's gotten her into trouble. How it's played a role on this trip. How Charlie probably knew to anticipate it. She's not defying habit. She's being the old Lena, wild and tempestuous and careless. Something's not right. I have to remind myself three times that *I selected Cha-cha.* She did not find us. Everything will be okay. Still, with everything that's happened, I'm reluctant to trust anyone.

"Are you sure this is a good idea?" I whisper, but Lena just waves off my question with an intolerant sigh. Then she quickens her step to match Cha-cha's, and we're turning down one dark alley after another until I no longer remember which way we came from, or how to get back to the main road where we could find a cab. Finally we turn into a low-lying, unmarked building. I hesitate until Lena ducks inside, then pops back out to motion me forward. It's nearly ten p.m.

"Let's do this," she says. Cha-cha's already in there, putting in a request with the DJ. Eerily, Western pop is blaring through the speakers in the form of Lady Gaga, Miley Cyrus, and Taylor Swift. *Party in the USA* is blaring loudly, and two Caucasian guys are rocking out to it, slurring the lyrics about half a beat after they're due. "I don't know about you," Lena confides, "but I'm a huge fan of any song that rhymes 'crazy' and 'famous.'" I laugh. It's ridiculous; she's right. Lena walks to the bar and orders shots and hands me one and I decide, *To hell with it.* I can't control old Lena but I can control old Aubrey, and who I don't want her to be, even if I'm not sure yet who I do want her to be.

I take the shot, only mildly bothered that this tab is going on my credit card, with its rapidly waning credit. Lena takes hers and goes back for another one, and alarm bells go off. "Take it easy, okay?" I caution.

"Live a little, Aubrey," Lena says, tossing her head impetuously, her hair streaming down her back. "That's what we're supposed to be doing tonight, isn't it? Just say yes." She takes my face between her hands and holds it there. "You're so beautiful, Aubrey. Just say yes to everything for a while."

It sounds dangerous. But I do it anyway. I nod, my face still inside her palms. Lena lets go when the bartender delivers the receipt; she signs my name and pockets the paper, waggling the credit card in my direction. "For later," she tells me, smiling broadly. Then she pockets my card, too, and I try not to worry about what she plans to use it for. I watch her climb on top of the bar and I lean my head backwards, staring at the ceiling, allowing everything to roll off me as the music plays. When I put my head down, everything's different. I've let go.

Letting go is a hard thing. It makes you feel vulnerable. But this is not to be mistaken for weakness. It takes strength to be vulnerable. That is what I've learned from Lena.

I don't want to drink too much. I'm not used to it, and tonight I need to maintain control. I sip on a sparkling water and watch her dance onstage with Cha-cha, this girl we met only an hour or so ago. Lena is beautiful up there, fearless, raw, her blond hair streaming about. It's what makes her so lovely. It's, I'm sure, why Charlie loved her. Why another guy will love her again someday, someone far more worthy, I hope, than he was. She deserves that.

"You didn't see me, I was falling apart . . ." The National plays as Lena leans into Charanya and sways, unsteady on her feet. I sit by myself at the bar, watching them. Watching her, watching over her. My watch says 10:37 p.m.

It can't be right. That's so early—we've been here for at least an hour. I look closer. My watch has stopped, for sure. The second hand is barely limping along. I'm overcome by the sudden, irrepressible need to know how much time is left. How much time is left to expire before we can consider ourselves safe. Lena stumbles onstage and almost falls. I stopped counting after her third shot. She must have had at least one or two more. Charanya, just as drunk, supports her with one arm. A jolt of suspicion rocks my frame. Who is this girl, and why is she here? What would cause her to leave her job in the middle of the evening to come with us? Just a wanton desire to get drunk on our dime? Or something much worse?

Fear wends its way up my spine, wraps its bony fingers around the base of my neck, and squeezes hard until I'm choking. I can barely breathe. The air in the room feels heavy, the room feels smaller than before, and I need to leave. I have to. I run up onstage and grab Lena, hoisting her arms around my shoulders and prying her away from the leech who is trying to grab her back. The faces around me look sinister, and it occurs to me that I may be feeling that first shot and may be acting irrationally.

But maybes are enough to warrant action in this distorted world, where suddenly every minute and every person can attain heightened significance. Lena and I meet eyes at the end of a song, a Bruce Springsteen ode to Youngstown, *"them smokestacks reaching like the arms of God / Into a beautiful sky of soot and clay,"* and I'm so nostalgic for home, and so afraid of what's about to happen, that I almost burst into tears. Seeing me, Lena has something register in her own mind, and her distant expression shifts into something more present. She yanks away from me and jumps off the stage rather than taking the stairs, a move that nearly results in her collapse. I hurry after her.

"I'm so sorry," she says desperately, her eyes wild. "I'm sorry for dragging you out here. I'm sorry you're stuck with me now. You'd be okay if it weren't for me."

"I still am okay," I tell her. "Listen. None of this is your fault." It's not entirely true but it's what she needs to hear, and I steer her toward the bathroom and past the stares of everyone around us, male and female alike. Once in the stall, she loses it. I follow her in. She cries hard, her face buried in a mound of toilet paper. She's perched on the lid of a toilet, apparently unconcerned by the stains that mar it.

"I'm sorry it's been so hard for you, Lena," I say, crouching in front of her. Part of me feels like I've done a bad job of expressing just how much I'll care if I lose her. "I'm so sorry. I wish I could make this different, you know that, right?"

"I know," she says, sobbing. She leans her head on my shoulder, crying into it. "I know. I'm sorry. I wanted tonight to be great. I wanted it to be extraordinary. I wanted you to see things differently after tonight."

"I see the entire world differently because of you," I say, and I mean it. "Three weeks ago, I was just, what, a random girl in Illinois who'd seen nothing and done nothing and it didn't matter, because I was just closed up inside my bubble. And now I want to see everything and experience everything. I know I can't have it, but at least I want it. I'd rather want what I can't have than never know any better. You're the cause of that. I swear to God, Lena. No matter what happens, you opened my eyes."

Lena laughs a little through her snot and tears, and I realize how ridiculously sentimental I sound. Then she looks down at her wrist, where the lamb tattoo is just poking out from under her bangles, a black scribble for all to see. She pulls off the bracelets and scratches at her skin, almost as if she wants to scrape off the tattoo itself. She scratches harder, and her skin turns red and raw. I grab her hand to stop her.

"Cut it out," I tell her. "You're hurting yourself." But she jerks away, scraping furiously at her skin.

"Lena! Stop! You're going to make yourself bleed." I pull her hand away and this time she doesn't resist.

"I want it gone," she tells me. "I don't want any sign of him left on me."

"So we'll fix it," I tell her. "But you're making it worse this way."

"I want it gone now."

I clutch her hands in mine, holding them steady so she can't hurt herself again. "We'll go tonight. We'll go right now, if we have time. We'll cover it up with something new." Lena nods and grabs for some toilet paper. She blows her nose hard and presses at her forehead with her index fingers, steadying herself.

"Okay," she says. She looks tired, like a balloon that's been popped. All of her manic energy from earlier has drained out of her. "And then I'm ready to go home. I'm tired of this. I just want to go home."

"I couldn't agree more." I'm overcome with relief. The thought of being in the airport is soothing.

"Just give me a second," she says. "I need to pee and clean up a little." She points at her soggy face. "I want to splash some water on my face. Wait outside?"

"I'll go find us a cab. You meet me out front." Lena gives me a shaky thumbs-up and I push out of the tiny stall and make my way through the congested bar. I don't see Cha-cha anywhere. Somehow her absence feels reassuring.

It takes me less than a minute to flag a taxi. I slide into the back seat and ask if the driver knows English. He makes a "so-so" gesture with his hands, so I hold up my finger and say, "Just a minute." The clock on his dash reads three minutes past midnight. It's the day when Lena is supposed to die. I find myself squirming in the back seat as I wait.

Three more minutes go by and I tell myself to calm down. Lena's probably adjusting her mascara or something—knowing her, she's had a spare tube in her back pocket this whole time. I smile to myself as I picture her making her way through our misadventures in Kerala and Bangkok, mascara intact. But as much as I tell myself that things are okay, I can't stop feeling antsy. It doesn't help that the driver is sighing and glancing in the rearview mirror every few seconds. At ten past midnight, I ask him to wait while I step out.

"I'll pay you a good tip," I tell him, wondering how in the heck I'm going to find extra tip money. I can't shake my increasing sense of foreboding. I push back into the bar, which has become more crowded in the last ten minutes. I make my way to the single-cell bathroom; there's a line leading up to it. People are shifting restlessly, and one person, annoyed, knocks on the door. I shove in front of all of them. At least one person yells something in Thai, but I ignore it. I pound on the door, hard. I'm nervous, truly nervous. My heart beats wildly, and my whole body is poised to react to whatever I might find in there. I wonder if I've been stupid — if Lena took something other than alcohol. If she's overdosed.

I pound more and jiggle the doorknob. The people behind me are less angry and more curious now. I'm about to try kicking down the door. I look all around for someone who might have a key and rack my brain about how I'm going to convey to them why I need to break into the bathroom — and then the doorknob moves and the door creaks open.

An angry-looking tourist steps out.

"Dude, learn to wait your turn," he snaps. "If you weren't a chick, I'd punch you in the face right now." I push past him anyway, cutting the line in order to do a thorough check of the room. It's empty. There's no Lena. I dash back out of the room, and my heart is pounding as I scour the bar. There are so many people in here now, but there's no sign of Lena. I find a barstool and climb on top of it, holding on to a stranger's shoulder for support.

The guy I'm holding on to thinks I'm going to start dancing or something; he cups his hands around his mouth and whistles. A few others group around and start to wave their fists in the air like I'm some sort of sideshow act. I feel my panic rise higher. I ignore them and scan the rest of the crowd. She's nowhere. She's nowhere even though technically it would be easy to disappear in here. Not for her, though: with her white-blond hair, she couldn't disappear if she tried.

Ten more minutes have passed, and one look out the window tells me my driver has already taken off. "Have you seen my friend?" I shout at the bartender, hoping he speaks English.

"Blond girl?" he says back, and I nod eagerly, my heart lifting. "Nope." He shakes his head. "Haven't seen her."

It's clear by now that Lena isn't in the bar. It occurs to me that maybe I've missed her, maybe she's on the sidewalk waiting for me; so I run back out into the night. The temperature has dropped and people mill around, bartering with beer vendors, waving glow sticks. No Lena. I sit on the sidewalk and rest my head on my knees, trying not to lose it.

I breathe. I think.

I decide to wait a while longer. I wait and wait and feel myself giving in to my terror and the stress of first searching for Charlie, then running from him. It's hard not to feel helpless without Lena next to me; I'm so used to her knowing what to do next.

A man approaches me, and at first I recoil; but then he squats down until our eyes are level. I can't tell how much time has passed. His face is lined with concern. "Miss? Are you okay?" I nod slowly. "Do you have anywhere to go?"

His question triggers something, the part of me that still remembers how to act in an emergency. I *do* have somewhere to go. The airport. I rummage through my bag and gulp a mouthful of air when my hand closes around my passport. Folded inside is my plane ticket. Lena's got hers, wherever she is. "What time is it?" I ask the guy.

"One fifteen."

"I'm fine." I thank him, rising to my feet. I'm overcome by a surge of purpose. Lena may have gone straight to the airport when she didn't see me waiting. She's probably been there, looking for me, all this time.

Ten minutes later I'm at the airport. I still don't see Lena; but if she came here to meet me, she's probably at the gate. The rest of the airport is too big and too busy for us to connect. Our flight leaves in just a few hours. I have no luggage, since pretty much everything I brought with me was stolen in Kerala, so I head straight for Security.

I don't like not being with Lena. It begins to remind me of the dreams I used to have as a kid, the ones where a friend and I were being chased by monsters; and then my friend would disappear, leaving me all alone. That feeling is worse than being chased. I want my friend back. More than that, I want to know that she's okay.

As I creep closer to the Security desk, the feeling of anxiety only increases. I shift from one foot to the other, staring past the line to see what's taking so long. A family with several strollers is holding everyone up. I sigh and grind my teeth, so obviously impatient that the man in front of me turns and gives me a withering look, his white caterpillar eyebrows high on his forehead. Finally I reach a guard. Ahead of me, conveyer belts are packed with gray plastic tubs of laptops, shoes, and coats. Everywhere I look for Lena.

"Passport and ticket," he demands in a put-upon tone. I offer him my passport, wincing slightly as he opens it up and runs one meaty thumb over the hole where Anand stabbed it. I hold my breath; I'm not sure whether a torn (or stabbed) passport is illegal.

"Left it on the cutting board," I say lamely. He doesn't smile. Instead he examines my ticket, turning it over a couple of times. His brow is furrowed in concentration; and behind me, several travelers clear their throats. My stomach drops. If the tickets Dana issued us are flawed — or worse, counterfeit — I could be arrested. I don't know why it's taken this long for it to occur to me; but now that it has, it seems obvious. Charlie could easily be working with Dana. Everything about this screams "Danger," but it's too late to stop it — it's already been set in motion. This guy already has my passport and is already staring hard at my ticket.

He turns it over again, squinting. And then he stamps it. Every part of my body shudders with relief, from my toes to my ears, which are flaming from nervousness. The guard begins to hand me back my passport and ticket; but when I move to take them, his grip tightens.

"Wait," he says. Silence. Time passes, but I don't feel it. He retracts my passport and flips it open again. Then he takes his walkie-talkie and mutters something quickly in Thai. "Wait here," he tells me again. Nothing in his face betrays what he's thinking. He holds on to my passport.

Now I'm certain beyond a doubt that something is wrong. But it's not my ticket he was mulling over, so what could it be? Was it really the hole in the passport that got his attention? A second later, two armed guards approach the line. Each takes one of my arms. Their grip is firm — even rough.

"What is this?" My voice is loud, terrified. My first instinct is to refuse to go with them, but they leave me no choice. Both men are large and muscular, and when they hustle me forward, I struggle to keep my balance. "Tell me what's going on," I demand, but they ignore me, pulling me past the conveyer belts into a small room lined on all sides with windows. Around us, people are staring. Given how crude they're being, I may as well be a convict. I close my eyes, fighting tears, and allow them to shove me into a chair. They bolt the door behind them. I can't hear anything, see anything. My panic is overwhelming. I try hard not to curl up in my chair and sleep. It's the second best escape.

It takes a minute for my senses to right themselves.

When they do, I hear the policemen around me shouting things in Thai.

"Please, will someone tell me what's going on?" I ask. Then louder, then two more times. Each time, I'm ignored.

Finally I lose it.

"My flight's leaving in less than three hours," I shout at the heavier cop, the one who held my arms behind my back until the office door was locked. "Will someone please tell me what the hell is going on? I need to get home." I'm furious; and still, my voice trembles, betraying my fear.

Another guard, the one who is bent over the desk in front of me, pauses; he's been rifling through paperwork. He levels me with a cold glare.

"You're not going anywhere tonight." He looks at me like I'm something disgusting. "You're under arrest."

28

Charlie

It's fucking unfathomable what aubrey thought she could do. She thought she could sneak around behind your back and get away with it, then break up with you on top of it. Too bad she was weak. Too bad she revealed her Achilles heel. She thought she could control you.

But you're in control.

You're still in control. No matter how hard it gets.

The fear in her eyes when you told her you'd stay with her. It made you want to show her she can't dick you over and get away with it. She won't get away.

For a while, she'll think she's free. She'll feel safe. It'll all be a mistake.

You've made simple plans for Lena. She was a burden to be discarded. But Aubrey is going to suffer.

For Aubrey, you've planned a fate far worse than death.

29

Lena

THE AIR IS STAGNANT AND HEAVY, as though it's been recycled by
a thousand bodies already. The tape that was used to bind me has
fused to my mouth. Every time I breathe, it creates a vacuum, and
I panic and struggle against the metal cords that cut deep into my
wrists and ankles. Screaming silently. The panic is worse than the
night terrors that used to paralyze me as a kid, worse than any kind
of physical pain, worse because I let myself believe for two seconds
that I was safe. That I could climb in that taxi with Aubrey and fly
away from all this and erase Charlie forever.

It's black where I am. Too black to see anything, even outlines of
shapes. I'm lying on cold, hard cement. I can't stop shaking. I tense,
then freeze. Footsteps are drawing close. They're feather-light, almost soundless. Still, I detect them in the vibrations of the floor, in
the rhythmic *thrum* just past my own desperate breathing. I widen
my eyes and still I see nothing and the cement presses against my
cheek and jaw and as the steps draw closer, I imagine all the ways
they could kill me.

A foot to my skull. (It is exposed; there's nothing to protect it.) A
knife in my back. (My back arches away from the invisible knife.) A

gun. (I press myself into the ground, begging its cement mouth to swallow me.)

The person draws closer and I sniff the air, trying to detect scents of him. Is it him? Is it Charlie, walking tiptoe like all the times he snuck up behind me and covered my eyes and kissed my neck and made me guess? All of a sudden, I know it: I've found Charlie, just as I had hoped to. I've ended the story that started three years ago. Meeting him was inevitable. Our relationship was inevitable. This moment was inevitable, I know now.

The person is next to me. I can feel his presence. I hear the creak of his knees as he squats low. I am still. My cheeks are wet with tears. I wait for the blow that will kill me. I pray for it, because waiting is too much misery.

I feel a hand on my back. My body folds in on itself. The hand moves to my back pocket. Then it's drawing away, and my pocket is lighter, its contents gone. I am lighter and heavier all at once.

The footsteps retreat.

I am alive, for now. But I wish I were dead. I decide that being dead would be better than anticipating death.

30

Aubrey

THE FIRST FEW TIMES I ASKED, they ignored me. Then I swore, pleaded, cried, yelled. I struggled against their arms until they had to contain me.

Finally, with my arms and legs bound by shackles, they said it: *Murder.*

"No." I shook my head. I yelled. "I had nothing to do with the plane crash," I cried. I said all the wrong things. "I had nothing to do with Charlie's death."

"So what happened on the plane? Tell us exactly how he died." Their voices were loud and insistent, full of vitriol.

"I don't know," I insisted. "I don't know if he's dead."

"But you just said—"

"I don't know!"

"Tell us about your association with Lena Whitney."

Tears, buckets of them, wet on my cheeks and chest, soaking the thin tunic I'd been wearing for days. I was sweating. I could smell my own stench. It smelled like panic and fear, but a thousand times worse, coupled with the fetid odors of the bodies that are packed around me.

I'm in Bang Kwang Prison.

All I smell is filth and rot. All I hear are the Thai policemen's words:

A body was found. A female tourist. Her throat slashed. Your credit card was on her person. Her passport read "Lena Whitney, of Boston, Massachusetts." Tell us about Miss Whitney, Aubrey.

And so I began:

We came to search for Charlie.

Charlie Price?

That's right. When do I get out of here? When can I go home?

Home? Your home is Bangkok now.

And around these words, the moans of the ill. The rattling of shackles. Bodies pressed upon bodies pressed upon the cold rails of the cage. It's not a cell, where they've thrown me. It's a cage, ten by twelve, packed with twenty-five bodies or more. We're lying on top of one another. There are no toilets, just a hole in the opposite side of the room. We're lying in our own filth. It must only be six in the morning at the latest, but no one's asleep.

Some of the girls have open wounds. There are flies everywhere. The odor nearly makes me pass out; I struggle to breathe through my nose. I badly have to urinate. It's been hours. I push my way to the hole. One woman elbows me; another runs her hand down my leg beyond the dark brown shorts they gave me. I jerk away from her and lurch into someone else, and then they're both laughing until others join in, and it feels like a hundred hands are grabbing at me. There's one other Caucasian in the cell; she's pressed up against a wall, watching from just outside the fray. I meet her eyes, pleading desperately for help, but she turns away and smirks. They've taken my other clothes. They've dumped me here without a word. They told me Lena is dead.

But they said Lena had red hair.

I said:

How can you be sure it was her?

They said:

Her passport photo matched perfectly.

In her passport photo, Lena had red hair, which makes sense since according to her, she used to dye it all the time. What's strange is that when I last saw her, just hours before the body turned up, her hair was blond. It's not much, but it gives me hope.

I move from the hole back to the front of the cell. I'll wait.

The problem is, I'm not sure what I'm waiting for. I'm not sure if I'll ever get out of this cell, or if they'll let us out to eat, or why everyone else seems to want to press up around these cold, metal bars as much as I do. Guards walk by us every few minutes but most of them don't turn, other than to spit or sneer. Mostly, I'm afraid. There are too many people in here, and I have the feeling that if violence broke out, no one would be very interested in stopping it. I can feel the others around me sizing me up, putting me into little boxes. I don't want to know which boxes. I have to believe the policemen will come for me—realize their mistake—but they dumped me in here to begin with. They threw me into this cell, into the waiting arms of these other women, without even letting me contact my parents.

I wait until I can't any longer, and I push my way back to the hole. It almost doesn't matter, because I can see that the walls are lined with filth, and many of the women have stains on the backs of their clothing. This place isn't a prison; it's hell. My face burns with shame as I pull down my regulation shorts, tug my tunic as far over my thighs as it will go, and squat. The hole is poised just over a plastic bucket; I almost vomit for the second time when I see its contents. I try to focus on my knees, not on the leering faces around me or what's below. When I do glance up, one girl in particular, young and pretty aside from a jagged scar running the length of her neck, meets my eyes. Hers harden; and before I can straighten up, she moves toward me and gives me a shove.

The hole isn't big, but it's big enough for a foot to slide down into the excrement below. I claw at the wall next to me, trying to right myself; and I'm just inches from slipping in when a strong hand closes around my wrist and pulls me away from the hole and to safety. Around me, the other inmates are laughing. I pull my shorts the rest of the way up, my ears burning. Tears push their way to the fronts of my eyes and threaten to spill over; but I blink them back, because even I know it would be suicide to establish myself as weak in a place like this. I try to tell myself that Lena isn't the only one with strength. *Lena, if she is alive.* Strength, willpower . . . they're not things some people are born with. They're entities separate from ourselves, there for the conjuring. You can conjure anything, make your mind believe anything about yourself if you try.

"Thanks," I whisper, even though I'm certain she won't understand me. The girl who helped me is standing across from me; but in this place, "across" means so close I can feel her breath on my cheek.

"You were asking for it," she whispers back in clear, perfect English. The relief on my face must be obvious, but it just makes her scowl harder. "No, bitch. We're not friends. I did you one favor. I talk to you any more, I'm dead. That's the way things are around here. You want food, you want to stay alive, then you gotta be on the inside. You gotta pay your dues." She turns from me and rattles off a string of Thai to another girl who has wedged herself in close.

I try to reclaim my spot near the front of the cell, as far away from the toilet hole as possible, but I meet resistance in the form of arms, legs, and backs that rearrange themselves in front of me no matter which way I move. I get it: I'm the new girl. I'm the one who has to stand in the back. For a second I wonder how long it will take me not to be the new girl; and then I'm overwhelmed by panic. I don't want not to be the new girl. I want to get out of here before I become that. But how can I, without anyone to talk to? To explain that this is all a horrible mistake?

By the time they come for me, I haven't slept for days. I've eaten only a few crusts of bread and a tiny bowl of rice, half of which I scarfed down before I realized it was maggot-infested. That almost wasn't enough to stop me. Almost. My hair is lank and greasy and my scalp itches. That's how they find me: scratching my scalp, huddled in the fetal position toward the back of the cell. By now I don't even bother to fend off the other women. No one's tried anything violent or extreme, but they like my whiteness. They like to touch my hair and skin, to provoke me: pull at my clothes and pry open my eyelids with their fingertips.

Some of them are crazy. Some of them regularly soil their clothes. Some pluck cockroaches off the floor and eat them whole. Some are dying of infected wounds. One moans so much and so constantly. Her leg is black with what looks like gangrene. She is clearly out of her mind with shock and pain and delirium. Still, no one comes for her.

It's why I'm so surprised when they come for me.

It's a woman, a Westerner. She approaches the cell, flanked by two guards. She calls my name. At first I think I'm imagining her. Conjuring her with my mind just like I've conjured any small bits of strength I still possess. Everything feels like a nightmare; my concept of reality has shifted since I left the airport. It seems impossible that I ever saw the inside of the Taj Hotel, ever sipped wine with Lena in a Parisian café or sat idly sketching in my tablet in the window seat of my suburban Illinois home. It seems strange and funny that college ever existed, ever mattered to me at all. The thought of it makes me laugh so hard, so loud, that I forget I heard someone say my name.

The guards bark it out again — "Aubrey Boroughs" — along with a flurry of angry-sounding words in Thai. I half drag myself to a sitting position. Some of the other women are hissing, and one kicks me. I scoot away, but my body feels like lead. I'm weak and nauseated. I think about standing — I try — but I collapse back onto the cold stone floor.

Then the girl who helped me before is yanking me to my feet and hauling me to the front, where the American woman's eyes are narrowed with concern. "I've never broken my rule until now," the girl says. "This is your only chance. Don't be an idiot." She gives me a hard shove toward the gates; the guards yank them open, pull me out, and slam the gates shut against the pulsing throng of bodies. So many of the women are listless. They're dispirited, ruined. But a few are fighters, and they're the ones who reach their arms through the bars even as the tallest of the guards beats them with a long metal club. They cry out, but they've felt it before; their bruises and scars say as much.

I allow myself to be shuffled down the dim corridor toward a small, barren room; and it's only now that I understand the magnitude of this prison and its horrors. My cell is just one of hundreds, the people within it a couple handfuls out of thousands. It was easy to miss when I came here in the middle of the night, half dazed with exhaustion and panic.

"Hello, Aubrey," says the woman, once I've been seated across from her on the opposite side of a low-lying wooden folding table that seems to have been set up for our meeting. A large window lines the wall to my left; it overlooks what appears to be the guards' station. A few of them are kicked back in their chairs, watching TV, their feet propped up on the desks in front of them. Others appear to be sifting through paperwork. Some civilians sit in chairs in a separate, sectioned-off area, the tops of their heads barely visible from where I sit. "I'm Dr. Paulson," the woman continues in a clear American accent. "I conduct psychological evaluations for Western women in the prison."

"Dr. Paulson," I start. "I didn't do anything. I don't know anything about Lena or Charlie. Please. You have to believe me." She holds up a hand to silence me, and her expression remains unchanged. But she beckons over a guard and speaks to him in perfect Thai. He turns; and a few seconds later he comes back with a bottle of water, which he offers to me. I accept it eagerly.

"I'm here because there have been some developments in your case," Dr. Paulson explains once I've had a chance to drink some water. "You know by now that you're a primary suspect in the events that led to the death of Charlie Price."

"I didn't—"

She holds up a hand to stop me, her voice firm. "Please don't interrupt until I'm finished," she instructs. "And remember, all of this is being recorded. It might be in your best interest to remain silent." I swallow hard, and the tears I've been holding back for the last several days—it's hard to tell how long I've been here—begin to spill over. Dr. Paulson's face remains impassive. "You're also being charged with the murder of Lena Whitney," she tells me. My stomach lurches, drops. "You were formerly only a suspect, but the prosecution has since had a witness come forward. She's given them a motive, and they've found the murder weapon. It's a pocketknife with your prints on it. There were strands of your hair on the victim's clothing. DNA tests confirmed it."

"My hair? We were together all this past week. And that pocketknife—no. Lena gave that to me to use once, on a boat, when we were in danger. Then I gave it back. I didn't—"

"I'm going to tell you one more time," Dr. Paulson says. *"Be quiet."* I take a long, shuddering breath. My head is spinning; I hadn't even known Lena still had the pocketknife. Someone must have found it on her person and used it to hurt her. Part of me, the part that still hopes she is alive, is floored. I didn't know it was possible to feel this frightened and alone until now. It's some internal gut feeling I can't ignore. Instinct is telling me she's alive.

"A young woman approached the Bangkok police this morning, claiming to have evidence pertaining to the murder. She identified herself as the girlfriend of Charlie Price. I'm here to talk to you about that." Dr. Paulson pauses as if to gauge my reaction.

"No," I whisper. My body is charged with adrenaline. "No. That's not possible. I'm—I was Charlie's girlfriend. And Lena, Lena was his girlfriend too." Another girlfriend? Is it possible that there was a third? But why wouldn't there be? Still, for her to implicate me . . .

"That is exactly what this girl said you would say," Dr. Paulson commented. "Tell me the truth, Aubrey. How do you know Charlie Price?"

"I was his girlfriend," I repeat. My head feels light, airy. I think back, trying to remember anything that might make her believe me, but my mind's gone blank.

"This woman claimed that Charlie had a distinguishing physical feature that a person who was . . . intimate with him might know about. Can you tell me what it was?"

I think hard. I scour my brain in an effort to remember a mole, a constellation of freckles, a birthmark, anything that might apply, but I come up empty. "I never had sex with Charlie," I tell her, my voice trembling. She raises her eyebrows.

"You never saw Charlie in a state of undress," she says, like she doesn't quite believe me. I shake my head. "And how long were you together?"

"A year," I say. "But we only saw each other occasionally. It was long distance." Dr. Paulson sighs and pushes away her notepad, balancing her pen on its tip with one forefinger.

"Aubrey," she says, and this time her voice is a shade gentler. "I'm on your side. It could actually help your case, if what this girl is saying is true."

"I don't understand."

"She's accusing you of aggravated stalking," Dr. Paulson continues. "She's saying you met Charlie once and created a false relationship in your head. That you wrote him letters, called him. That he asked you to stop but you didn't. That one time, you found out his hotel information and met him there uninvited. That you were very jealous of his other girlfriends."

"I was one of his girlfriends," I say. Dr. Paulson raises her eyebrows.

"Can anyone verify that?" she asks. "His parents? A friend?"

"I . . . never met his parents," I say feebly. "But he met mine! Mine can verify."

"Your parents aren't credible character witnesses," she tells me. "They're not going to persuade any judge. But you're missing the point, Aubrey. There's already a case stacked against you. This girl's statement—it's very compelling. We've spoken with Charlie Price's sister, and he's corroborated Charlie's complaints about the inappropriate nature of your behavior toward him. We've also uncovered evidence that you were in the United Kingdom at the time of Mr. Price's disappearance."

"What? I wasn't. I was home in Chicago," I insist. Dr. Paulson's eyes narrow.

"Your emails would indicate otherwise." She produces a printed-out copy of a flight confirmation: British Airways. "There are also several messages from Charlie to you that imply you were harassing him. In them, he asks repeatedly that you leave him alone."

"I wasn't . . ." I trail off, barely able to breathe. Then I know. "Charlie could hack," I say desperately. "He broke into my emails. That flight confirmation is fake!" Dr. Paulson narrows her eyes. I can tell she's irritated. Angry, even. I push on, my words tumbling faster and faster from my mouth.

"He had a friend, Adam," I remember suddenly. My body fills with relief. Adam will tell them the truth. He'll exonerate me. He'll show them this is all a huge lie. "We saw Adam when we celebrated my last birthday. And . . . I think I talked to him the weekend Charlie disappeared." I realize the second it's out of my mouth that this sounds incriminating, but I can't stop myself. I'm sweating, nervous.

"Adam Ruffino," Dr. Paulson says. It's a statement, not a question;

and the look on her face worries me, but I plunge ahead, hearing my voice grow more and more tense.

"Yes, call him. I have his number, I—"

"He's already been interviewed. He's not a credible witness on your behalf either. He can't be considered unbiased. I think you know why." Dr. Paulson's gaze is hard. "He'll be questioned further in the coming days." My heart pounds. Is Adam a suspect? Or is he a witness? It was Adam who led us to Kerala. Did Charlie use Adam, knowing I'd contact him in Mumbai? Or was Adam more directly involved? My thoughts are confused, racing.

"Regardless," Dr. Paulson goes on, "he says he technically never saw you and Charlie together. Not once. He was eager to defend you, but without being able to swear under oath that he saw the two of you together simultaneously, his defense is useless." I think back to that weekend in D.C. Adam and me on the sofa, after Charlie passed out. Me chatting with Adam at the bar while Charlie was in the bathroom. Heading to the bathroom myself, saying goodbye to Charlie, giving him a kiss on the cheek while Adam was still up front ordering drinks. Me falling asleep in Charlie's bedroom, only emerging after Charlie came in and passed out himself.

"But I was in Charlie's uncle's apartment that weekend," I protest.

"You could have snuck in. This girl, his girlfriend—she says you did that. That you went so far he almost filed a restraining order. She has letters from Charlie, emails complaining about your behavior."

My heart feels almost as though it's stopped beating. My hands are cold. It can't be true; Charlie would never do this. Why would he?

Unless.

Unless the other girl was suspicious. Unless she'd found out about

me and he wanted to deceive her, to keep her from knowing the
truth. To keep both of us around. Or unless she wasn't his girlfriend
at all—she could have been working with Charlie, setting up this
whole thing. "What else did she say?" My words are barely audible;
but Dr. Paulson shuffles in her bag and retrieves a sheaf of papers.

"This is a copy of her statement," she says quietly. "Read for
yourself."

It's long, maybe ten typewritten pages. The phrases that jump out
at me are cruel and so wrong that they make my hand—and the
paper within it—shake until I can hardly read anymore.

. . . *met Charlie one summer in New York. He was kind, invited her
in, helped her when she had nowhere to go* . . .

. . . *Delusional. Imagined she was his girlfriend* . . .

. . . *until she began stalking him. She concocted an elaborate history
of their "relationship." A fake anniversary* . . .

. . . *It was becoming more frequent, more aggressive. She showed up
at his door. Sent him presents. Wrote love notes.*

. . . *Charlie cheated on me, yes. With a girl named Lena. I found out
a year ago. He broke it off with Lena; we made things work. I forgave
him. Aubrey, though, she was very jealous of both of us.*

. . . *Charlie was about to press charges when he disappeared. I
wouldn't be coming here if I weren't afraid for my own life.*

My face, my body, they weigh a thousand pounds. I am too confused to ask questions, too panicked to think. I can't move.

"There's more," she tells me, and I wonder: *How could there possibly be more?* "According to this girl, Charlie told her that you were
involved in a hit-and-run." She pauses, as if to assess my reaction.
"She turned in a whole collection of clippings related to it, clippings
containing alleged confessions and apologies from you. I checked

the clippings against your sketchbook, which was confiscated at the time of your arrest; a handwriting expert says they check out." I am trembling violently now, and tears wet my face, although I can't remember ever having started to cry.

"You have another option," Dr. Paulson continues. "If you're convicted of these crimes, Aubrey, you won't be extradited to an American prison. The system here is very corrupt. It's likely that you'll stay here in Bang Kwang for the remainder of your life." She pauses, taking a breath. "Unless," she goes on, "you believe what you're saying. If you believe this elaborate lie you've concocted, there is hope."

"It's not a lie," I tell her. But my voice is feeble, shaky. "It's not." But I don't have anything to prove it. I think back to all the times Charlie and I were together. I think back to that weekend in D.C. To the first time we met. *We're dating now,* Charlie had said. Hadn't he? My brain is so fuzzy, so thick with fatigue. Now I can't remember.

All the times Charlie never answered my calls. Never returned my correspondences. Do I have anything to prove he engaged in a relationship with me? An email, a text? My emails are automatically deleted within thirty days of receipt. I routinely clear my text log to free memory in my phone. Even if I did have something, would it matter? I think hard. My body goes rigid. I don't have anything. There is nothing. Not even a present, because he only ever gave me a cake on my birthday. I'd been hurt that there was no card.

But did he give me a cake on my birthday?

There was a cake. I can remember it, plain as day. "Happy 18th, Aubrey! With love, Charlie" had been written across it. But I can no longer remember him giving it to me. Helping me blow out the candles. Kissing me on the cheek and digging in, feeding me a bite. That's what should have happened. But I can't remember.

"I'm confused," I mumble. "I need to rest."

"There's no time. We only have a few minutes," Dr. Paulson says. "Do you understand what I'm saying? You have an out. You could be transferred back to America, Aubrey. To a mental hospital, if the judge rules you criminally insane. It's not much, but it's your only hope."

I can't breathe, I can't think, I can't swallow, I want to die. If only Lena were here. My best option is a mental hospital in America. A life confined to a mental hospital, or a life in a Bangkok prison.

It is too much to bear. I lay my head on the table, blinking at the glass window, where policemen, guards, and visitors mill about.

It is a fate worse than death.

But it's what I deserve. I see it now: Charlie only gave me what I've deserved this whole time.

I stare through the window. I blink. I sit up.

"What is it?" Dr. Paulson asks. She sounds surprised. My back is straight; every hair on my neck is standing at attention. One girl in the waiting room looks familiar.

"Is that her?"

Dr. Paulson doesn't answer.

"It's her, isn't it?" I point. "That? There. Her." I try to stand and barely manage, but my shackles are too heavy for me to take a step forward. I struggle, leaning heavily against my chair.

"Sit back down," Dr. Paulson orders. One of the guards moves toward me. But the answer is written all over Dr. Paulson's face. Even before the girl stands up. Even before I see her long mane of thick, black, wavy hair. Even before she turns to the side, her beautiful features illuminating her jaded dark eyes.

Even before I grab the witness statement and tear through the pages to the very end.

Before I make out the signature: *Charanya Buajan.*

Before I scream, loud and long, and lunge for the window.

They take me away even as I yell, "She did it! She killed Lena," screaming it over and over, loud and long. But before they do, she turns all the way. She meets my eyes. And she smiles.

31

Lena

I AM STILL ALIVE. Come and find me.

Aubrey will come for me. I feel it. When she does, we'll make Charlie pay.

ACKNOWLEDGMENTS

My sincerest thanks above all to my agent, Stephen Barbara, who has been wonderful in every way: from envisioning a future for Charlie, Lena, and Aubrey in the novel's inception; to giving me outstanding editorial advice; to being my strongest advocate as well as a terrific friend. Many thanks also to my editor, Margaret Raymo. It's been an honor to work with someone as dedicated and passionate as you. I am grateful to you for taking a chance on Charlie and for shepherding my story to publication. A big thanks to everyone at Houghton Mifflin Harcourt who worked hard to support this novel and make it beautiful.

My friends went above and beyond for me throughout the revision process. In particular I am grateful to Laura Bernier, and to my writing group for your profound insights in the early stages of the manuscript: Marie Rutkoski (who provided thoughtful comments on several drafts), Jill Santopolo, Eliot Schrefer, and Marianna Baer. You can't know how much I appreciate your warm welcome into the group and your honest feedback. I am incredibly lucky to have such talented writers by my side.

Thank you to my dear friend Rachel Hutchins, a brilliant author who has read each of my books with zeal and has offered wise insight. You read and caught errors in the latest and most crucial stages of revision, a task few would embrace.

My brother, Alex—also a writer and a passionate reader—read my first draft with his usual intelligent, critical eye. There's a reason I've asked you to read early drafts of every novel I've written! Thank you as well to my mom and dad for being consistently devoted readers.

I am enormously grateful to Chris Carboni, who challenged me to see my story in a different way and confront the holes and questions I'd hoped to ignore. Thank you for always setting the highest expectations for me, and for fully believing I can meet them.

Last, thank you to Caroline Donofrio for reading Charlie and loving it, as well as for coming through in the clutch with an author photo I really like.